WINTER IN
WISTERIA

Wisteria Witches Mysteries

BOOK #12

ANGELA PEPPER

CHAPTER 1

Mount Woolbird
Morning of December 3rd
Zara Riddle

The weather was perfect for picking snowberries. The sky was cloudy but bright, and the ground was white. It had snowed the night before—just a light dusting in town, but deeper on Mount Woolbird, the peak that overlooked the Wisteria Zoo.

It was a coven tradition to meet on the mountainside and pick snowberries on the morning after the first snowfall. The berries only grew on the east side of the mountain, and they only lasted a few days.

My sixteen-year-old daughter, who was driving, pulled the car into the zoo's outermost parking lot. This was where the coven had agreed to meet before hiking up the mountain.

Snow crunched under the tires of our shared car. The white stuff covered the yellow parking lines, so we couldn't tell where the spots were.

My daughter asked, "Where am I supposed to park? I can't see the lines."

"You don't need to park. You're just dropping me off."

"But where?"

"Anywhere you want. It's a free-for-all."

She grumbled. Zoey was the sort of teenager who preferred boundaries, even for something as simple as parking. I appreciated that because it meant I got to be the zany one. We balanced out.

She finally pulled up next to the only other car in the lot, and wished me a good day. She would be meeting her best friend, so I planned to get a ride home with one of the other witches. I grabbed my empty ice cream pail from the back seat, told her to have a great day, and stepped out.

The driver of the other car was leaning against the hood of her car and sipping a steaming beverage. She was a young witch from my coven, Fatima Nix.

Fatima waved goodbye to my daughter as she drove away, then turned to me, smiling.

"Hi, Zara!"

"Hi, Fatima. Happy belated birthday."

She blinked. "Huh? My birthday was last week."

"I know. That's why I said *belated*."

"Oh! Happy belated birthday to you, too."

"My birthday was in July, Fatima."

"I know," she said slowly, as though I were the dense one. "That's why I said *belated*."

"Of course," I said, nodding. "Thanks."

"You look... spicy," she said.

I was dressed in red from head to toe.

"Thanks," I said. "You look... warm."

Fatima Nix typically wore animal-print clothes covered in pet fur, and big, white-framed glasses that were always falling down her tiny nose. Today, she also wore a fuzzy brown winter jacket made of artificial fur that had seen better days. She looked like a teddy bear that had been put through the wash multiple times.

"I am warm," she said. "The weather's perfect. I like the first part of winter."

Fatima had just turned twenty-two, but could pass for younger, thanks to being under five feet tall. When I first met Fatima, at the vet clinic where she worked, she had actually been under four feet tall, but she had grown since then. Not from a natural growth spurt, like a regular person, but from returning to the height she had been before a few bad spells. The spells had been her attempt to make herself taller, but they had inverted from bad juju and done the reverse. It was never wise for a witch to use magic to alter her body.

Fatima had dark hair, olive skin, and wide-set, sparkling brown eyes.

Her witchcraft specialty was communicating with non-humans. She had a sympathetic connection with pets and other animals.

If anything, she was a little *too* sympathetic toward animals. Fatima had been quick to take the animals' side during my recent dealings with the local union of Capuchin coat check monkeys. The Capuchins were essentially bandits. They showed up at parties without being hired, tossed a few jackets into a magical closet, then demanded overtime pay plus tips. Everyone knew it was a racket, but the monkeys never got in any real trouble because they were so adorable.

As Fatima and I made small talk, snowflakes began falling, catching in my eyelashes. The world around us had the secret hush that only came after a fresh snowfall.

We talked about the perfect weather, as people are obliged to do when the weather is perfect.

The short witch used her magic to pour coffee from a thermos into a Dreamland Coffee takeout cup, which she then floated over to my hand.

"My aunt sent coffee for everyone," Fatima said.

"Maisy's not coming?"

"She couldn't get away from work. Both of the locations were short-staffed today."

"That's a shame," I said, resisting the urge to jump in the air and click my heels. Fatima's aunt, Maisy Nix, got on my broomstick in a way that nobody but my mother could.

Fatima looked around the empty parking lot. "Where's Zinnia? Is she coming in her own car?"

"My aunt can't make it today. She had to help Margaret Mills deal with her children's snakes. They got loose in the heating ducts." I shuddered. "They've been breeding up there. They love the darkness, and the warm air."

Fatima nervously toyed with the top button of her teddy bear jacket. "What about Margaret? Is she coming to pick snowberries?"

"She's got a snake farm in her heating ducts, Fatima. I just told you. Zinnia went over to..." I heard the irritation in my voice, and I stopped myself. Fatima didn't mean to be so dense. Who would choose that? She was simply one of those people who didn't make conjectures.

Fatima pulled out her phone and looked at the screen. "Margaret Mills messaged the chain to say she can't make it."

"Oh?" I pressed my lips together as I played along.

Fatima frowned as she read the message and relayed it. "She says there's a problem with some of her children's pets." She looked up at me, her wide-set, sparkling brown eyes showing concern. "Do you think she means the snakes?"

"I'm guessing that's it."

"And Ambrosia Abernathy isn't coming, either."

"I knew about that," I said. "She's hanging out with my daughter today. That's why Zoey dropped me off."

Fatima looked over at the parking lot's vehicle entrance. "Do you think we should wait and see if anyone else from the coven is coming?"

There were only six of us in the coven. Four of them had officially bailed on the meeting, which left the two of us. Fatima's math skills were as lacking as her ability to make conjectures.

I glanced over at the mountain trail, which looked steep, then down at my coffee, which had no lid. I could use magic to keep my drink from spilling on the hike, but the spell also trapped the aroma, and everyone knew the aroma was half of the pleasure in drinking coffee.

"I suppose we could wait," I said to Fatima. "I don't mind hanging back here in the parking lot for a bit. We could give them ten more minutes."

"Okay," she said brightly. I couldn't fault the young woman for her amiable disposition.

I sat next to Fatima on the hood of her car. She'd charmed the hood with a warming spell so that it served as a radiator, pleasantly heating our bottoms. Being a witch had its perks.

I sipped my coffee while I took in the gorgeous view. From our position, we looked out over the entire zoo, as well as most of the town, and the blue sea beyond. From this distance, Wisteria appeared to be just another charming seaside town, lightly dusted with picturesque white snow. The tallest building, City Hall, looked particularly striking as its windows glinted in the morning sun.

After ten minutes had passed, Fatima said, "We've waited long enough." She put away the coffee thermos, and retrieved a trio of wicker baskets from the passenger seat of her car. She stacked two together for herself, then handed me the third.

"You can use this for your snowberries," she said. There was a twist to her smile that hinted at mischief.

"Thanks, but I brought a plastic ice cream bucket."

"It has to be wicker," she said, a little too gravely. "The snowberries must be able to breathe at all times, or they'll asphyxiate and turn to mush, screaming the whole time." She pushed her big, white-framed glasses up her small nose and gave me a knowing look. "They're the most dramatic of all the berries."

"Are you sure we should be picking berries that scream? Zinnia says they're not very useful, and most of the spells that call for them say you can substitute cranberries."

"It's tradition," Fatima said with an emphatic chin lift. "You can't have Christmas dinner without snowberry jelly."

"If you say so." Wicker basket in hand, I walked toward the sign that marked the start of the trail. She jogged to get ahead of me, and then led the way. In her puffy, furry jacket, wobbling to keep her balance on the rocky terrain, the short witch looked even more like a teddy bear.

She called back over her shoulder, "Keep your eyes open for woolbirds."

"Ha ha," I said. "Very funny."

She didn't laugh.

We'd been walking for a while when a four-legged creature emerged from the woods ahead of us and crossed the trail. It was smaller and stockier than a deer, and covered in pale, curly fur.

"There's one now," Fatima said in a hushed tone. "A genuine woolbird."

Woolbirds were real? I thought woolbird was just an antiquated term for sheep. I should have known.

This creature resembled a sheep, but was the size of a miniature goat, like the type you might find at a petting zoo.

"It's adorable," I said.

The woolbird approached, seemingly curious about us. Its fur looked very soft and appealing. I very much wanted to pet it.

"They are cute, but be careful," Fatima said.

"How careful do I need to be? Do they spit poison in your eye? Is their wool a neurotoxin?"

"They're perfectly safe to pet, but you need to..." Fatima turned to face me. "Uh-oh." She dropped her baskets. Her hands went to her mouth in a theatrical gesture.

I sensed movement behind me, then a cream-colored blur rammed the backs of my legs.

While I'd been looking at one woolbird, a second woolbird had attacked me from the rear.

I blinked, and suddenly I was staring up at blue sky. I was flat on my back in the snow.

Fatima came to my side and loomed over me, her dark hair falling around her face. "Are you wounded?"

I continued to lay in the snow. "Just my dignity bone."

She frowned. "What bone is that? Is that the one in the elbow that people say is a funny bone, but isn't funny at all?"

"Don't worry about it. My dignity bone has been wounded plenty, and I always survive."

She was still leaning over me when her glasses slid off her nose, into the snow. She jerked her head up, squinted at something in the distance, then called out, "Hello!"

I propped myself up on one elbow and turned my head. Nobody was there. Even the pair of woolbirds had disappeared.

"Who are you talking to?" I asked.

"Your sister," Fatima said. "She was there, but now she's gone."

"Are you sure about that?" I grabbed Fatima's glasses from the snow, cleaned them, and handed them up to her.

"Pretty sure," Fatima said, pushing her glasses into place. "She shifted into a small, dark animal and ran off."

"A black fox?"

Fatima nodded. "Pretty sure," she said again, scrunching her nose.

"That does sound like my sister. Maybe she's working on something undercover and doesn't want to be seen." Persephone Rose was one of the town's detectives.

She reached down and helped me up. We both dusted the snow off my clothes.

"I'm wet and bruised already," I said. "Who knew picking snowberries could be so dangerous?"

"Zara, I *did* tell you to keep your eyes open for woolbirds."

"Yes, but you didn't specify that they were *real*. Let alone that they sneak up behind you."

She blinked rapidly. "You always have to defend your back when you're in woolbird territory. That's why I stayed in front of you. It's tradition. The newest witch goes in the rear."

"Now you tell me."

Since I didn't have anyone to watch my back, I cast a spell for a virtual set of eyes in the back of my head. It was a protection spell that would alert me if anything else tried to sneak up behind me. Modern-day witches with children used the spell while grocery shopping, to protect their Achilles heels from kid-propelled shopping carts.

I looked around for the pair of woolbirds, but they were nowhere to be found. No black fox, either.

Also missing was my snowberry container.

"Fatima, have you seen my basket? Don't tell me the woolbirds took it."

"They eat anything paper or wicker," Fatima said. She handed me one of her two baskets. "Be more careful with this one."

I put together the clues. We'd started with three baskets for a reason. "Fatima, is it a coven tradition for the newest witch to go in the back so she can get knocked down by a woolbird?"

She beamed. "Yes! You figured it out!" The smile fell off her face. "Are you mad? You can't be mad. It's a tradition."

"Good ol' tradition. I guess I'm not mad at all, since it's a tradition."

"Yay!" She clapped her hands and beamed again.

Ah, the blissful ignorance of people with weak sarcasm detectors. I wondered how Fatima would hold up under my mother's constant barbs.

We started up the mountain again.

When we reached the patch of jingling snowberries, Fatima started picking right away, filling her wicker basket.

My mind wouldn't settle. I was curious about why my sister had been on the mountain, and why she'd avoided us. I pulled out my phone and called her.

Persephone Rose answered, sounding breathless. "What's up, Zara?"

"Are you on Mount Woolbird right now?"

"Where?" Without waiting for an answer, she said, "No. I'm at home. Why?"

Just then, a bird flying overhead let out a loud squawk.

I still had my phone to my ear when a second squawk, identical but on a slight delay, came from the speaker of my phone.

Busted. My sister was not where she claimed to be, at home. She was on the mountain, and not far from where I stood.

"Persephone," I said in a teasing, sing-song voice. "I heard that. Are you going to tell me you have a bird in your house? That squawk sounded bigger than a budgie."

She cleared her throat. "Zara, I'm in the middle of something. I'll have to call you back."

"You'd better," I said.

While I'd been on the phone, my witch companion had been happily harvesting the snowberries we'd come for. Fatima hummed a pleasant tune while she worked.

The berries were a deep crimson red, and made a peculiar sound. They had no bell mechanism that I could see, but they jingled like bells in light breezes, and when picked.

I got to work filling my own basket. I even joined in with the humming, and was pleasantly surprised that my tongue knew the tune even though I did not. With witches, some things were simply in the blood.

I was pleasantly lost in the experience when I suddenly realized we weren't alone. We'd been joined by two people, an older woman and a young man. They had that semi-transparent quality of ghosts, and, more surprisingly, I knew both of them.

The older woman ghost was Mrs. Pinkman, who had lived in my apartment building back in my former city.

I was thrilled to see her again, then saddened. She'd been alive when we'd said goodbye, and now she was not. This would be a bittersweet reunion.

The other ghost was a young man named Nick Lafleur. He was a handsome young zookeeper. I'd spoken to him about his interesting job once or twice. I knew him through his sister, Naomi Lafleur, who was a junior staff member at the library where I worked.

Nick the Ghost was frowning and rubbing his head. He was flickering in and out of focus, which was odd.

Mrs. Pinkman, on the other hand, was as solid as a ghost could be. She'd been holding Nick's hand, but when we made eye contact, she released it and ran toward me. To my surprise, she hugged me. I felt nothing, since she was a ghost, but it was a nice gesture all the same. She pulled away, put her ghostly hands on the sides of my face, and gave me a good look over.

"Mrs. Pinkman," I said. "What a surprise."

She gazed at me mutely, as expected. Ghosts didn't talk. It was unusual for them to directly communicate even this much.

I glanced over at Nick, then back at her. "What are you doing here?"

Her expression grew sad, and her eyes glistened with tears. She nodded in the direction of Nick.

"You're here because of him?"

She didn't communicate anything.

I talked it through out loud. "Nick's from around here, and you're a long way from home, Mrs. Pinkman. Do you two know each other? Are you related?"

She gave me two thumbs up, which could have meant anything. Ghosts were terrible at charades.

Fatima came over to my side. "Zara? Who are you talking to?"

"An old friend," I said.

Fatima wasn't able to see ghosts, so I explained what was happening, careful to use neutral language that the two spirits would not find alarming. In my experience, ghosts had some idea they were dead, but existed in a denial state, and didn't take well to being told they were dead.

Nick the Ghost wandered away. Mrs. Pinkman stayed by my side, watching me talk to Fatima.

"So, they're both dead?" Fatima asked. "D-E-A-D, dead?"

I winced. "In a manner of speaking," I said delicately.

Mrs. Pinkman didn't freak out. She shrugged, which surprised me. She seemed to understand she was dead, and wasn't bothered by it.

Fatima pulled out her phone. "I'll call my aunt," she said. "Maisy will know what to do."

"Not so fast," I said. "If we're calling anyone, it should be Ambrosia. She's the only one in the coven besides me who can see spirits."

Fatima already had her phone to her ear. "Maisy's not answering."

"Hang up," I said. "You and I can handle this ourselves."

"Really? Me and you?"

Mrs. Pinkman was watching us with a bemused expression. Nick staggered around aimlessly nearby, still flickering in and out of focus. Mrs. Pinkman grabbed him by the hand, waved for me to follow, then started walking up the mountain.

"Mrs. Pinkman wants us to go up there," I told Fatima. "Do you know what's at the top of this mountain?"

"There's nothing up there, except for a log cabin. That's where the after-hours zookeeper lives."

"The after-hours zookeeper? That's Nick Lafleur, right?"

"Yes." She kicked at some snow. "Lucky duck."

I stared at her, wide eyed. "You think?" Given that he was currently a disoriented ghost, he didn't seem so lucky to me.

Fatima sighed. "I'd kill to have his job."

Kill?

I sucked in air between my front teeth. "Maybe you should keep that little tidbit to yourself."

"Why? Being the after-hours zookeeper is a great job. It's no secret. Everyone knows that."

"I mean the part about you being willing to kill for it."

"Okay," she said. "It's our little secret." She winked at me.

I took a long look at the young witch. "Maybe you should stay down here with the snowberries while I go up to the log cabin on my own."

"Nah," she said, shrugging. "I'll come with you, Zara. I can't see the ghosts, but I can always watch your back."

"Thanks. I feel so secure."

"You're welcome!"

We headed up the hill.

CHAPTER 2

Detective Persephone Rose

The black fox streaked through the white snow to the edge of the zookeeper staff parking lot, which was lower on the mountain and had no view, unlike the lot where Fatima and Zara had met up thirty minutes earlier.

Two dozen cars were parked in the staff lot, but only one was covered in two inches of fresh snow. The snowy car was an otherwise unremarkable sedan, the kind a police detective drove.

The black fox sniffed the perimeter. No suspicious smells. No people around—for the moment.

The fox completed the survey before darting into the nearby bushes.

Seconds later, Detective Persephone Rose stepped out of the snow-dusted shrubbery. She was dressed in the same clothes she'd worn the day before. Under her jacket, her dark-pink blouse was deeply wrinkled—not from being magically folded during a supernatural transition, but from lying in a heap on the floor of Nick Lafleur's log cabin. That was where she had spent the night.

Persephone popped open the trunk of the sedan, grabbed the snow remover brush, and started clearing the snow off her department-issued sedan. She worked quickly, wary of being seen.

She was seen. A blue jay watched from a tree branch high above, then flew away on silent wings.

Persephone was already sweaty from the trek down the mountain, and grew more damp as she swept away the snow. She kept flushing with a mix of pleasure and embarrassment as she replayed the events of the previous night.

Nick Lafleur's pick-up lines had been so obvious and corny. He was ridiculous. But cute and blonde, with a great body. It all balanced out.

She mentally replayed the phone call she'd gotten from her half-sister moments earlier. Her smile turned to a frown.

A cloud passed overhead, dimming the weak winter sunshine. The sweat on the back of the young detective's neck chilled.

She yanked open the car door, tossed the snowy brush on the passenger seat, and started the engine.

As the car warmed, the windshield wipers swiped left and right, clearing the melting snow.

She sat very still, hypnotized by the rhythmic sound of the wipers.

There was a knot growing in her stomach that was more than morning hunger. Something was wrong, but she couldn't put her finger on it just yet. Persephone knew in her heart that she'd done something bad, but it hadn't quite reached her head.

A case began forming, but her internal Lawyers of Justification fought back with their argument.

Yes, the Lawyers of Justification said, *if last night's situation had been reversed, there would be no doubt the detective had done something wrong*. No doubt at all. A *male* police detective inviting himself into a *female* citizen's secluded log cabin? Wrong. So many shades of wrong.

But, her lawyers argued, Persephone wasn't a male officer, and Nick Lafleur was no damsel in distress. Therefore, although the lawyers couldn't argue that she'd been entirely in the right, certainly she hadn't been too far into the wrong. Last night's events had happened in the gray zone between right and wrong. In the twilight of morality.

Furthermore, how could something that was wrong feel so right? She blushed. It hadn't seemed wrong at the time.

Persephone put the sedan in gear, exited the staff parking lot, and drove toward town.

The road was slippery, thanks to half-melted patches of snow. She kept her speed low in spite of a desire to get away from the scene of the... indiscretion.

The knot in her stomach grew tighter.

She passed an oncoming ambulance with lights flashing but no sirens.

The Lawyers of Justification went on coffee break.

Persephone realized there was only one reason she'd lied to her sister. Gray zone or not, she'd been on the wrong side of it. Then she'd lied, making it worse.

Her phone buzzed with an incoming call. The phone wasn't in the same pocket where she'd replaced it after the call from Zara. Not even close. Her supernatural nature was to blame. A shift to animal and back again moved around one's pocketed items, clothes, and even makeup.

Normally, a surprise like that would make the fox shifter laugh at the absurdity of magic.

But today, feeling as shamed as she was, Detective Rose was not exactly on top of her game. The phone buzzed just as the car rolled onto a sheet of ice. Rather than gently tapping the brakes, the shock made her slam the pedal, sending the car into a dangerous tailspin.

As Detective Persephone Rose spun helplessly on the icy road, her disgust with herself only grew. She'd screwed up. Royally.

Most people would say that a young man like Nick Lafleur got only what he asked for and not a penny more.

But Persephone wasn't like most people. She had a badge, and she'd made an oath.

She was supposed to do better.

She was supposed to *be* better.

Detective Persephone Rose's emotions careened out of control, sliding into the ditch, along with her car.

CHAPTER 3

Xavier Batista

While Zara and Fatima were on Mount Woolbird, and Persephone Rose was calling a tow truck, back in Wisteria, Xavier Patrick Esparza Batista was waking up with a terrible hangover. Given that he was only twenty-five, waking up with a hangover was not that unusual.

The young Wisteria Permits Department employee, who worked at City Hall with Zinnia Riddle and some other supernatural folks, rolled out of bed with a groan. He blamed his hangover not on the alcohol but on his lack of supernatural powers. It wasn't fair that he had to suffer hangovers when so many others he knew did not, thanks to their better-than-human powers. It wasn't fair at all. And the hangovers weren't even the worst of it. The worst was knowing he was a Red Shirt, an expendable member of any adventure party.

Xavier pulled on a pair of sweatpants, and went upstairs in search of medical attention for his all-too-human condition.

In the living room, he found his roommate, Ubaid O'Connor, sitting on the couch with her back to him. She didn't seem to hear him come up. The television was off, but she was staring at the dark screen. She twirled a strand of her pale blonde hair and tucked it behind one delicate ear.

Ubaid and Xavier were first cousins, but few would guess by looking at them. Both were skinny, and shared a set of Irish grandparents, but she was fair and he was dark, thanks to his Mexican heritage.

Ubaid's unusual first name was Pakistani in origin. She'd been named after a friend of the family—a doctor who had gone on to pay for the girl's medical training. This wealthy family friend had shown no interest in young Xavier, which had been disappointing to Xavier, but also a relief. Medical school sounded intense.

"Hey," Xavier said.

At the sound of his voice, Ubaid shot up from the sofa like a snapped rubber band. She whirled, and the ends of her feathery blonde hair fluttered like gossamer threads, or cobwebs.

Xavier yawned and scratched at his sternum lazily. What was it about rubbing yourself somewhere on your center line shortly after waking? Chin, chest, crotch—all were good scratching, but never the knee, or elbow, or anything off center.

Ubaid had one angular, pale hand at her chest. She stammered, "I-I thought you were out." Her light-colored eyes were sharp and accusatory. She dropped her hand and began tugging the ends of her long sleeves down over both hands—a nervous tic she performed frequently. Xavier had heard that sleeve-tugging was a trait common to some sort of personality disorder—his girlfriend had told him as much, but he couldn't remember which disorder it was, and didn't care. It was probably one of those flaws that only other girls noticed or cared about.

"You weren't out?" Her eyes were still sharply on him.

"Out?" He was stumped. Why would anyone want to be *out*? Thanks to the pounding in his head at that moment, Xavier couldn't imagine being anywhere, let alone *out*. It was *bright* out there, where the sun was, especially with it glaring off the snow. The mere suggestion made his eyes hurt.

He shuffled toward the open-plan kitchen in search of water, giving Ubaid a wide berth, just in case she had malicious plans to grab him by the arm and drag him outside. Like him, she had no supernatural powers, but she was stronger than she looked, and the cousins had a long history of mutual torture.

"Nah," he said, finally answering the question. "I didn't go out."

"But I thought I heard you go out the garage door a while ago," Ubaid said, giving her frayed sleeves another pair of tugs. "I heard something when I was making myself a second cup of coffee. I happened to look at the clock, and I remember it was nine-fifteen." Her voice was higher and squeakier than usual. "You didn't go out at nine-fifteen?"

"Wasn't me," he said. "If you heard the door, it must have been our *other* roommate."

She made the gag face that had become part of their twisted in-joke. The "other roommate" they referred to was the ghost of the previous tenant.

Earlier that year, another young man had suffered a tragic demise in that very apartment. The death had been officially ruled an accident.

Yeah, right.

The sort of accident where a person's head *accidentally* falls off and then *accidentally* rolls itself into a trophy cabinet.

Xavier hadn't known the victim well—though he did work with the man's sister—but he knew the decapitation had been no accident. Xavier's eyes were wide open these days. Since his trip to another world earlier that year, he had learned a lot about magic, as well as how things worked in Wisteria.

When the victim's apartment became available, Xavier didn't think twice before snapping it up. Any place could be haunted by ghosts, so why not go with the best deal? Since the "accident," the place had been not just cleaned but fully renovated. The former above-the-garage bachelor pad was now a two-story home. The entire lower floor, once a parking spot for the landlord's unused second car, was now Xavier's spacious bedroom.

And what a bedroom it was. When the weather warmed up again next spring, Xavier would roll open the big garage door and...

Well, that was as far as Xavier had gotten with his plans. He would open the big door and... throw a party, probably. A spring party. It didn't matter *what* he did; what mattered was that he had a garage door on his bedroom and he *could* do something cool with it. Xavier's life wasn't exactly on the upswing, but soon it would be. He currently worked a boring administrative job at City Hall, but he had a few other irons in the fire.

Xavier opened the fridge, took out the near-empty water jug, poured the scant drops into a glass, and started refilling the pitcher at the sink.

He and his cousin hadn't been roommates for long, but he'd already noticed a few flaws. Ubaid squeezed the toothpaste tube from the middle—never mind that it was *her* toothpaste and not his—and she never refilled the water pitcher. He would bug her about it eventually, but not this morning. Not when he wanted a favor.

Ubaid was a doctor, and Xavier knew she could help with his hangover. But he couldn't simply ask. He didn't like asking for favors. It was humiliating, and people could say no. Or they could say yes, and then he'd owe them. In Xavier's view, if someone were to do something nice for him, it had to be their idea.

"My head feels really bad," he said, as though talking to himself. "I should take some Dayquil." He leaned on the kitchen's island, a small grouping of cabinets that separated it from the living room, sipping his lukewarm tap water.

Ubaid, who had returned to the couch, her thin legs folded in a pretzel shape, practically bristled at the idea. "Don't be stupid," she said. "That's not what Dayquil is for. If you're hungover, all you need is hydration, electrolytes, and time."

"Sure, Doc." He set down his empty glass and licked his lips. "You're probably right, but this water isn't cutting it. I'm gonna take a chance on Dr. Dayquil."

He started rummaging through a drawer that contained all the random junk that didn't belong anywhere else. He knew there was no Dayquil in there.

Ubaid sighed. "Don't take anything." She got up and headed toward her room, which was on that level, along with the entrance, bathroom, and common spaces. Her bedroom was tiny, so she paid less than half of the rent. "I'll get you a banana bag."

He protested, but not really.

A few minutes later, he was hooked up to an IV fluid bag. The "banana bag" contained vitamins and minerals that gave it a pale yellow color.

Xavier stretched out on the couch and closed his eyes.

He was drifting into sleep when something dropped on his stomach. A pile of unopened mail.

"Make yourself useful," Ubaid said. "Go through the mail and pay your bills."

"You don't have to be so controlling," he said, not for the first time.

She bristled. "I don't want you wrecking my credit rating now that we're sharing an address."

"That's not how credit ratings work." Xavier was only twenty-five, and didn't know when to stop drinking vodka shots, but he did know about bureaucracy and credit scores.

She sniffed. "Open that stuff anyway."

Xavier pawed through the mail. None of the envelopes were for the new address, as they'd just moved in. They bore stickers showing they had been forwarded from his previous address.

One envelope jumped out at him. It was unremarkable, except for two words in the sender's address: Police Academy.

Was this it? The upswing he was waiting for? Had one of the irons he'd put in the fire become red hot at last?

Xavier's hands were moist. The envelope curled in his hands as he ripped it open.

Had his application to the police academy been accepted?

He forced his eyes to focus as he scanned the sheet, holding his breath.

His chest felt buoyant, his hangover long forgotten. Xavier was filled with points of light. He was high on hope, but then, when he tripped over the word "unfortunately," there was only freefall.

He cursed, crumpled the paper and tossed it over his shoulder.

Their loss. If the police academy didn't know a good candidate when one applied, clearly they were an inferior institution and didn't deserve his efforts.

Ubaid picked up the paper ball and began reading it, exactly as Xavier had known she would. She was as nosy as she was controlling of the television remote.

She plopped down on the end of the couch, on top of his feet. Xavier didn't bother pulling his feet away. He liked the pressure of a body on top of his. It kept him there, in the room, and not spiraling into a vacuum of despair.

She said nothing about the rejection, and seemed to be reading the same short paragraph over and over in a way that annoyed him.

"It says no," he said. "That's all it says."

"This isn't a no." Ubaid looked him in the eyes and shook the wrinkled page. "It's not a no, Xavier. This is the universe telling you to find another dream."

He scoffed.

She held eye contact. "What about medical school?"

"That was your dream, not mine." And besides, he didn't have the academic skills. They both knew it, but sometimes Ubaid forgot. For a doctor, she could be dumb.

She kept her head held high, as though willing strength into her weak cousin's backbone. She blinked, then said, "You don't have to be a doctor. How about an EMT?"

Xavier grunted. He thought about the guys he knew who were EMTs, and how much he disliked all of them. The job itself might not be so bad, but the coworkers would be the worst.

He muttered noncommittally, and Ubaid started talking about the courses he could take to upgrade his skills and become an EMT.

He half listened while he leafed through the rest of the forwarded mail.

There was another institution he'd been waiting to hear back from, but their letter wasn't in the stack. He had no interest in the rest, so he tossed the pile aside.

Ubaid was looking at him expectantly. She must have finished her sales pitch for EMT training.

"I'll think about it," he lied. His feet, still trapped underneath her, were going numb. She was heavier than she looked.

"You'll think about it," she repeated with a snort. "Fine. Sorry for trying to help. You can keep working at the Permits Department until it's time to collect your pension, like any other *nothing person*."

He winced, stung by her nasty words.

"Nothing person" was what some in the know called those without supernatural powers. But not just *anyone* without powers. Being a nothing person wasn't like being a muggle. A nothing person was someone who *knew* about magic, who knew that extraordinary people were everywhere, yet didn't make any compensatory efforts to rise above their nothingness.

The insult, paired with the derision in her voice triggered his fight reflex. When it came to Xavier's fight reflex, it didn't take much.

He yanked his feet out from under his cousin, jumped to a standing position on his end of the sofa, and raised both fists. The top of his head brushed the ceiling. He felt ridiculous, but he couldn't help himself.

"I'm not a nothing person," he growled. "I'm not. I'm going to be something."

His arm pinched. He was still attached to the IV fluids. The plastic catheter was digging in, and it hurt, but distantly. He didn't have to feel anything if he didn't want to.

Ubaid simply leaned back and gave him a smug, satisfied look. "Keep telling yourself that."

He glared down at her. Ubaid O'Connor was a brilliant young doctor who knew just enough to *think* she knew everything, but she didn't.

See: Exhibit A, the mangled toothpaste tube she squeezed in the middle like some sort of barbarian.

See: Exhibit B, Xavier Batista, *not* a nothing person.

He would show her. He would show her as soon as he got the results of his blood test.

"You'll see," he said.

"When?" She smiled cruelly. Her pupils were darker than they should have been, but he didn't notice.

He had planned to wait for the other letter, the one with the blood test results, and then show her. He didn't want to tell her now and spoil the surprise, but that smile of hers was unbearable. His fists were like rocks now. He would never hit a girl, much less his cousin. Not with his fists. But he would hit her with the truth.

"You'll see *when my blood tests come in,*" he said.

Her smile faded. Her eyes got very small, and very dark. In a hushed tone, she said, "You didn't."

Neither of them had to clarify about the blood tests. She knew exactly what he was referring to.

There were certain organizations that analyzed blood for DNA information. Most of these tests were used by people who were curious about their ancestry, or wanted to connect with lost family members. But there were organizations that tested... deeper. A person might use such a service to discover traces of supernatural powers in their bloodline. It was considered taboo and foolish for any person with knowledge of the magical world to do such a thing, so he had done it in secret.

Ubaid shook her head. "Tell me you didn't," she said.

"It's anonymous," he said. "What's the harm?"

Her nostrils flared, her face reddened, and a vein on her forehead pulsed with rage. Her eyes were so black now that Xavier almost noticed. "You idiot! How could you possibly believe it's anonymous? Just because they say it is?"

Xavier had seen his cousin riled up, but never like this. His fists remained raised, though now his ridiculous stance on the couch felt more defensive than offensive.

Ubaid's head moved jerkily as she spat out more words. "I can't believe I'm even related to you. How could you willingly send your blood to some corporation? You're putting our whole family at risk!"

"It's *my* blood," he said.

"Nobody's blood is their own," she said, practically growling. "Blood is..." She trailed off, her furious eyes unfocused.

"Huh? What do you mean my blood isn't my own?"

Something changed in her. Ubaid's head lolled to one side as the fight left her body. "Never mind," she said tiredly. "What's done is done. We'll deal with whatever happens. I'd explain it, to you, but you're too stupid to understand."

"I'm not stupid. I'm smarter than you. In a few days, I'm going to know exactly what bloodlines are in our family, and you know what? Even if there's something good in the O'Connor line, I'm not going to tell you."

She didn't seem bothered by this.

He drove the point home anyway. "Enjoy not knowing what you are or who you came from. Enjoy not knowing, forever." He kicked out his feet and landed triumphantly on the seat cushion, arms crossed. Clearly he had won the conversation.

They sat in silence a moment, then Ubaid, who'd calmed down, spoke softly. "Statistically speaking, if it turns out you do have powers, you're far more likely to die a violent death."

"I know." His stomach lurched. She wasn't wrong. Powers attracted trouble. He thought of something one of his witch coworkers always said: *Secrets revealed, trouble unsealed.*

Ubaid said, "Even if this idiotic idea of yours does work, and you do find out what's in your blood—"

"Our blood," he said. "Both of ours." They both knew and agreed, without saying, that their set of shared Irish grandparents had been the most unusual ones in the family.

"Even if it does work, you're still an idiot."

"I know."

She sighed and crossed her arms.

He uncrossed his, checked that the banana bag was empty, then yanked the IV from his arm. When the line came free, for a split second, his arm had a hole in it. A dark, deep, dangerous hole. Then it filled with blood.

There was a knock at the door.

Ubaid shrieked and jumped up, the same as she had when he'd come upstairs. She really was on edge today. He wondered if she was worried about someone coming for her. She'd been adamant about setting up the most overpowered security system he'd ever seen.

Xavier got up to answer the door, pausing to rub his arm as he looked at his cousin.

"You know, you can talk to me," he said. "Any time. About anything. I'm actually a pretty good listener."

26

She frowned. "What are you talking about? Get the door."

He walked over to the door, reached for the handle, and paused.

His thumb twitched. His heart was thundering. He'd expected the IV fluids to help him feel strong, but he felt anything but strong now. The tiny hole in his arm burned like a bullet hole. He wanted to go back to bed and hide under the covers, to hide from the awful, bright world. His mouth was gummy and he had stars at the edge of his vision. Could he feel any weaker if he tried?

There was another knock, this time louder.

He didn't like the knock. He didn't like this situation.

Literally *anything* could be on the other side of the door, and Xavier Batista was a *nothing person*, with no powers except his puny human fists.

But what could he do about it?

He jerked the door open angrily.

CHAPTER 4

Zara Riddle

Fatima Nix and I followed the two ghosts up the mountainside. It was quiet up there, and the air felt crisp and thin.

The ghosts' destination was obvious when we reached it. As Fatima had suggested, Nick had led us to his residence, the after-hours zookeeper's mountainside cabin. It was a postcard-pretty rustic log structure with a steeply pitched roof. A cord of split firewood was stacked neatly under the eaves. There were no lights on inside, and the dark windows reflected the snowy trees around us.

I caught sight of the four of us in a window reflection —two ghosts, plus a rumpled teddy bear and a woman dressed entirely in red. The lady in red was me. I wore a red knit cap over my red hair, which cascaded in waves onto the shoulders of my red coat, which I wore over a red jumpsuit. When my closet had picked out the monochrome outfit that morning, I'd assumed everything was red to match the berries we would be picking, but now I had a bad feeling there might be blood in my near future. Lots of it.

The ghost of my old friend, Mrs. Pinkman, who'd been at my side, evaporated without warning. The other ghost, Nick Lafleur, walked through the door into the log home where he lived. Or, should I say, *used to* live.

Fatima knelt down and murmured softly, facing the snowy ground.

"What's that spell?" I asked.

"No spell," she replied. "I'm talking to a snowball vole."

"A what-now?"

"I'll introduce you." She reached into a hole in the snow and pulled out a furry rodent the size of a gerbil. It looked similar to the European snow vole, but instead of being pale gray, it was pure white, with dark red eyes.

"Hello," I said with a friendly wave. "Have we met before?"

The red eyes stared back, unblinking.

Fatima shook her head, which I took to mean the snowball vole wasn't a human-to-animal shifter, let alone anyone we knew.

Fatima tilted her ear toward the creature, then reported to me. "This undomesticated female tells me something bad happened around here. There's bad juju in the air, and she can smell blood coming from the cabin."

"What else? Did she see anyone fleeing the scene?"

Fatima murmured to the creature some more, listened, then said, "She's not talking. Either she didn't see anything, or she's too scared to say."

"Or she's the attacker," I said. "Check her little incisors for fresh meat."

Fatima gasped. "How could you suggest such a thing?"

"If there's one thing I've learned about investigations, it's that you can't rule out any suspects just because they're cute."

Fatima narrowed her eyes at me and whispered, "I won't treat her like a suspect. She's an innocent woodland creature."

"That's what they all say." I put my hands on my hips. "You want to do good-cop, bad-cop? I can work with that. Hand her over. Let me question the eyewitness. You can translate, or interpret, or whatever it's called, while I put on the ol' squeeze."

Fatima held the vole to her chest protectively. "No."

I wiggled my fingers in the universal gesture for gimme-that. "Come on. Stop hogging the eyewitness." I took a step forward.

The vole squeaked and then jumped from Fatima's hand. It landed on all four paws, then curled into a tight ball, like an armadillo, and rolled away down the hill, not unlike a snowball. I could see how the snowball vole had gotten its name.

"Thanks, anyway!" I called after the tumbling ball of white fur. "Come back if you think of anything else."

I turned back to Fatima, who was holding her cupped palms to her nose and inhaling deeply, like a person sniffing fresh-baked sourdough bread.

I didn't ask what *that* was about, but she answered my unspoken question anyway. "Their musk is very pleasant," she said. "Smell my fingers?"

"No, thanks. I have a blanket policy of never smelling anyone's fingers, especially when offered."

We both looked around. The log cabin had a great view, isolated from the rest of the world. Fatima and I appeared to be all alone, stationed on the only path in and out. There was no vehicle access. It was quiet and peaceful there, nestled in the woods. A little too quiet for me, which said a lot, considering I was a librarian.

Fatima stared at me expectantly, the way new hires at the library did. Even though the young witch had gotten her powers a few years before I had, due to my late blooming, she expected me to give the orders.

"I guess we should start with the basics," I said, rubbing my hands. "Let's look into that bad juju your smelly snowball friend mentioned. Let's see if it shows up on our witch Doppler."

Fatima nodded.

Working in tandem, we pooled our powers. We linked arms and cast a generic threat detection spell. To nobody's surprise, the log cabin before us glowed.

"The bad juju is focused on the cabin," I said.

"I know, she said, sounding mildly offended. "I can't see any ghosts, since I'm not Spirit Cursed, but I can see threat detection spells just fine."

"Spirit *Charmed*," I corrected.

Ignoring my correction, she said, "At least it's just a mild threat. The danger is passed."

"So it seems," I agreed. The glow was faint. I'd seen a similar color of glow elsewhere, but couldn't place it. It might have been on my coworker, Frank Wonder, when he was waiting for me to discover one of his pranks. His glow hadn't been the exact shade of the cabin, but it was hard to say. Indoor lighting changed magic colors.

Fatima set down her wicker basket of berries, which she'd had hooked around her elbow while handling the vole, and wrung her hands.

My hands were empty, my basket long forgotten back in the berry patch. The Riddles would be having regular cranberry jelly with their turkey this Christmas.

Neither of us stepped forward. As recently as a few months back, my curiosity and desire to help would have driven me into the cabin at top speed. Lately, my innate eagerness had been tempered by a number of dangerous situations.

Fatima cleared her throat and kicked at the snowy edges of the vole's hole. "Awkward," she said.

"We should go into the cabin," I said. "Don't touch anything. We don't want to disturb the crime scene."

The petite, dark-haired witch gave me a startled look. "You think it's a crime scene?"

"Don't you? Look at the facts: Two ghosts, the scent of blood, the bad juju in the air. Maybe it's not a first-degree murder scene in there, but those ingredients sure don't add up to a picnic."

"I try not to jump to conclusions."

"Yes. I've noticed that about you." I raised a hand and pinched my thumb and finger together, as though physically pulling a point out of the air itself. "Fatima, it's not wrong to put two and two together sometimes and make a conjecture, even if it seems like a wild one. That's called lateral thinking, and it's good for problem solving." *Listen to me, sounding like I know what I'm doing. Zara tries to be a good mentor.*

"Okay," she said slowly. "I'm going to try." She scrunched her face momentarily. "Okay. Here it is. I have a wild conjecture that the blood came from an animal that Nick was bandaging."

I couldn't help but snort. "You think a zookeeper brought an injured animal all the way up here to his personal residence? Instead of using the zoo facilities?"

Fatima jerked her head and took a small step back. Her wide-set, brown eyes shone with tears behind her oversized glasses. She looked away quickly. "No," she said poutily. "Don't put words in my mouth."

I'd hurt her feelings. Now I deeply regretted my snort. *Zara is too sarcastic to be a good mentor.*

"Sorry I was dismissive," I said. "That was a perfectly valid conjecture you made, and I appreciate you sharing it with me."

She kept looking down as she kicked at the snow, filling in the hole the vole had come from.

The cabin before us was no longer glowing. The threat detection spell had worn off.

Enough with the caution. I moved toward the cabin's front door.

My companion didn't move.

"I'll keep watch out here," she said.

"If you're that scared, you can totally wait out here. Fine by me."

She chewed her lower lip. "You're going to tell everyone in the coven I'm an Overly Cautious Witch."

I shrugged and kept going. "There are worse things to be called," I said over my shoulder.

I used magic to open the log cabin's door without touching it, and entered the residence. I smelled the blood immediately.

CHAPTER 5

The cabin interior was rustic, matching the exterior. A lamp and a side table were overturned, indicating a struggle. A body lay on the wood floor at the center of the room. It was Nick Lafleur, on his back, wearing jeans and no shirt. He was surrounded by a moat of blood. The copper-scented puddle was still expanding.

"There's a lot of blood in here," I called out to Fatima. "More than you'd expect for just one body."

"What do you mean?"

"Let's just say that if Nick *did* bring a zoo animal inside this cabin for medical treatment, it must have been an elephant."

Fatima remained several steps outside the door. "But the zoo doesn't have any elephants. Our climate is too cold. We did have one elephant, years ago, but people protested."

"Are you pulling my leg?"

"The knitting club tried making the elephant custom sweaters, but then people realized that forcing such a noble, intelligent animal to wear ugly sweaters was even more cruel than letting it shiver."

"But people do that to chihuahuas all the time."

"And it's not dignified for them, either. However, if you give small dogs a lot of compliments, they'll feel cute in their sweaters."

"Good to know. My point about the elephant is that there's too much blood in here. It's like a blood fountain went off. I can't figure out—oh! He's breathing!"

"Who? What's happening?" She called out more questions, but my hearing shut off and Fatima became background noise.

Despite lying in two bodies' worth of blood, Nick was, against all odds, still breathing. No wonder his ghost had been confused, blinking in and out. The young man wasn't exactly jumping around, but he wasn't dead, either.

I rushed to his side and yelled back to Fatima, "Call an ambulance!"

"Already done."

"Good thinking."

"It wasn't me." The cabin doorway darkened. Fatima had come to the threshold, and was peering in meekly. "Someone else must have called an ambulance," she said in a hushed tone. "There's a crew with a stretcher coming up the trail. They'll be here in a few minutes."

"That's great news, but I don't know if Nick has that long." There was so much blood. I checked his airway and muttered to myself, "Then again, what do I know? He should be dead already, but he isn't. Maybe he'll make it a few more minutes. Maybe he'll outlive all of us."

The shadows in the cabin changed as Fatima left the doorway. I heard her yelling to the EMTs, urging them to hurry.

I certainly could have used her powers to pool with my own at that moment for a healing spell or two, but she was being an Overly Cautious Witch. This was exactly why we witches harassed each other for being OCWs. When the chips were down, you wanted to know you could count on your coven.

But there was no time to be upset at Fatima.

A man was dying, and since I couldn't exactly do magic in the presence of random paramedics, I had to act now.

His airway was clear, and the source of the blood flow was a head injury just behind his temple. I could see skull, *ick*, but no brain, *phew*.

I hesitated. *Zara tries to be a good witch, but Zara doesn't know how to fix a head wound.*

Why hadn't I been studying more? Back at my house, I had a reference tome about medical magic. The book held a number of spells for repairing wounds of all sizes. For the past month, it had been sitting on my nightstand, under a stack of other unread magic books. I should have been studying each evening, instead of reading the spy thrillers and Gothic romances that had come out with fall's new releases. Curses on the non-magical publishing world for being too bountiful.

I reached down slowly. Was it the left hand or the right that I was supposed to apply over the victim's heart? If I got it wrong, I'd reverse polarity and accelerate the damage. My uncertainty made me pull back, but not before a drop of sweat fell from my forehead and into Nick's open, unseeing eye.

He didn't blink.

"Sorry," I said, in case he could hear me. "I really want to help you, Nick, but you know what they say: *A bit of knowledge is a dangerous thing.* I'm afraid I know just enough to either save your life or, um, finish the job someone else started."

He didn't respond. His unseeing eyes pointed at the lofted, rustic log ceiling. His breathing was growing more shallow.

If only I could turn back time. In the early days of my powers, when I hadn't known anything technical about healing, I'd been guided by pure instinct. I'd saved several people from life-threatening injuries. But now that

I understood how complex the living system was, with all its levels of magic, that knowledge was paralyzing.

Zara tries to be a good witch, but Zara hasn't memorized the pathway for converting lactic acid to pyruvate.

Nick's eyelashes fluttered. He groaned, and a bubble of foamy saliva formed at the edge of his mouth.

"Help me," he gasped.

His plea was like a spell. My mind went blank, first with terror, then with calm. My confidence flared, like a birthday cake candle that refused to be blown out. And why wouldn't I be confident? I didn't know everything, but I was one resourceful witch. Just last week I'd fixed a leaky pipe under my kitchen sink, all by myself.

That was it!

Nick's head wound was essentially a plumbing problem.

I didn't know how to fix a head wound, but I did know a spell for mending rusty pipes, and blood vessels were like pipes. Sort of.

I was aware that, unlike household pipes, blood vessels were lined with a hydrophilic layer one cell thick, carrying a quantum charge that no modern scientific instruments could measure; but, on some level, *plumbing was plumbing*.

I cast the pipe repair spell, closed my eyes, and applied both hands to Nick's chest.

I felt Nick's chest quiver, then fall. It didn't rise. He had stopped breathing. I opened my eyes. His face was pale, wax-like.

"Come on," I said, pumping his chest. "Come on, Nick. You're a big, strong guy. We're going to get you through this. You can—" My pep talk turned into a strangled cry. My throat was so tight. I wanted to strangle myself for what I'd done moments earlier, standing around outside, talking to voles and quibbling with Fatima while Nick gushed like a blood fountain. I should have rushed in. I should have run after the ghost, full-tilt up the mountain instead of ambling along like a tourist.

I pounded his chest. "Come on, Nick! You make a handsome ghost, but it's not your time."

He didn't breathe.

The pipe-mending spell, however, was working. The head wound had stopped spurting blood, and the flesh was pulling itself together.

The spell was working a little *too* well. I cast a counterspell, pinching off the mending effects before the wound could close entirely. The paramedics would need*some* explanation for the blood.

He still wasn't breathing.

I took a big breath, leaned down, and blew air into his lungs, resuscitating him the old-fashioned way.

After three good puffs, he started breathing on his own. A tear of relief slipped down my cheek.

Before I could congratulate myself too much, he began shaking.

Not good. The pipe under my sink hadn't done that.

More foamy spit bubbled from his mouth. His whole body was quivering.

I held his face in my hands. "Hang in there," I said. The golden stubble on his cheeks was prickly but sparse.

His eyes were tightly closed. His molars squeaked as he ground his teeth together.

His head wound was healing, and he was breathing, but he was still in pain.

I cast a calming spell at double dose.

The shaking subsided by half. I cast the spell again, at quadruple strength, and he went limp. His pulse was weak, but he kept breathing.

What an emotional roller coaster!

Fatima returned to the doorway. "Zara, the paramedics will be here in less than a minute. Do you, uh, need any help?"

I laughed under my breath. Her reluctant, way-too-late offer to help reminded me of my daughter's friends in our previous city. Francie and Jade were always offering to help, but only once they were sure the dinner cleanup was done.

"You might as well stay where you are," I said to Fatima. "There's no point in both of us tracking through all this blood."

She leaned her upper body into the cabin and looked around. "This is a great cabin. What do you think happened in here?"

I patted Nick's bare shoulder as I scanned the surroundings.

If I hadn't saved him, I could have used my powers on his ghost and had our answer. But I had saved his life—for now, anyway—and so we had a mystery.

"I love this cabin," Fatima said. "I love, love, love it. That blood could get scrubbed out. Do you really think it's a crime scene?"

I gestured with my chin at an overturned lamp. "Something happened. There are signs of a struggle."

"You mean this lamp?" The rustic lamp, which had been on its side on the floor, floated upward magically. Fatima was levitating it, and she grunted from the effort. "It's heavier than it looks," she said.

"We shouldn't mess around with stuff," I said.

"I'm not touching anything with my hands."

"But you're disturbing the scene."

"I'm not the one taking a bird bath in a blood puddle."

"I'm not..." She wasn't wrong.

"That's why it's so heavy," she said, rotating the lamp in the air. "The base is hardwood. Arbutus, I think. What's that?" She let out a strangled cry.

The lamp dropped to the floor with a loud thud. "Ew," she said. "There was blood and hair on the corner of the base."

"Are you sure?"

"It looked like meat."

"Now we know where the head injury came from."

A chilly breeze came in through the open door.

The breeze caused something high overhead to begin swinging, and the movement caught my eye. The cabin's roof had a steep pitch, and the ceiling lofted all the way up, following the roof line. High above us were a half-dozen ropes, some with knots and some with rings, hanging from the open rafters. The breeze had caused them to sway.

"Maybe it was an accident," I said. "Look up there."

"Huh? Ropes? What are those for?"

"Exercise." I patted Nick's bare shoulder. "He didn't get this chiseled body from zookeeping and fresh mountain air alone. Nick must have been exercising up there on the rings when he fell." I pointed out a potential pathway. "If he was swinging when his hand slipped off a ring, he could have fallen on that coffee table head first. I'm guessing the lamp was there."

"Huh," she said. "You're good at this crime scene stuff."

"I learned from the best."

"That's got to be exactly what happened." She made a dusting-off gesture with her hands. "People in this town think everything is a big conspiracy, but sometimes weird accidents do happen."

There was a flash of movement behind her. A blue jay landed on Fatima's shoulder. The bird looked around, surveying the blood and the accident scene, then flew away. Fatima didn't react to the bird or explain it to me.

I would have asked, but the paramedics were already rushing in.

Two male EMTs at the front of the group were tripping each other in their excitement. I had met a few paramedics over the years, and most of them were fantastic, caring people. I'd noticed, however, that the ones who worked with the regular hospital in Wisteria were very excitable.

"First," the guy in the lead cried out as he rushed at the body, his boots sliding through the slick puddle, spraying red mist all over me. "First!"

CHAPTER 6

I stood in front of the log cabin, watching the paramedics making their way back down the snowy mountain with Nick on the stretcher.

The paramedics had reported to me that the victim was unconscious but stable, which made me feel hopeful. Nobody wanted to see a young man in his prime struck dead by a freak accident... except possibly Fatima, who wanted both his job and his cabin.

I didn't want to be suspicious of my fellow witch, but I had to at least entertain the idea that she might have killed him and made it look like an accident. She could have arrived at Mount Woolbird much earlier than our planned meeting time, hiked up, done the deed, then been back to the parking lot before the coffee had cooled.

Whatever had happened earlier that morning on the mountainside, it was peaceful there now. The snow had stopped falling, but the valley before us was still hushed in its white blanket. I was accustomed to quiet places, being a librarian, but it was a different kind of quiet on the mountain. I kept hearing the sound of my own breathing. I tried to breathe less noisily, but paying attention to my breathing only made me feel claustrophobic.

Fatima returned from the woods, where she'd disappeared to a moment earlier to "canvas the local wildlife," or so she'd said.

She crunched through the snow as she joined me in front of the cabin. She looked down at the retreating paramedics. "Those guys were not very professional."

"You think?"

She sniffed. "My boss, Dr. Katz, wouldn't let them wash dogs for free."

"How is Dr. Katz, anyway?" The veterinarian had saved my father's life. While the bill had been settled long ago—thanks to my vampire mother—I still felt a debt toward the man.

"He's fine," Fatima said. "All he talks about these days is the new calendar. He says it's going to be the best one ever."

I laughed. "Best one ever? I guess he cut out my photo shoot with Boa."

She gave me a puzzled look. "Huh? He didn't cut yours. Your picture is going on the October page. It's going to be the photo of you sitting in the pumpkin patch, with Boa on your shoulder."

"I made the cut? Wow. My career as a calendar model is finally about to take off. Goodbye, library, hello stardom. Is it too soon to start looking for an agent?"

Fatima nodded absentmindedly and stared after the paramedics, whose heads were now disappearing from view on the other side of a rise.

"I really don't know about those guys," Fatima said. "They're not very well trained for EMTs."

"You mean it's not standard protocol to yell 'First!' and slide through puddles of blood toward the victim?"

She wrinkled her nose. "They didn't even ask us what we were doing here."

"Oh. Well, you can't blame them for that. I used a bluffing spell or two. I told them there wasn't anything unusual or noteworthy about us being there, and that they weren't feeling suspicious."

"Huh?" She tilted her head to the side as she peered up at me. "You use that spell to mind-control people?"

"All the time. Isn't that what it's for?"

She blinked at me, then repeated her accusation. "You use that spell to mind-control people?"

"It *is* a bluffing spell. Bluffing is a type of mind control."

"But..." Her face reddened.

For someone who may or may not have killed a man to get his job, Fatima Nix sure played up the role of being morally superior.

She sputtered and stared at me.

"I guess I do get into people's heads from time to time," I admitted. "But only when necessary. I swear I only do it for good reasons." I coughed. "Well, mostly for good reasons. And that *is* what the bluffing spell is for."

"There's a big chasm between bluffing and mind control."

"A gray area, maybe, but not a *big chasm*."

"There's a high cost to abusing spells for your own personal gain," she said. "No wonder bad things always happen around you, Zara. You've got the bad juju."

"I do *not* have the bad juju."

She cast a threat detection spell directly at me.

I immediately blocked it.

"My juju is just fine," I said with finality.

She muttered something that included the word *know-it-all*.

"I never claimed to know everything, Fatima." I held out both hands. "I'm simply a novice witch, taking things one day at a time. I use bluffing spells the way I'd use white lies—to avoid complicating matters. I don't go around giving people mind wipes the way the Department does. So what if I use a few fibs here and there? I'm not exactly the Chief of Magical Misinformation."

"The what?"

"The Chief of Magical Misinformation. That's what I call the DWM's top person in charge of fake cover stories, whoever that is."

She smiled, and the tension that had been gathering between us dissipated. "Good one. Those underground people *always* lie, even when it's not necessary."

"They are the worst." My gorgon friend who worked there, Charlize, was the one exception, but that went without saying.

"The worst," she agreed.

"Speaking of which, the Chief of Magical Misinformation may have his or her work cut out for them. I did use the bluffing spell successfully, but those paramedics may not be as stupid as they look." I pointed a thumb at the cabin behind us. "They must have noticed the volume of blood in there."

"It did look like a *lot* of blood, even from the doorway."

I meandered over to the wood pile and took a seat on the chopping block. "Does Nick have powers?"

"Not that I know of." She took a seat on a stump next to me. "But a lot of people keep it secret if they do. Not everyone has the full support of a coven, like we do."

I nearly laughed out loud. "Fatima, being *in* a coven isn't the same as having the *full support* of a coven."

"Huh?"

"Never mind."

Just then, the vole returned, rolling up to Fatima's feet in snowball form.

Fatima picked up the white rodent and brought it to her ear. "What's that? You don't like the scary lady?"

"Scary lady?" I sniffed. "I'm sitting right here. I can hear you."

"The vole doesn't mean you, Zara. She came back because she remembered something she wanted to tell us."

"Do tell."

"Hang on." Fatima listened, nodding. "There's a scary lady with dark hair who's been coming 'round the mountain lately."

"Coming 'round the mountain? Like in the song?"

Fatima frowned at me.

I hummed the song.

Fatima remained confused. *Not a fan of folk music, apparently.*

I stopped humming and asked, "Did your little friend happen to get a name?"

"Most human-assigned names mean nothing to animals."

I let that go, even though I knew otherwise. My cat Boa knew her own name very well, along with several other English words. She had very good comprehension, except when she was being told not to do something.

I asked, "How about a description of this woman? Besides having dark hair?"

"She smells unnatural, like she covers her natural scent with a synthetic."

"If this lady was here this morning, it might have been my sister." Persephone Rose was a fox shifter, so it stood to reason that a tiny rodent might be scared of someone like that.

Fatima listened some more, then reported, "The scary lady wasn't here this morning. Not in person."

"Okay," I said slowly. Our informant hadn't been very helpful so far, but it wasn't like we had much else going on. "Does the vole know anything about Nick Lafleur, such as unusual activities, or special powers?"

"No."

"So, that's it?"

Fatima lifted the vole toward me. "She says you can pet her a little, as long as you're gentle."

"Why not?" I held out my hands.

Fatima passed me the furry rodent. She weighed next to nothing, which was good, since her claws were very sharp, pricking like pins on my palm.

I stroked her silky white back tentatively. I'd held rodents before—mainly Zoey's class gerbil, Young Edward, who had stayed with us most weekends when Zoey was in third grade—but this was different. I felt nervous and self-conscious. I had never cuddled a rodent upon getting verbal consent through a third party pet psychic.

As minutes passed, the awkwardness increased. How long was the petting supposed to last? If I set her down too soon, would she be offended? My play sessions with Young Edward the Gerbil had always ended with him nipping me or going to the bathroom on my hand. Was that about to happen?

I looked down at the vole. She blinked her red eyes at me with what I guessed was pleasure, then lifted her chin for a scratch. I scratched. The vole's eyes rolled upward.

I was sweating now, and I could hear my own breathing again. A lack of conversation was making this interaction extra uncomfortable.

"My daughter also likes chin scratches," I said casually.

Fatima chimed in, "Chin scratches are the best. Digital massage releases scent from their musk glands."

"Uh... nice." I made a note to wash my hands as soon as possible.

The vole rolled onto her back in my palm, baring her white tummy. The underbelly looked soft and tempting, but I knew better.

"Nice try," I said to the vole. "I have a cat. I know a trap when I see one."

The light shifted. Detective Theodore Bentley was standing next to me. He had used his vampire speed to sneak up on us.

The handsome vampire raised an eyebrow at my new friend. "Making friends with the locals, I see."

The vole leaped from my hand to the ground. With a whip-like flick of her tail, she was gone, disappearing into a snow tunnel.

"Don't leave on my account," Bentley called after the vole. "I've got peanuts." He dug into his pocket and tossed a few on the ground. The vole didn't return.

"That was a snowball vole," I said. "I've seen a lot of interesting wildlife today. Did you know that woolbirds are real?"

"Yes. That's why this glorified hill we're on is called Mount Woolbird."

Fatima got up from her stump and offered her hand formally. "Good to see you again, Detective Bentley."

"Same to you, Ms. Nix. I wish it were under better circumstances." He shook her hand, then moved toward the log cabin door at regular speed, pulling a pair of gloves from the pocket of his gray wool overcoat. "Let's see what we're dealing with in here."

I jumped up to join him, but he stopped me with one hand. "I was using 'Let's see' as a figure of speech."

"Fine. If you don't want me around, I'll go away."

He moved in a flash, hooking his arm around my waist, and pulling me to him. He leaned down and spoke huskily in my ear. "Make no mistake, I *do* want you around. But you are a distraction at the best of times, and, at the moment, that outfit of yours is not helping."

"Oh?" I leaned back, looked up into his silver eyes, and batted my eyelashes. "Seeing a woman dressed in red does something to you?"

"Not just any woman. You, Zara."

My name on his lips sent a shiver down my spine.

Then he was gone, inside the cabin. I nearly fell over.

Fatima gave me a knowing look but said nothing.

CHAPTER 7

While Bentley did his detective thing inside the log cabin, Fatima and I returned to our seats on the stump and chopping block respectively.

I scooped some snow to rub my hands clean of vole musk, then cast some spells to clean the remainder of Nick's blood from my outfit. The best cleaning spells included one ingredient a witch had with her at all times: spit.

My closet had chosen well, particularly the jacket. Its swirling pattern hid bloodstains better than a movie theater carpet hid soda spills.

When Bentley finally emerged from the log cabin, his jaw was clenched, his cheeks were pale, and his movements were stiff.

Seeing him so grim affected me immediately. The playful energy from earlier disappeared. There was pressure on my chest, like I was carrying a box of old, heavy books, pressing into my rib cage.

Since we'd started dating, things kept changing. I used to enjoy seeing Bentley shaken up. I used to mess with him on purpose, doing whatever I could to elicit that same facial expression. But now I dreaded seeing him stressed by a new case, and not just because it meant his focus would shift away from me. His job took a toll on him, and the longer we dated, the more the darkness of his world seeped into both of our lives.

That winter morning on Mount Woolbird, he closed the log cabin's door as though it weighed a thousand pounds. He slowly removed his gloves, staring ahead blankly.

I forced a smile onto my face and into my voice. "Quite the mess in there, isn't it? There'll be a big cleanup job waiting for Nick when he recovers. I'll have to pass along a business card for Ruth's cleaning service."

Bentley nodded, glanced around, then asked, "Where's Zoey?"

"She's doing something with the Abernathys today. Something normal, like making shortbread cookies. I'm sure both of the girls are steering clear of trouble."

His silver eyes narrowed. "Those two aren't the ones who always turn up at crime scenes."

I jerked my head back. "This is a crime scene? Are you sure?"

"Not sure, no. What do you think happened?"

Fatima waved her hand like a student in class.

Bentley shot me an amused look. I was relieved to see his sense of humor wasn't entirely gone.

He said, "Yes, Ms. Nix?"

"Zara told me her conjecture that it was a freak accident. Am I using that word right?"

"I understand what you mean," he said. "We call it a theory. What's the theory?"

I stayed quiet and let Fatima answer.

"Zara had a theory that Nick was exercising on the ropes hanging from the ceiling, and he fell and hit his head on a lamp. Did you see the lamp?" She sucked in air, then whispered, "It had blood and hair on the edge."

"I saw the lamp you're referring to, and it did."

Fatima added, "It looked like *meat*. You should put that in the report. There was scalp-meat on the lamp."

"We call it *tissue*," he said, then looked at me.

I shrugged. "The whole freak accident thing was just a theory," I said. "What do you think?"

"I think... there's more to this case than meets the eye," he said. "Tell me how you two came to be involved in the discovery of the victim." He looked at Fatima instead of at me.

"Zara saw two ghosts," Fatima said. "We were picking snowberries, and then she started talking to herself. That's what it seemed like, anyway."

"I am familiar with that phenomena," he said.

"But she was talking to the ghosts," Fatima said. "One was from where she used to live, an old lady, and the other one was Nick, except he must not have been a real ghost yet because he wasn't a hundred percent dead." Fatima turned to me. "Is that right? Can a person be dead and also not dead?"

"It happens." I'd also experienced it once personally.

"That's how it all got started," Fatima said. "We followed the ghosts up here. Well, I followed Zara, who followed the ghosts. Then I kept watch while Zara worked on Nick and got him to stop bleeding." She took a quick breath, then asked, "He's going to need lots of time to recover, right? He probably won't be able to get back to work for a while. How long do you think it will take? The zoo will have to hire someone else to watch over the animals at night."

Bentley shot me a look, one eyebrow raised.

"Apparently, the job of after-hours zookeeper is a desirable position," I said. "Fatima has mentioned multiple times now that she'd *kill* for such an opportunity." I smirked. "Multiple times." I pointed her way and mouthed the words *prime suspect.*

Bentley almost smiled.

We were interrupted by the sound of a group of voices, coming toward us. A crowd of a dozen people, some in zoo uniforms, were making their way up toward the log cabin.

"I guess the two of us should be going," I said. "We'll leave you to it."

"Thank you both for your help," Bentley said.

Fatima had wandered away, and was kicking snow off a flat patio.

Bentley watched her a moment, then asked, "Is she looking for clues?"

"If only," I said. "I bet she's planning out patio furniture placement for when she takes over Nick's life."

"You don't think she might have...?"

"Stranger things have happened."

His eyes darkened. "Keep an eye on her," he said. "Keep your friends close and your enemies closer."

"Like you do?" I batted my eyelashes his way.

Without missing a beat, he replied, "Exactly."

CHAPTER 8

After Fatima dropped me off at home, I ran upstairs and filled the tub with hot water plus soap, bubble bath, Epsom salts, essential oils, and a rubber duckie that had been magically encharmed to dispel bad juju.

I'd removed all Nick's blood from my clothes and my body, but I still felt its residual energy on me.

I was in a hurry to climb in and soak, but not too big a hurry to prepare a pile of snacks on the Frisbee we used as our tub plate.

The pipe-repair and calming spells I'd performed on Nick had left me with a fierce protein hunger, so I piled the Frisbee high with various cheeses, salami, pepperoni, and hard-boiled eggs. Plus one strawberry Pop Tart. It was a superstitious yet enjoyable tribute to the home's former owner.

About an hour into my soak, with the empty Frisbee floating near my feet, I nodded off.

I fell into a dark, dreamless slumber.

I didn't wake up until Zoey came into the washroom and announced that she'd made dinner.

"You're home?" I asked groggily.

"Am I?" She pinched her forearm. "I feel solid enough. I must be home, since I'm not an astral projection."

"Smartypants." I tossed the rubber duckie at her. She sidestepped my missive easily. The duckie soared over her shoulder, then squeaked as it bounced down the hallway.

In a flash, she changed into fox form, and ran off in pursuit of the rubber duckie as it continued bouncing down the stairs.

Another mother might have yelled after her shifter daughter to mind her sharp nails on the wooden stairs, but I knew there was no point. Thanks to the creatures who shared my home, the steps were more scratch than wood already.

* * *

My daughter and I had a nice dinner together, starting with a first course of shortbread, which she'd made that day with the Abernathys. She told me about her day with Ambrosia's family, and then I told her about my own misadventures.

"Then Fatima dropped me off here, and I had a bath," I said, finishing up the tale. "Now you're all caught up."

"Where's Mrs. Pinkman now? Is she here?"

"I haven't seen her since she disappeared, up at the log cabin. Nick's ghost went back into his body, and Mrs. Pinkman went to wherever she needed to go."

"I think she must have gone to a good place. She was a nice lady." Zoey pursed her lips in distaste. "Except for her choice in pets." Our old neighbor Mrs. Pinkman had been the owner of Marzipants, the budgie who had tormented Zoey as a child. The creature had left an impression on Zoey, who had dressed up as the vile bird for Halloween.

I asked, "Do you think he's floating around in the spirit realm with her?"

"No way." Zoey smirked and pointed downward. "He'd feel more comfortable with the other demons."

"Can you picture him with a tiny little pitchfork?"

"All too well." She gathered up her last forkful of dinner. She hadn't touched her cookies yet, saving them for dessert, unlike me. "Why do you think Mrs. Pinkman came all the way here?"

"I suppose it's possible she knew Nick Lafleur, though I can't imagine how."

"It's us that she knows. She must have come to see you."

"You figure?"

Zoey shrugged. "Maybe she'll stick around. Like a guardian angel."

"That wouldn't be so bad. I could use someone to help me smarten up when I'm stepping out of line, and to watch my back."

She gasped in mock offense.

"Besides you," I said. "And anyways, I could use a new buddy around here, since you're practically an adult now. You're driving, you've had your heart broken by your first boyfriend—"

"I'd hardly call him a boyfriend!"

I continued, "And now you've got a new best friend you're always hanging out with. I'll have to break the news to the Abernathys that you're not available for adoption."

"Don't think it hasn't been discussed."

I frowned. "I hardly see you anymore as it is, and soon you'll be graduating, then off to college." Speaking louder, for the benefit of any spirits that might have been listening, I said, "Mrs. Pinkman is welcome to stick around as long as she likes."

"So that's it? You're going to replace me with a ghost"

"It wouldn't be much of a replacement. Ghosts can't talk. I guess that makes her... an upgrade?"

"Ha ha."

I poked at the peas on my plate. They kept falling off my fork, but I was too stubborn to mash them or use magic. We were having chicken pot pie. I remembered eating chicken pot pie with Mrs. Pinkman, in her apartment. She'd tried to teach us how to patiently capture peas by stabbing them one at a time with the tines of our forks.

"It was nice to see her again," I said softly. "There's part of me that believed that after we moved away, everyone we knew would continue on exactly as they had been, forever. In stasis. Unchanging. It's hard to think about those people dying. I know it's weird, but I almost feel like I killed them by abandoning them."

Zoey raised her eyebrows at me. "You think you're that important?"

"No. Of course not," I said quickly. "My ego is normal sized. Well, normal-ish." I used magic to levitate the remaining peas into my mouth. They were cold and didn't taste very good. I'd never liked peas. Zoey was still watching me, eyebrows raised. I shrugged. "It's just a feeling I have. A vague but shameful feeling that occasionally takes solid form as a dumb idea, like that our moving away killed people."

"Is this vague but shameful feeling a witch thing?"

"A woman thing. Or maybe a human thing. But mostly a woman thing."

Zoey was quiet for several minutes, then asked, "What about the snowball vole?"

I set down my fork and pushed my plate away. "I didn't say anything to you about voles." I sniffed my hands. All I could smell was my bath products. "Don't tell me you can smell it on me."

"Okay. I won't." She stuffed a shortbread cookie in her mouth and started clearing away the dirty dinner dishes.

"Zoey, can you smell it on me? Do I really smell like vole?"

"Yes."

"I'm so embarrassed. I swear I washed up. Repeatedly."

She wrinkled her nose. "In all fairness, their musk is pretty strong."

"Does it ever bother you, having such a strong sense of smell?"

She paused and looked down at our dirty plates for a moment before saying, "Why would I be bothered by something that's natural and part of me?"

"Right. Of course. I know it's part of your shifter nature to have a powerful sense of smell. I'm being such a thoughtless witch just by asking you about it. No wonder there's a rift between witches and shifters."

She didn't comment.

"Present company excluded," I said. "No rift between us. In any case, I didn't mean to offend you."

"I'm not offended."

"Are you sure? Sometimes when I ask you about shifter stuff, you get your hackles up."

She raised an eyebrow. "My hackles?"

"Not literally." I bobbed my head back and forth, recalibrating. With a playful smile, I said, "Well, sometimes literally. You do have hackles, and I have seen them up."

"You're not wrong," she said, smiling as she resumed clearing away the dinner plates. "For the record, I can barely smell vole on you. When I asked about it, I was technically fishing."

I sniffed my hands, not that it did my non-shifter nose any good. "There was a snowball vole near the log cabin. Fatima talked to it, or, should I say *her*, then she suggested I pet her, which I did." I crossed my arms and rubbed my biceps. "It was weirdly intimate."

Zoey raised one eyebrow playfully. "Careful. That's how you get more house pets."

Right on cue, Boa, who must have entered the room silently, rattled her food dish. As the dish rocked, she meowed with the anguish of a cat who has just walked into the kitchen and discovered her human servants feeding themselves and *not* Her Royal Highness. She followed up the howl with a sweeter request. The fluffy white feline still had the limited verbal powers she'd acquired by eating a clockwork bird, so she asked for her preferred food by name. "Ham?"

Zoey frowned at the cat. "I fed you right before I went up to get Mom out of the tub," she said. "Do you really think my memory is that bad?"

"Ham?" Another rattle of the food dish. She could be relentless.

Zoey sighed and started preparing more food for our youngest family member. It was impossible to say no to that sweet little face.

Neither of us had plans for the rest of the night, so we got comfortable on the couch and had a quiet night in.

We watched movies and ate popcorn, not unlike a normal family, such as the Abernathys. However, unlike normal families, we had to pop two enormous bowls of popcorn because our resident telepathic wyvern couldn't share nicely. It wasn't so much his talons that were an issue. It was more the fact that he insisted on sitting right in the serving bowl, with his popcorn. Ribbons claimed it was the most natural and enjoyable way to consume the fluffy treat, and that we should try it sometime, perhaps using the bathtub to accommodate our "unnecessarily large human bodies."

Zoey and Ribbons were still watching a horror movie when I retreated to bed.

After some light reading, and an exchange of flirty text messages with Bentley, I was out like a light.

I dreamed about Nick Lafleur. His head injury was completely healed, and he was the picture of vitality. He was teaching me how to brush the zoo's zebras with a curry comb, and he was shirtless.

* * *

Sunday morning, I woke up feeling a twinge of guilt and sense of danger. My blankets were twisted up. I'd had too many dreams about shirtless guys who were not my boyfriend.

I was still sleepy, so why was I awake?

There weren't any ghosts in my room. Everything seemed to be in place. All objects were where I'd left them the night before, including a medical magic reference book lying open on the bedside table. I'd managed to read three whole pages before nodding off.

The room was dim. I was sleepy, but it was conceivable that I might get up for the day, despite it still being dark outside.

The doorbell rang.

Who would ring my doorbell at seven o'clock on a Sunday morning?

Rather than waiting for Zoey to do her job, I ran downstairs and yanked open the door.

The visitor was Fatima Nix. She was wearing her furry jacket, and looked like she hadn't slept at all since the day before.

"Hi, Zara," she said. "I know it's early..." She trailed off.

"You'd better have coffee and danishes, and a good explanation," I said.

"We can get coffee on the way," she said.

I tapped my foot, waiting for an explanation. If this was another berry-picking operation designed to get me run over from behind by goat-like creatures, she was going to have to work a lot harder to trick me again.

"We have to go to the hospital," Fatima said.

"*Sure* we do."

"Dr. Ankh wants to see us."

I crossed my arms. "It is way too early on a dark winter morning for that to be even remotely funny."

She shivered and pulled her fuzzy teddy bear jacket tighter. "It's the truth." She plucked at some faux fur, leaving a bald patch on her sleeve. "Dr. Ankh wants to talk to us about Nick, and about how we found him. She said to come in this morning."

"Before or after breakfast?"

"She didn't specify."

I stepped aside and waved her in. "*After* breakfast, then. Unless someone is inviting you to a brunch they're serving, it's assumed you'll be coming after eating."

"Is that a rule?"

"Do you happen to know otherwise?"

"I don't know if Dr. Ankh would like that. She's a scary lady. Even scarier than the mayor."

"I can be scary when I'm hungry, so let's eat first, then go."

Fatima wrung her hands together in front of her stomach. "You can eat when there's something icky you have to do?"

"I can always eat. It's one of my superpowers."

"It is?"

"Since before I was a witch." I waved my hand impatiently. "Come in, already. The house doesn't like it when people stand on the porch with the door open, letting all the warm air outside. You wouldn't want to offend my house."

She hesitated at the doorway, ducking her head forward and peering in tentatively. "I haven't been here since your Halloween party. Is everything back to normal?"

"Normal? No. Far from it. But there aren't any interdimensional hallways that suck people in and out of the kitchen through pneumatic tubes, if that's what you mean."

That seemed to be enough reassurance for her. She came in and we went to the kitchen.

I whipped us up some breakfast, gourmet style. I didn't even use the microwave. I stirred the packet of instant Hollandaise sauce on the stove, like a chef.

Fatima watched me keenly. "Is that Hollandaise from a packet?"

"Sort of. I also put in a packet of orange powder that Zoey forgot to put in the macaroni casserole a few days ago." I gave her a warning look. "Don't knock it 'til you try it."

"It... smells good."

Boa jumped up onto Fatima's lap and started rubbing all over the young witch frantically, as though she never got any attention from us and had to rely on the kindness of visitors.

"Tell me all about it," Fatima said to the cat.

The two of them seemed to be having a conversation.

Fatima giggled and said "No way! They do what?"

I focused on making breakfast and pretended I wasn't bothered by my cat's disloyalty, but I was.

I cooked up two big ham steaks, and gave Boa none.

As we were eating, it came out that Boa had only told Fatima positive things about her new life with the Riddle family.

"She's so happy she finally found her furever home," Fatima said, petting the cat on her lap with one hand while she adeptly ate with the other hand, as though she ate every meal that way.

"Is that all she told you?"

Fatima bobbed her head. "She wants you to know she's extremely grateful for everything you've done to make her feel like part of the family. You take very good care of her."

Boa, still curled up on Fatima's lap and purring loudly, blinked at me. The hardness around my heart melted away instantly.

"Ham," the white cat, ever so sweetly. She glanced down at my plate and licked her lips.

"You win," I said to the cat as I cut off a third of my ham steak to put in her bowl.

We finished breakfast and prepared to visit the brilliant yet rude Dr. Ankh.

CHAPTER 9

Fatima's car was already warming up when we stepped outside my house. The engine was very quiet, but it was running, along with the windshield wipers that swiped away the occasional snowflake.

"Nice spellwork," I said.

"Huh?"

"Getting the car warmed up for us. I didn't even notice you casting the remote start."

"Oh, I didn't cast anything. The car has a mind of its own."

"Like my house?"

"I don't know if it's as powerful as your house. Not many things are. I just got it, and I'm still learning its quirks."

The vehicle was bright white, and the paint finish was pearlescent, like Fatima's glasses. It had no distinguishing features or manufacturer logos. It looked neither big nor small, new nor old, sporty nor sensible. It was flashy yet forgettable. How intriguing.

"Fatima, when you say you just got this car, do you mean you got it this morning?"

"No. I've had it for a few weeks now."

"Is this the same car you gave me a ride home with yesterday? Why don't I remember it?"

She stared at me a moment, frowning, then said, "Oh! That must be the cloaking spell. It's very mild. I'm surprised you didn't see right through the glamour yesterday. Are you sure your magic is working okay?"

I sniffed. "We did have an eventful day yesterday. I had other things on my mind."

She narrowed her eyes at me. "Maybe you should get your aura checked."

I narrowed my eyes at her. "Maybe you should get *your* aura checked, young lady."

I opened the passenger side door. The door swung open as though weightless, gliding like a feather on a breeze. I slid into the passenger seat, which fit my body better than any body deserved.

Could a person fall in love with a car? Could that person marry that car so they could be together forever?

I felt a little guilty for the second time that morning. First, I had been mentally cheating on Bentley in my dreams, and now I was cheating on Foxy Pumpkin with another car.

Fatima slid into the driver's seat. As she settled, the leather seat made popping and whirring sounds. The whole seat adjusted to her short frame, cupping her body and lifting her so she could both reach the pedals and see over the steering wheel.

"Fancy," I said. "Custom fit."

"The automatic booster seat action is over the top," she said, wrinkling her nose. "I'm not *that* short."

"Of course you aren't," I lied. "How does one come to be in possession of such a fine automobile?"

"I got it from Margaret's boyfriend, Bill and Harry. I mean *Barry*."

"He's building custom cars again? That man sure knows how to stay busy. If you don't mind me asking, how much?"

"It's a prototype. Barry gave it to me in exchange for my honest feedback. You like it?"

"Yes. Maybe a little too much. I feel like I'm cheating on Foxy Pumpkin. Does your car have a name?"

"Nilla. That's short for vanilla. I call it that because of the color."

"But your car is white, and vanilla is brown."

"Huh?" She gave me a dismayed look.

"Vanilla beans are brown." I used my hands to mime a long, thin bean. "The pods are harvested from an orchid, and they're brown."

"I should have known that." She moaned and smacked her forehead. "I'm such an idiot."

"It's an honest mistake."

She held her face in her hands. "I'll have to come up with a new name for Nilla. Then I'll have to do the whole safe-naming ritual all over again."

"Maybe you don't have to," I said. "Vanilla ice cream is always white. In fact, the word vanilla may be on its way to officially becoming a contronym. Most people use it to mean *plain* or even white. For example, if someone were to describe the two of us, me and you, and said that one of us had vanilla-colored skin, which one would they be talking about?"

"You're pale, and I'm more brown, so they would be talking about you, if they said vanilla."

I pushed up my jacket sleeve to show her the inside of my forearm. "In the Riddle family, we call this shade 'marshmallow.' By midwinter, it's dangerously close to 'skim milk,' but, even in the summer, it never looks anything like a vanilla bean."

She frowned, then blinked three times as her expression relaxed. "Oh! I get it. You and I are two kinds of vanilla. It can mean brown, or white. Wow, Zara. You really know how to win!"

"What do you mean, *win*?"

"You know exactly how to put words together so that you can trick people into thinking you must be right. I bet you never lose an argument."

"That's debatable."

She smiled, put Nilla in gear, and we pulled away from my house.

"So, about Dr. Ankh," I said. "She's a bit..." There were so many adjectives. It was hard to pick one. "Unsettling?"

Fatima rubbed her forehead with the back of her hand. "I know, right?"

"At least we're not going in to see her alone. We have each other's backs."

Fatima gulped audibly.

"Don't be such an OCW," I said.

She clenched her jaw and kept her eyes on the road.

* * *

We arrived at the town's hospital—the one that was above ground, and that most people believed was the *only* hospital.

I wasn't very familiar with the place. I had only been there once before, and I hadn't exactly taken the scenic tour on my way out.

From the exterior, it was a typical small town hospital, built in the same era as the town's library. The style was Brutalist—all chunky rectangles, raw concrete, and stern, flat roof lines.

The interior was much more cheerful, and showed signs of ongoing renovations. People bustled around noisily. It was Sunday afternoon, so the place was full of visitors and kids.

Fatima, who was already walking at a slow pace, paused by the gift shop. "We should bring Nick some flowers," she said.

"Flowers? Sure. Why not. I'll chip in for half. Sure, I already saved the dude's life, but why not throw in a get-well-soon gift? Nobody can say I'm not a *full service* witch."

"A what?"

"Never mind." I handed her some money.

The gift shop interior was the size of a postage stamp, so I stayed outside next to the foil balloons while Fatima went in to pick out a bouquet.

A dark-haired, forty-something Asian man in a business suit came by, chatting with a female nurse. He saw me, did a double take, then winked at me and kept walking. I didn't know him, but he seemed to know me.

The man stopped and stood not far from where I was, still talking with the nurse. He looked over and smiled at me a few more times before giving me a nod as he left.

When the nurse he'd been talking to came back my way, I stopped her and asked, "Can you help me with something?" I would be asking her to violate patient confidentiality, so I cast a bluffing spell to put her at ease. And also to get what I wanted.

Maybe Fatima had a point about me using the bluffing spell to manipulate people.

But it was too late for take-backsies. The spell had taken effect.

"I can help you," the nurse said.

"Who was that man you were talking to just now?"

"Only the sweetest patient we've ever had," she said.

"And does the sweetest patient ever have a name?"

"Ethan Fung. He's a policeman. A detective. Or at least he was."

"I thought that might be him," I said.

I'd never met the man, but I'd heard plenty about Ethan Fung. He was an old friend of my aunt's, and he'd been the town's detective before Bentley took over the job.

"You know, it's funny," the nurse said. "He was stuck in here for weeks with multiple serious injuries, but now he doesn't even have a limp. It's like magic."

"Some people heal faster than others."

"Lucky him."

Lucky, indeed. He was lucky to have survived an ordeal at the hands of a sadistic killer. Not so lucky to have gotten broken apart like a Kit Kat bar in the process. According to Zinnia, Detective Ethan Fung had no powers beyond bravery and brilliance, but this story about his magical recovery said otherwise.

"What was he doing here at the hospital?" I asked the nurse. "Is he working on an investigation?"

"I don't think so. He just got back in town from a long vacation, and he brought us all gifts from his travels." She sighed dreamily. "He really is the sweetest patient we've ever had. And he's single. Can you believe it?" She sighed again, this time with more yearning. "I wish he could see me as more than just a nurse. It's a shame when people look at you, but don't actually see you."

"You're right. That is a shame." I took another look at the woman, this time as more than just a titleless book of information.

Her ID tag read Shari Heminger, and had been decorated with metallic rainbow stickers. The woman was about forty, my height, and also a redhead, but with tight, springy curls. In fact, there was a tight, springiness to all of Shari's body parts, from her turned-up button nose to the bosom that filled out her aqua-green scrubs. She had bright, aquamarine eyes that matched her scrubs, and healthy skin with lots of nice freckles.

Any man who didn't notice a woman like that either had no taste for redheads, or wasn't looking.

"Maybe it's my scrubs," Nurse Shari said. "The female nurses who wear pink scrubs and bright lipstick get more attention, but redheads can't wear pink. It's wrong."

Oh, no, she didn't!

"Do I look wrong to you?" I waved my fingertips at myself, clad in pink from head to toe. My closet had chosen well, yet again.

The springy redhead swished her lips from side to side and didn't answer.

"Shari, forget all those so-called rules. A redhead can wear whatever she wants. Even pink."

"Really?"

"Yes. And, as for Detective Ethan Fung, if you want a man to see you, you have to get up in his face and *make him* see you."

She stared at me, slack-jawed. "I have to *get up in his face*," she repeated, her aquamarine eyes glazed. Dreamily, she said, "I have to wear pink scrubs and bright lipstick, and make Ethan Fung see me."

Oops. My dating advice had been boosted by the bluffing spell. I was hypnotizing this woman into throwing herself into a man's field of view the same way I would. Not that there was anything wrong with that.

Out of the corner of my eye, I saw Fatima coming out of the gift shop with Nick's flowers. I hurriedly sent Shari on her way before Fatima could bust me for using spells for questionable reasons. Interfering in matters of love was specifically taboo for witches.

"Perfect," I said of the bouquet.

"These are tiger lilies," Fatima said. "*Tiger* lilies, because he's a zookeeper."

"Plus they smell like hot dogs," I said. "Men love hot dogs."

She sniffed the lilies. "They *do* smell a bit like ham."

"And that's why I can't have lilies in my house. They're toxic to cats, and Boa would eat them for sure."

"You're a good cat mom," she said.

My heart buoyed in my chest. It was always nice to be complimented on your parenting, even if it was regarding a cat.

We checked the hospital directory, and headed toward the Intensive Care Unit to see Nick and meet with Dr. Ankh.

Fatima was very quiet in the elevator.

The tiger lilies in the bouquet were trembling.

"Don't be nervous about Dr. Ankh," I said. "I've got your back."

The lilies kept trembling.

Fatima bit her lower lip. "I always get the crazy feeling those doctors from the underground want to take us apart and find out what makes us tick."

"That's not crazy," I said. "They would absolutely do that. In a heartbeat."

Fatima gulped.

The elevator doors opened.

CHAPTER 10

We found Nick Lafleur and Dr. Ankh in one of the rooms of Wisteria General Hospital's ICU.

Nick was lying unconscious in a hospital bed. His hair was bright and golden, free of blood. The wound on his head had been cleanly bandaged. His face, golden hair, and body—or at least the area that wasn't covered by a green sheet—had also been cleaned up.

The room itself was cavernously large, the walls lined with medical equipment on rolling stands. The air smelled of plastic, chemical antiseptic, and also tea tree oil.

The blonde doctor leaned over Nick's head, checking the edges of the bandage.

Dr. Aliyah Ankh had an oval face, a narrow nose, and large lips that were both thick and wide. Her features were slightly alien, not conventionally attractive, yet hard to look away from. She could have passed for a high fashion model. I could imagine her in a catalog campaign for lip-plumping lipstick.

She didn't glance up when we entered, but I guessed by the change in her posture—from relaxed to even more relaxed—she knew we were there. Ignoring us was a total power move. It was exactly what I'd expect from someone who'd made disparaging comments about my "mixed" family tree.

"Dr. Ankh," I said. "I almost didn't recognize you without your squid costume."

The last time we'd seen each other had been at the Monster Mash, when she'd been eager to turn my aunt into a vampire with one of her elixirs. Another Riddle woman might have changed powers that night, if I hadn't been there to intervene.

Dr. Ankh kept inspecting Nick's bandage, which looked clean and impeccably placed. Her hand seemed to move independently of her body, which was utterly still. Her fingers were delicate, and longer than those of a typical person. I'd seen her bare toes before, when she'd been in a hot tub at Castle Wyvern's spa, and they were nearly as long as a regular person's fingers, but her actual fingers were something else. *All the better to perform experimental medical procedures with.*

What was she? Did she even belong in our world? I'd asked around, but my friends at the DWM weren't talking, and nobody in the coven had the dirt on her.

Without looking up, she started talking, speaking in her lilting, sing-song voice, "Zara, I have been meaning to check in on your mother's sister. I do hope she made a full recovery following the events that transpired at Castle Wyvern."

Fatima and I exchanged a look. Dr. Ankh was in no rush to get to the Nick business. No rush at all. Therefore, it had been a solid move, after all, for us to have eaten breakfast before coming to see her. Fatima had been doubtful about my decision, so now I turned to the young witch and made a told-you-so expression.

Fatima didn't pick up my nonverbal communication at all. She made her usual I-am-confused expression.

"My mother's sister," I said, repeating the doctor's odd phrasing. "That would be my aunt, Zinnia Riddle. I'm happy to say she's still alive in every way."

"Zirconia did report as much," Dr. Ankh said. "When she was here last month. Shame she had to leave before we could visit the spa together."

"I'm sure my mother will curse us—I mean bless us, with a visit again soon enough."

"How is Zinnia's size?" Zinnia had been shrinking, wasting away, haunted by a tragedy from her past, until she'd hit rock bottom thanks to a giant Pain-Body Demon.

"Back to normal size," I reported. "We even checked her with a tape measure, and she's full height. Either that or she lied on her driver's license."

"Fascinating." The blonde doctor glanced up at us briefly, her thin skin smooth and expressionless. Based on her appearance under the hospital room's bright lighting, I would put her age at fifty. Given her alien features, it was hard to pin her down, but she had to be somewhere between twenty and ninety.

Dr. Ankh blinked her strange, lavender eyes at me. "What is the situation with that inbred mutt behind you? Does it require medical attention? Its fur is bedraggled."

I turned, looking for a dog. There was only Fatima, who had been hiding behind me in her ratty faux-fur jacket.

Fatima stepped forward meekly. "It's just me, Dr. Ankh. I'm not a dog."

"That is disappointing," the good doctor replied. "I had hoped Zara had brought me a new hybrid creature."

"Just a couple of regular witches," I said.

"Oh, well," she replied.

"Fatima got the message you wanted to see us about something," I said. "But if you're busy, we can drop off these flowers for Nick and get out of your hair."

Dr. Ankh held up one long, gloved finger, ordering us to wait as she finished her inspection of Nick's head by tousling his golden curls.

When she was done, she pulled off her gloves slowly, then asked, "What did you two do to him?"

"N-n-nothing," Fatima stammered.

"He was already bleeding from the head when we found him," I said. "My word is my bond."

Fatima didn't offer her bond. Fatima was only twenty-two, and there was some controversy about whether or not the oath even worked on people who were younger than twenty-four. Something about their brains still developing. As with most things magical, it was not a hard-and-fast rule. Also, as with regular promises, it only meant as much as the giver wanted it to.

"After that," Dr. Ankh said. "What did you do to this young man *after* you found him?"

I shrugged. "Magic stuff. A little of this and that. I was only doing what I could to help him."

"A little of this and that? Could you be more specific? What strain of spellwork did you unleash upon my patient?"

I looked down and scuffed the floor with my pink shoe. Would I tell Dr. Ankh I'd used a spell meant for fixing rusty pipes? No way. I did want to help the doctor assess and treat her patient, but that didn't mean I had to reveal all my trade secrets.

Waving one hand vaguely and hunching my shoulders, I said, "I used the strain of spellwork where you put your hands on someone and they get better. Healing stuff. Hard to say after the fact exactly what was going on in my head at the time. Fog of war and such. With the healing magic, it's often purely by instinct." I was close enough to the truth that I wasn't hampered by the oath I'd just sworn.

"Witches," Dr. Ankh spat out, her large lips curling with distaste. "You do not understand how anything works, and yet you continue to use the powers anyway. You take and you take, and you do not know what you do."

I straightened up. "Hey, lady, I don't know how my car runs, either, but I still drive it around."

Fatima chimed in, "Me, too."

Dr. Ankh spat out one word: "Hobbyists."

Hobbyists? I made eye contact with Fatima, who pressed her lips shut and nervously plucked more fake fur out of her jacket.

The doctor continued, saying, "You may have caused damage to the patient's eye. As you can see, the surrounding skin is inflamed. It is quite discolored."

She beckoned me to come closer, so I did. I was able to see what I hadn't noticed from the entrance. Nick had a black eye.

"That's a real shiner," I said. "By which I mean ecchymosis. When the capillaries are damaged by trauma, localized bleeding travels into the surrounding interstitial tissues, causing all sorts of funky bruise colors." *Thank you, three pages of the medical magic book I read last night.*

Dr. Ankh's honey-brown eyebrows rose with a hint of amusement. "I know what a *shiner* is, Zara. The question is, did you give it to him?"

"Not that I know of. I always remember when I punch someone. I always put a notch in the brim of my pointy witch hat for each successful knockout." The oath allowed for some degree of joking, if it was done with good intentions, such as lightening the mood.

The doctor dodged my joke without missing a beat. "Did you use your 'this and that' magic to treat the eye region?"

"Not specifically. I didn't notice it, under all the blood."

"If you did not strike him, nor accelerate his eye region's inflammatory response by inducing time slippage at a cellular level, then the damage is approximately thirty-six hours old. It was acquired several hours before the head wound. The bruise pattern matches that of a fist."

"So, let me get this straight," I said, mostly for Fatima's benefit. "You're saying that, according to his wounds, Nick got punched in the eye Friday night, and then Saturday morning he fell on a lamp and nearly bled to death? The poor boy's had a rough weekend."

Dr. Ankh's lavender eyes narrowed. "He may not have fallen. Look." She grabbed the sheet and whipped it off. "Tell me what you see."

The blood-soaked jeans he'd been wearing the day before had been removed. Along with his underwear. Poor unconscious Nick was sporting nothing but a faded tan line. I looked away instinctively.

"Look," Dr. Ankh said impatiently. "You are not a child. You have seen the human form before."

"Not this one."

"This one is not irregular," she said. "He is no different from Michelangelo's famed statue of David, except for a few details."

I stared up at the ceiling. "I hadn't noticed."

An awkward moment passed, then I finally forced myself to look.

Dr. Ankh said, "You'll see there is no bruising anywhere, except the eye."

"You're right. There's a lot of skin, and none of it's bruised."

"If he had fallen hard enough to produce the wound on his skull, he would bear additional marks."

She was right. His body was as flawless as it was toned, at least on the front.

"What about his back?" I asked.

She grabbed the young man's hip and shoulder, and quickly rolled him over with a facility that made Fatima gasp. Or maybe it was the sight of Nick's bare backside, which was as Michelangelo-worthy as the front. Not that I cared about Nick Lafleur's manliness and flawlessness in *that way*. I was only checking him for bruises. Like a professional.

"No bruises," I reported in a detached tone. "No marks whatsoever. Not even a suspicious mole."

Behind me, Fatima asked in a squeaky voice, "Are you saying it wasn't an accident? He didn't fall on his lamp and leave a chunk of scalp meat on it? But that had to be what happened. There's no other explanation."

I gave my companion a closer look. She was sweating profusely. Was it from wearing the heavy winter jacket indoors, or was she hiding something? She wanted Nick's job at the zoo, and his home.

I looked away and brushed off the suspicious frame of mind. Fatima Nix was a suspect, technically, but only on paper. I didn't truly feel suspicious of her in my heart.

Then again, I had been wrong about people before.

Dr. Ankh flipped Nick like a piece of toast, making him butter-side up again. "All I can say for certain in my report is that, aside from the head wound, there is no physical evidence suggesting that any other part of the patient was injured, except for the eye, which happened on Friday night. We do not yet know what happened to him. I am working on doing my part, which is why I asked for you to come see me *first thing* this morning." She stared at us, then through us. "I can see by the orange flecks on the corners of your mouths that you do not take your duty seriously, and that you chose to stuff your faces before coming here."

Fatima and I rubbed the dried remnants of orange sauce from the corners of our mouths guiltily.

"I can only make note of what is in evidence," Dr. Ankh said. With a flourish, she replaced the sheet over Nick's bare body. "I will be submitting my report to the Department, including the key fact that the indiscriminate use of magic by a pair of hobbyists may have altered the healing process and obscured evidence."

"I didn't touch him," Fatima said.

"You were there," Dr. Ankh said.

"But Zara didn't do anything, either," Fatima said.

"Except save his life," I said.

Dr. Ankh tilted her head and said nothing.

I couldn't take it anymore. "Hey, lady, I'm not looking for a key to the town, or an official commendation for my tireless efforts to round up the bad elements in this town and prevent the next apocalypse, but a little less suspicion might be nice."

The ageless doctor rubbed her chin thoughtfully.

I pushed my shoulders back while I cringed inside. I very rarely called people "hey, lady," but this woman brought something out in me. Perhaps it was a manifestation of the "mixed" breeding that made up my lineage. That could have been it. People had a way of living up to others' expectations, even when the "people" was me.

"You do make an effort," Dr. Ankh said, still rubbing her chin.

Fatima wiped more sweat from her brow.

Dr. Ankh stopped rubbing her chin and tilted her head in the opposite direction. "You have helped the police on more than one occasion."

"I have," I agreed.

"With that in mind, I believe you may be able to assist with something specific. It might atone for the damage your untrained magic may have caused."

With my sarcasm set to level nine, I said, "Oh, well, since you put it so nicely, how could I refuse?"

She continued unabated. "I did find something that may be of interest regarding the matter of his bruised eye." She handed me a slip of paper. It was a receipt, stained with blood. "This was in the pocket of his jeans. The time stamp corresponds to the window of time during which he may have sustained the eye socket injury."

I levitated the paper an inch above my hand to avoid touching it. "What do you want me to do with this?"

She stared at me. "You could have it framed, and hang it above your fireplace," she said dryly. "Or you could pass it along to your colleagues at the police department."

My cheeks burned immediately. I wasn't the only one in the room who could dish out the burns.

I plucked the stained receipt from the air and stuffed it in the jacket of my pink overcoat.

"Will do," I said curtly, turning to leave.

Fatima had already set the bouquet of tiger lilies on a rolling stand, and was two steps ahead of me heading for the exit.

My fellow coven member and I said nothing to each other until we were safely in the elevator, at which point she exhaled while saying, "I'm so glad that's over."

I retrieved the receipt from my pocket and looked it over.

I considered my options for all of five seconds, then turned to Fatima and said, "It's not over yet. Our next stop is Becky's Roadhouse."

CHAPTER 11

Fatima Nix did not want to visit Becky's Roadhouse. Not for an early afternoon cocktail, and definitely not to play amateur detective. She had no interest in asking around about Nick getting into a fight there on Friday night. She wasn't even mildly curious.

"It's not our job," she said, keeping her eyes on the road ahead while scowling. "You're supposed to give that bar receipt to Detective Bentley. That's what Dr. Ankh said."

"And I will give the receipt to Detective Bentley, along with the report of whatever we find out at Becky's today."

"Would that be admissible in court?"

"That's a good question. Honestly, I'd be more concerned if we lived in the sort of town where homicide cases actually went to court. In my limited experience, most homicide investigations end in violent bloodbaths."

She kept driving, her eyes on the road, her lips scrunched.

"What's wrong?" I asked. "Is my casual mention of bloodbaths eroding your sense of adventure?"

She shot me a wary look. "Did my aunt put you up to this? You, mentoring me? Are you trying to help me find my bravery?"

"Sure," I said. "Let's say I'm mentoring you." Fatima's aunt, Maisy Nix, had requested no such thing, but it was always generally implied that witches ought to help each other level up.

Fatima slumped behind the wheel. The seat squeaked and popped as it magically adjusted itself, compensating by boosting her small frame even higher.

"Okay," she said with the heaviness of weary resignation. "We can go to the bar and ask about Friday night. But if there's any sign of trouble, I'm dropping a smoke screen and high-tailing it out of there."

"I would expect nothing less." Under my breath, I added, "From an OCW."

She pretended not to hear me.

* * *

Fatima steered Nilla into the parking lot for Becky's Roadhouse, a charmingly ramshackle dive bar on the outskirts of town.

The founding owners of the bar had recently retired, and the place had been taken over by a rough-and-tumble regular customer, a woman named Becky Anderson.

Around the time of the business handover, Charlize, my gorgon best friend, and I had been drinking in the bar with Becky and her friends. After a few rounds of tequila, I had jokingly suggested a name change for the establishment.

The joke stuck.

The place was now officially called Becky's Roadhouse Bar and Grill. It said so on the sign.

A second banner beneath the new sign read *Under New Management*.

A third banner read *Deep Fryer Oil Now Changed Regularly*.

Fatima parked in a snow-dusted spot near the entrance, pushed up her big, white-framed glasses, and said with a huff, "I changed my mind. I'll wait in the car."

"Don't be silly. You have to come in with me. Even if you don't want to interrogate anyone, you can casually chat with the regulars."

"What regulars? It's not even open."

She was right. It was still early on a Sunday, and the bar didn't open for a few more hours. The other cars in the parking lot must have belonged to the staff.

"It's open enough for us," I said. "I know the owner. She must be here. That's her Bronco over there."

"How do you know that's hers?"

"It's a big truck with monster tires, with Becky's Roadhouse stickers on the sides, and it's parked in the spot with the sign that says 'Becky's Bronco Parking Only. Interlopers will be Beckified.'" I reached for my door handle. "Come on."

"Are the people who work there scary?"

"The human staff are a bit rough around the edges, but there's all manner of vermin pitter-pattering around in there. You can talk to them with your pet powers."

"Huh? Did you say *vermin*?"

"You'll see. Becky doesn't mind the vermin because they keep the cockroach numbers low. Come on."

"No, thank you."

"Don't make me say it."

Fatima frowned and stared straight ahead, pouting.

"Fatima," I said. "You're being a real Overly Cautious Witch right now."

She cracked like I knew she would. She threw off her seatbelt as angrily as any person had ever thrown off a seatbelt.

We walked through the melting snow to the bar's heavy wood door, pushed it open with a mighty creak, and entered the dim establishment.

Becky's Roadhouse wouldn't be open for a few hours, but a few members of the staff were already bustling around, sweeping up broken glass from the night before and changing the dangling streamers of fly strips. You wouldn't think flies would be such an issue in the dead of winter, but flies in Wisteria were persistent—both the visible and the invisible ones.

The proprietress herself was standing at the bar. "No early birds," she growled at us without looking up.

Becky Anderson was large and tattooed. She could throw a refrigerator across the local sinkhole without breaking a sweat. Sure, it had been a mini-fridge, but still. *You* try throwing a mini-fridge across a sinkhole and see how that goes.

"We may be early birds, but we're not regular customers," I said. "You don't have to serve us."

Becky looked up and broke into a grin when she saw that one of the early birds was me.

She exclaimed, in her gruff voice, "If it isn't my former cellmate!" She leaned forward, her beefy, tattooed elbow on the bar. "How's it going, Princess Buttercup? Have you been staying outta trouble?"

"Trouble has a way of finding me."

Becky let out a bellow of laughter. She reached for a bottle. "You're okay, for a couple o' early birds. How about a whiskey shot for you and your furry friend, on the house?"

Fatima hunched over, staring at her boots as she plucked another spot bare on her jacket.

"I'd love one," I said. "But my furry friend is driving, so make hers a soda."

Becky poured a pair of shots, and a glass of soda for Fatima, who accepted the glass with trepidation. I shook my head at the younger witch. Since when did she have any reason to fear a slightly grimy glass? She was a witch, and her saliva had both antibacterial and antiviral properties. A witch could spit on her hands and clean it of anything. Well, anything weaker than vole musk.

For the record, I did not spit on my hands at the library. I used the normal hand sanitizer, like a normal librarian. I even complained about it making my papercuts sting, even though I didn't get papercuts anymore. One had to keep up appearances.

I introduced Becky to Fatima—names only, not powers. Becky hadn't yet opened up to me about where her strength came from.

We made small talk about the snowy weather, then about the bar business. Becky didn't care for the cloud-based accounting software the previous bar owners had been using, and had switched to a different service. The monthly fees were higher, but it did come with toll-free support, and she liked hearing the different accents of people when she called the line.

I waited for the conversation to reach a lull before pressing on with the business of finding out who had given Nick Lafleur his black eye. It stood to reason that the same party who punched him might have been responsible for harming the man the next morning at his cabin.

"He was from Tallahassee," Becky was saying, speaking about the accounting service, not Friday night's events. "Real nice accent."

"I'm glad the new software is working out for you," I said.

"But that's not what ya came here to talk about. What's on your pretty little mind, Princess Buttercup?"

"It may be none of my business," I said, "but did anything unusual go down here on Friday night?"

"Unusual? I dunno. It was quiet, on account of the snowfall warning. We did have the ukulele sing-along group." Becky nodded at the ukulele she kept on the wall behind the bar. She was a big fan of the uke, and folk songs. She could *and would* play any Simon and Garfunkel song upon request, or even without a request.

Becky grabbed the ukulele and began playing "A Hazy Shade of Winter." It was an abridged version, only two minutes long. Her voice managed to be both gritty and ethereal.

When she finished, I clapped politely. I zapped Fatima until she joined in.

"But that's *also* not what ya came for," Becky said sagely. She replaced the uke on the wall, between a pair of antique bear traps. "Tell Becky what ya really want."

I smiled. I did enjoy it when Becky referred to herself in third person.

"A young man named Nick Lafleur was here Friday night," I said. "Do you know him? He's in his early twenties, works at the zoo, and I guess you could say he's attractive, in a wholesome sort of way. Blonde. Chiseled body. Model material, but catalog modeling, not runway." I waved my hand to distract from the blush rising on my cheeks. "You get the picture."

Fatima said nothing. She hoisted herself all the way up onto a bar stool, where she watched me talking as she gingerly sipped her soda water.

"The pretty boy," Becky said. "Yah. He was here Friday night. He got himself into a fight, too. I didn't say nothin' before, when you asked, because it's not exactly unusual. They're called bar fights because they happen at bars."

"Do you know who he was fighting with?"

Becky poured two more shots and gestured for me to drink before tossing back hers.

When the glasses were empty, Becky said, "The pretty boy got into it with that dark-haired kid who works at City Hall." She chuckled. "The kid clocked him real good. He's wiry, but he's fast. Last name's Batista. First name is something Spanish, but they don't say it that way."

"Do you mean Xavier? Xavier Batista? That's who punched Nick?"

"If Xavier's the cocky one who's always sticking his chest out like a rooster."

That was him, all right. A more apt description could not have been made.

"I actually saw Xavier Batista on Friday night," I said. "At the Shady Lanes. He must have come over here after we finished bowling." I licked the remnants of whiskey off my lips. My head was pleasantly buzzy. "Any idea what they were fighting about?"

"Nope. Don't ask, don't care. Stay outta trouble. That's my motto."

Fatima found her voice and chimed in, "That's pretty much the exact opposite of Zara's motto."

Becky nodded. "That's why trouble keeps findin' her," she said to Fatima.

"Zing!" Fatima said.

The two shared a chuckle. Ah, the mild mean-spiritedness of new acquaintances bonding over the trouncing of the shared friend who introduced them.

After they finished their entertainment at my expense, the proprietress offered me a third shot. I wisely declined. I was already reeling from the first two, plus the news that my aunt's coworker might be involved in something unseemly.

I thanked Becky for the information and the hospitality.

I tried to pay for the drinks. Becky threatened to beat me senseless if I didn't accept her hospitality.

Fatima and I left, Fatima leading the way at a pace too fast for her short legs.

Outside, the crisp winter air smelled particularly fresh after the stale beer of the bar.

Snow was falling again as we got into the car.

Once we were buckled in and our fancy seats had adjusted, I said to my companion, "So? What do you think? Did Xavier punch Nick on Friday night, then go to his cabin and try to finish the job Saturday morning?"

Fatima swished her lips from side to side a moment, then said, "Xavier Batista has his flaws, but he's not a killer."

"Look at you, making conjectures! We'll make a detective out of you yet."

"I'm serious." Her brown eyes filled with tears. "I know Xavier. We have some friends in common. He's nice. You can't tell anyone about Xavier punching Nick."

"Fatima! Are you sweet on Xavier?"

"No." She blinked back the tears and pushed up her oversized, white-framed glasses. "It's just that he's a nice guy, and he doesn't deserve to get in trouble."

"He doesn't deserve a *little* suspicion? Maybe he shouldn't have punched someone in the eye."

She said nothing as she put the car in gear and started driving.

The falling snow turned to crystal-filled water droplets on the windshield before being swept away on silent wipers.

She was quiet on the drive back to my house.

It had only been two hours since she'd arrived at my house that morning to take me to Dr. Ankh, yet it felt like considerably more time had passed.

I sensed her stewing. I'd rarely seen Fatima worked up. She was passionate about her personal projects, such as the eradication of the common flea, but most of the time she was quiet and easy-going.

Her face muscles twitched as she argued about something in her head.

I guessed it was about the idea of Xavier being involved in a crime. People like Fatima had a lot of empathy, but sometimes it could be too much. There was such a thing as being empathetic to a fault. It was just like Fatima to take up a cause that nobody asked her to.

She pulled up to my house, still silently stewing. Her glasses were sitting crookedly on her face, and her dark hair was as disheveled as her ratty jacket. She looked small and wrong inside the luxurious car, like a hairball in a marble sink.

Seeing her that way made me feel sorry for her, and then disappointed in myself. I really had given her a hard time all weekend, considering she'd done nothing wrong. She'd wanted to pick berries, not get tangled up in other people's drama.

"Hey," I said softly. "You *did good* today. By which I mean you did *well*, and also that you performed good deeds. Can you give me a smile and let me know we're okay?"

She scowled. "Get out of the car."

"Not until you tell me what's bothering you."

"It's *you*. You're bothering me. Get out."

I'd been feeling soft toward her, but the angry outburst did something to me. My hackles went up.

"Are you serious, Fatima? First of all, I made you breakfast, and you complained about the color of the Hollandaise sauce. Then, at the hospital, I gave you money for half of Nick's bouquet, and I don't think I got any change back. I did all the talking with Dr. Ankh so you didn't have to, then I took you out for a free drink. You got to see a new place and meet new people. Nobody bit, scratched, or zapped you." The last part wasn't entirely true. I'd zapped her myself, but not so much that I needed to correct myself. "I'd say, all in all, we had a pretty fun day out."

She turned to me, her brown eyes blazing with anger behind her skewed glasses. "You and your ghosts," she spat out. "You and Ambrosia both, with all your ghosts." She shook her head slowly, disapprovingly, which made her look much older than her twenty-two years.

I pulled my head back, knocking the passenger side window. "My ghosts? Mine?"

"You're both Spirit Cursed," she said, eyes still blazing, her voice taking on a raspy edge. "Death follows you. Death awaits you. Death is all around you."

My cheeks burned. "Me? You're blaming *me* for the existence of death?"

She said nothing. Her eyes said it all.

"Listen, honey. Death is part of life," I said. "If you're angry about existence, take it up with someone else. Don't take it out on me."

The passenger side door opened of its own accord. Fine by me!

I stepped out. "And another thing," I said, getting worked up enough for my hand to start waving around as though it also had a few things on its mind.

The car door slammed on its own, cutting me off before things really got heated.

CHAPTER 12

Moments later, I was still standing on the sidewalk, fuming about Fatima, when another car rolled up. It was Foxy Pumpkin, the vehicle I shared with my daughter, and Zoey was driving. Ambrosia Abernathy, our coven's newest member and Zoey's best friend, was in the passenger seat.

"Hi, girls," I said as they stepped out. "It's not what it looks like. I was just," I waved in the direction that Fatima had gone, "getting to have the perfect last word in an argument. You can only do that when the other party is gone."

Zoey gave me a thoughtful look. "That's exactly what it looked like."

Ambrosia nodded. "I figured the same thing." She looked me up and down. "You're wearing a lot of pink. I thought redheads couldn't wear pink."

"Pink is trending in the redhead world," I said airily.

Zoey chimed in, "Is that a costume? Are you supposed to be cotton candy?"

"Ha ha," I said. "Make fun of me all you want. That's all I'm good for today."

The teen girls exchanged raised eyebrows, then looked down at the snow.

"Here's a question for you," I said to Ambrosia. "Has Fatima Nix ever said anything derogatory to you about being Spirit Charmed? Like that you're cursed, and that death is always around you?"

Ambrosia winced and glanced around. In a hushed tone, she said, "We don't know for sure if that's even what I am?" Ambrosia's voice rose up at the end, turning her statement into a question. Her habit of talking in upspeak had improved lately, along with her confidence, but wasn't entirely gone.

"You've got to be Spirit Charmed," I said. "Besides me, you were the only other witch who saw the Shadow, and you tagged along with us into my aunt's memories. You can see ghosts, just like me."

"But *am I* just like you?"

"I do realize those are some pointy boots to fill, but why not?"

Zoey cleared her throat. "Perhaps this discussion could take place inside a house." She pointed at our porch. "How about that one? It looks nice."

* * *

We sat in the living room, which had recently had its furniture rearranged. The house must have been doing some redecorating, as I hadn't moved the chairs and sofa around, and it wasn't something Zoey did. The new layout was not ideal for watching movies, but perfect for a social conversation between three people. The only area that seemed unfinished was a wide-open patch near the front window. The imbalance made the room feel like it was holding its breath, waiting for someone or something else to arrive.

"I think that space must be for our Christmas tree," Zoey said. "If we put one right there, next to the window, people will be able see the twinkling lights from outside."

"We could get a big tree this year," I said. "A real one that smells of the forest, and drops needles and everything. We're not in a tiny apartment anymore."

Zoey looked wistful. "It was a good apartment, though. I used to love decorating for Christmas."

"We brought all the decorations with us, so you can love decorating this place, too." I tapped my fingers and surveyed the imbalanced living room some more. "Is that fireplace new?"

Zoey answered, "We had a fireplace last week, but it was smaller. This one is much better for hanging stockings." She addressed the ceiling. "Nice work, house!"

Zoey turned to her friend and started telling her about our collection of tree-shaped air fresheners, which we'd brought with us on the move, as well as the ornaments she'd made as crafting projects over the years.

I watched the exchange with motherly happiness. They were becoming such good friends. Had I done this? I'd encouraged my daughter to make friends with the local teen girl who drove a hearse, and whose family ran a funeral home, but I'd only been partly serious.

When I met the girl myself, we'd both been independently looking into the death of Harry Blackstone, back before he merged with his brother Bill and became Barry. Ambrosia had suspected me of killing him—me!— since his ghost was often around me. After that, the two of us had a magical dust-up, and the young witch impressed me with her powers—by which I mean she knocked me out hard with an inebriation spell.

Ambrosia Abernathy looked exactly like the sort of kid who might have an interest in lurking around graveyards. She had an unnaturally pale complexion and a round face, like a full moon. Her eyes were dark and large, thickly rimmed with dark eyeliner and bruise-purple eyeshadow. Her natural hair must have been as dark as her eyebrows, but she bleached it a shade of titanium. The kids had all sorts of new terms for her look, but back in my day, she would have been called a goth, and her hair would have been black instead of nearly white.

Zoey finished telling Ambrosia about our Christmas rituals, and asked, "What about your family? Do the Abernathys have a lot of traditions?"

Ambrosia, who was staring at the empty patch by the window, seemed to not hear the question. When asked what was on her mind, she said, "Your house has something else planned for that spot."

"Like what?" Zoey asked.

Ambrosia shrugged.

"Some help you are," I said. "Look around. We've got a new, bigger fireplace for hanging stockings, green velvet curtains—also new, I think—and a cozy conversation pit here for socializing. You have to admit that a Christmas tree would be the most logical addition to the room."

"The correct position for a Christmas tree is in the *center* of a front room window," Ambrosia said. "It's traditional, or at least that's how we do it at my house. That spot is off to the side."

"You're right," Zoey said. To me, she said, "Ambrosia's right, and you're wrong. She knows about normal Christmas traditions."

I playfully tossed a pillow at my daughter. "I don't like this new dynamic where you and your friend gang up on me."

Zoey lobbed the pillow right back, and the three-way pillow fight began.

Ambrosia and I had magic to boost our tosses, but Zoey had her fox-like cunning. She got me right in the mouth with one of Boa's catnip toys.

I spat out the dank, vaguely minty cat toy, which was in the shape of a lobster. "You win," I cried. "Zoey is the winner of the living room stuffed-items toss."

We got settled down again, and opened some cranberry-flavored sodas for refreshment.

Ambrosia, her moon face serious once more, wanted to know why I'd asked her about Fatima insulting her powers.

I started telling them what I'd been up to that Sunday morning. I explained everything: the interview at the hospital with Dr. Ankh, Nick's shiner, the bar receipt, my investigation at Becky's Roadhouse, the suspicion on Xavier Batista, and then my blowout with Fatima in her luxurious car.

Boa passed through the room, sniffed all of our soda cans, walking over us like we were furniture, then left.

Ribbons flitted through, muttering about a popcorn hangover, then left to see what Boa was up to.

When I was done telling the girls why they'd found me in an agitated state on the sidewalk, Ambrosia nodded and said, "I didn't want to say anything at the time, but when we pulled up, I did notice you were drunk."

I rolled my eyes. "I only had two shots at Becky's. Practically nothing. Witches metabolize alcohol rapidly. Oh, but why am I telling you that? You're the expert on getting people drunk, though you do it by magic, and without their consent."

Ambrosia fidgeted. "I thought we were past that."

I took in a deep breath and sighed. "We are. You're a good witch, Ambrosia. Better than most. Dealing with spirits is tricky business, and you wouldn't have been given your charms if you weren't up to the task." I shook my finger at her. "Don't let Fatima Nix or her aunt, Maisy, or any of the others tell you otherwise."

"Did Fatima really say that we're cursed?"

"Yes. And I don't think she came up with that idea all on her own."

Zoey made a tsk sound, the way she did whenever she thought I was being mean about Fatima.

"Come on," I said to my daughter. "She's not wearing the pointiest of witch hats."

"People are smart in different ways," Zoey said. It was just like a person who was smart in *every* way to say that about other people.

"I'm glad Fatima is in the coven," Ambrosia said. "She makes the rest of us seem brilliant."

"The rest of us *are* brilliant," I said. *Oops*. I'd accidentally paid a compliment to Margaret Mills. Too late to take it back. Somewhere across town, Margaret's ears were probably ringing.

"I think she must be insecure," Zoey said. "Fatima's not as powerful as you two, so she has to find fault in your skills to make herself feel better." She hugged a pillow to her chest. "I'm smart at school, and everyone knows it. Some people are intimidated. That's why most of my friends until now have been the mean girls who think they know everything."

"I'd argue with you," I said, "but that is a perfect description of Francie and Jade, the two Tanyas, and even Brianna, to some degree."

Zoey gasped and dropped the pillow into her lap. "Mom, I've got it. Fatima is your Brianna."

Ambrosia, who was familiar with the antics of Zoey's old friends back home, nodded slowly. "Fatima is the new Brianna," she repeated.

"So, I'm just supposed to put up with her, or move to a new town?"

Both of the girls shrugged.

There was a cool breeze on the back of my neck.

I knew that feeling.

A ghost had entered the room.

CHAPTER 13

I wasn't the only one who noticed the ghost entering my living room.

Ambrosia's eyes bulged and her head jerked back. She stared at the air over my shoulder.

Zoey couldn't see ghosts, but she did notice the energy in the room had changed. She watched her friend expectantly.

Ambrosia leaned over and hissed at Zoey, "It's happening."

Zoey bounced up and down excitedly on the couch. "What's happening, Ambrosia? Do you see her? The ghost?" To me, she said, "I thought Mrs. Pinkman was haunting around here earlier today. I swear I could smell her perfume. I went out and picked up Ambrosia so she could be my seeing-eye person."

"You picked her up?" I asked. "Why couldn't she drive herself over?"

"The hearse is getting some repairs."

"I thought she drove that thing because it was reliable."

Zoey shrugged. "Even the most reliable car needs repairs."

"Or maybe she drives a hearse to make a fashion statement, and she only *tells* people it's because it's reliable, because she doesn't want people to think she's a poser."

Another shrug. "People lie to themselves and others about the strangest things. Even you."

"Do not."

"Mom. You claim that all of your clothes are comfortable when I know for sure they are not."

"Like what?"

"How about your hoop skirts with all the crinolines? Some of them weigh over five pounds."

"It's nice to lose five pounds at the end of the day. It's pure bliss to take off a corset and a hoop skirt, and put on sweatpants. Being liberated makes you appreciate liberation in general. What could be more comfortable?"

Zoey rolled her eyes.

We returned our attention to the haunting in progress.

Ambrosia raised a shaking finger and pointed in my direction. "I see something. Someone. I see an old lady."

I crossed my arms. "An old lady? You had *better* be talking about Mrs. Pinkman, and she'd *better* be standing right behind me."

"Describe her," Zoey urged.

"She has white hair, and it's tied up in a bun," Ambrosia said. "She's wearing one of those old lady smocks, and rubber gardening clogs."

"That's Mrs. Pinkman," Zoey said. "You're definitely Spirit Charmed, just like Mom. What a coincidence that, out of all the thousands of specialties, you both have the same one."

"I had it first," I said.

Zoey turned to me. She didn't have to turn far. The three of us were seated in a perfect triangle. "Mom, why is Mrs. Pinkman still around?"

"I do have a theory," I said. "Remember how she used to get into regular arguments with Hortense Hutchins?"

"Those two," Zoey said, shaking her head.

I explained to Ambrosia, "Our old apartment building had a lot of elderly ladies living on their own. You'd think they'd all get along, because they were so sweet and harmless, with their baking and their patio gardening, but there was always drama. It was as bad as high school, except with no parents to step in and sort it out. Hortense Hutchins loved her bible, and Minerva Pinkman was always rolling her eyes whenever bible stories came up."

"Was she an atheist?" Ambrosia asked, her eyes still fixed on the ghost.

"If you're implying that Mrs. Pinkman is refusing to move on out of sheer stubbornness, a refusal to believe in the afterlife, then you're catching on to my theory. Good work."

"I don't think that's how it works," Zoey said. "You can't just refuse to move on because you don't believe in it. Can you?"

I shrugged, and turned to Ambrosia. "Perhaps there's a witch in the room who can sift through the spirit's memories for a clue."

Ambrosia's jaw dropped. She held one hand to her chest. "You want *me* to mess around with the ghost of your friend?"

"Not *mess around*," I said. "We've already prepped you with the rezoning spell, which is probably why she didn't shoot up your nostrils instantly. You haven't tested your powers since the modification. Now's your chance."

Ambrosia squeaked out, "Now? Right now?"

"If not now, when? At least I can vouch for Mrs. Pinkman. You're not going to see anything too horrific inside her memories. I can't say the same about whatever random ghost pops up next."

Ambrosia clasped her hands together in front of her chin, looking very small and young, which she was.

"You can do it," Zoey said to her friend. "You have to see if the modifications worked. I remember what it was like before Mom altered her powers. Whenever she got a new ghost, it would take over and change her personality. Sometimes for the better, but it was still unsettling."

I pulled my knees up and rotated in my chair to face Mrs. Pinkman.

"Mrs. Pinkman," I said. "Do you understand what we're talking about?"

She smiled sweetly and pointed to the empty space in front of the window.

"Nod once if you can understand me," I said.

She looked behind herself, then pointed at the window again.

"Good talk," I said, then turned around again.

I said to Ambrosia, "We could play charades with her all day, but we won't get anywhere. At times, they seem to know where they are and what's happening, but it's fleeting. You'll have to use magic. Do you want me to walk you through it again? Do a refresh on the rezoning spell?"

Ambrosia unclasped her hands and shook them out. "I can do it," she said.

In unison, Zoey and I said, "Of course you can."

Ambrosia said, "But not if you're both watching me. Can the two of you," she waved her hand dismissively "go somewhere else?"

"We'll go downstairs," I said.

Zoey wrinkled her nose. "It's too dark in your lair, and the days are already short enough now that it's winter. Can we go outside?"

"Sure. We can go for a walk," I said. "Or we can go shopping at Mia's. I bet she has a new antique that would fit perfectly in our empty spot."

"Just go," Ambrosia said. "Go before I lose my nerve."

I got up. "Fine. First I'm kicked out of a car, then my own house. This is my life now."

Zoey got up and patted me on the shoulder as she walked past me. "You love it. You were so bored last month, when nothing weird happened to you."

"It's true," I admitted. The only real magic excitement I'd had in November was casting the giant spell to alter Ambrosia's powers the way I had altered mine. And even that was a way bigger deal for her than it was for me.

We left Ambrosia to her task of charming the stubbornly atheistic spirit of Mrs. Pinkman.

When we got outside, Xavier Batista was walking in our direction, on the other side of the street, carrying a cardboard tray with a trio of takeout coffee cups from Dreamland.

I waved and cried out, "Hey, neighbor! How's it going?"

He stopped in his tracks abruptly. Splashes of coffee escaped from the tops of the takeout containers and dribbled down the protective sleeves.

"Uh, hi, Zara," he said. "Hi, Zoey. Wow. You two sure look alike."

"What's with the coffee?" I asked. "Don't you have a coffee maker in your new place?" Xavier and his cousin had recently moved into a renovated garage across the street from my place. Zoey and I had brought over a housewarming gift of various jams and nut butters.

He lifted the tray an inch. "I do have a coffee maker, but we're out of filters."

"You can use paper towel in a pinch."

"We were also out of paper towel. And coffee beans."

"So you went out and got coffee beans, filters, and paper towels so you don't encounter the exact same problem tomorrow?"

His tan-colored cheeks reddened. He dropped his gaze to the steaming takeout cups on his tray. "Uh..."

"Don't let my mother shame you," Zoey cut in. "If you could see some of the things I've found in our coffeemaker..."

She had a point.

"Xavier," I said slowly. "Do you have a minute to chat about something a little more serious than coffee?" I wanted to confirm he'd punched Nick Lafleur Friday night, and hopefully confirm he had an alibi for Saturday morning.

"Sure," he said. "Any time. Do you mean now?"

Zoey let out a moan of pure mortification. She liked hearing *about* my investigations, but she didn't relish witnessing the process. She was a mature and responsible teenager, but she was still a teenager. She was scandalized by anything out-of-the-box her mother did.

Was this really the time and place to question Xavier?

I remembered what Fatima had said about me gathering information in a non-official capacity, and the invalidity of any evidence I might find.

No, I wasn't going to mortify my daughter further, or mess up the investigation.

I would pass the bar receipt along to Bentley, along with the tip that Xavier probably punched Nick on Friday night. I would let the detective deal with it, assuming Nick's injury had been more than a freak accident in the first place. I would be a good witch and mind my own affairs. Besides, I had enough on my hands with Mrs. Pinkman.

"Never mind," I said to Xavier. "It can wait until our next bowling session."

Zoey exhaled in relief.

Xavier looked disappointed. "Are you sure? I'm not doing anything important."

"Aren't you hanging out with your girlfriend? Liza Gilbert?"

His eyes widened. "How did you know? Are you reading my mind right now?"

"Relax. It was just a guess. You've got three coffees. One for you, one for your roommate, and one for Liza."

"Two hazelnut and one vanilla," Zoey said. She tapped the side of her nose. "Keen sense of smell." She liked casually mentioning aspects of her powers around people who were in the know. She said it made her feel more normal.

Xavier rubbed the back of his neck and gave us a sheepish look. "Must be nice for you Riddles to have all those powers you've got. I wish I could, uh, do stuff."

"Careful what you wish for," I said.

He blinked once, then pulled his head back and snorted. "Easy for you to say." He backed away, shook his head, turned, and walked off at a brisk pace without saying goodbye.

"We offended him," Zoey said.

"Without even trying," I said.

"It's probably for the best you didn't ask him about fighting with Nick Lafleur. Xavier does live across the street from us, and it would be awkward to bump into him regularly after you accuse him of homicide."

"It's not even homicide," I said. "Nick isn't dead. It would only be *attempted* homicide."

"Can't you just wait until Nick wakes up, and ask him who hit him on the head?"

"We could, but what if the person snuck up and hit him from behind?"

"Ah," she said. "Then Detective Bentley and Detective Rose will have their work cut out for them." She grabbed my arm and tugged me toward the car. "Come on. I'm driving," she said.

"Fine by me. While you drive, I'll call Bentley and pass along the information about the bar fight, and let him know Xavier's at home now in case he wants to drop in."

"And flirt with him."

"That, too."

CHAPTER 14

Xavier Batista

Ordinarily, a neighborly chat with the two younger Riddles would have made Xavier's whole day, but he walked away from the Sunday mid-day encounter with a storm cloud over his head. All because Zara Riddle had teased him to be careful what he wished for.

It was easy for her to say, now that she had incredible powers of her own. It was like a genius insisting that other people were smart in their own way. It was like a wealthy person telling an impoverished person to cheer up because having heaps of money wasn't as much fun as it looked. It was a pat on the head and a "there, there." It was an affront to Xavier's deepest desires, not to mention his dignity.

What she'd said had been, to her, casual chit-chat.

What he'd heard was, "Be content with your lot in life as a nothing person. Be grateful the rest of us let you live and breathe, instead of crushing you under our heels like the cockroach you are."

He stomped up the stairs to the upper story entrance to his home. The steps rattled beneath his heavy plodding.

After a moment of frustration with the needlessly complicated lock system Ubaid had installed on the door, he banged it open with a forceful shove.

Ubaid was standing in the kitchen, eyes wide in terror. "It's just you," she said, holding one thin, long-fingered hand to her chest. "I thought goblin hordes were at the door."

He grumbled out a few raw sounds.

"Someone woke up on the wrong side of the bed," his cousin and roommate said. "At least you have coffee." She plucked hers from the tray. "I have to run off to work. Got called in." She grabbed her coat and the big medical bag that doubled as her purse and went everywhere with her.

"Have fun at the lab with Dr. Ankh, breeding those flying monkeys."

"Ha ha," she said, sailing out the front door. "We're out of toilet paper," she called back over her shoulder.

Xavier went to the kitchen, refilled the water pitcher that Ubaid had left empty, and then brought the two remaining cups of takeout coffee downstairs to his room.

Liza Gilbert was stretched out on Xavier's bed in her underwear, scrolling on her phone. She barely looked up.

Liza was the person who'd been knocking on the door on Saturday morning, after Xavier and Ubaid's argument about him sending in his blood for DNA tests.

Twenty-four hours ago, Liza had shown up unannounced, with bagels and cream cheese. She had assumed—correctly—that there would be no fresh food at the house.

Now, twenty-four hours later, she was still there at the house. It was the longest stretch of time the two had spent together since being held captive by timeline-policing sandworms in another world.

Ever since the incident, Liza would get anxious about being in an enclosed space with Xavier for too long, citing

PTSD. Her therapist thought it was something else, but what did therapists know?

Lately she'd been getting more comfortable being around him for long periods. It should have been pleasant, but it wasn't. Xavier was starting to realize that scarcity had been part of Liza's appeal.

Now she was lounging on Xavier's bed as though it were her own. At least she was only wearing underwear. He rarely got tired of looking at her.

"She's so fake," Liza was saying, her focus still on her phone screen. "These pictures have been filtered and enhanced so much, she doesn't even look like herself."

"Who are you looking at?" He put the coffee cups on the dresser, pushing around magazines to clear space.

Liza paused before saying, "Larissa Lang."

"Isn't that the actress who used to be married to—"

"Yes," she snapped. "But that's not why I'm looking at her account."

"Then why are you looking at her account?"

Liza ignored him and kept scrolling.

"Stop looking at her if she bugs you so much," he said.

"Meh meh meh meh meh meh," she said, mocking him.

Xavier grabbed the phone away. Liza squealed and tried to get it back. He held the phone out of reach with his long arms. She tickled him. He tackled her. She twisted her body out of his grasp.

Xavier played weak and let her get the upper hand. She pinned his arms. She was straddling him, tickling again, and things were getting interesting when there was a loud knocking sound.

Someone was on the other side of the garage door, banging on that instead of the upstairs entrance.

Liza jumped off the bed and started pulling on her clothes. "Who's that? Can they see in here?"

"I dunno," he said, covering both questions.

The garage door had frosted glass panels. A silhouette of one person, a man, was visible.

Xavier fumbled around on his dresser, looking for the remote garage door opener. He couldn't find it, so he crossed over to the wall and pressed the button. The mechanical garage door's overhead motor lurched into life.

Liza squealed. "I'm not dressed yet! Now you're letting in the cold air!"

The frosted glass door rolled up slowly, revealing a dark pair of men's dress shoes, gray wool suit trousers with a sharp crease, and then the rest of the man. It was Detective Theodore Bentley, looking calm, cool, and savagely stylish in gray as usual.

Xavier knew a little about the detective. He was new in town, he used to be married to a super-hot actress named Larissa Lang, and now he was a vampire. Plus he was dating the hottest witch in town. Some guys had all the luck.

Bentley said nothing as he casually assessed the contents of Xavier's garage-bedroom, which was looking more disgraceful by the second. Unmade bed. Piles of laundry, dirty and clean. Dirty plates from meals. Stacks of workout magazines with muscled men on the covers. The last item was the most embarrassing, given Xavier's scrawny physique. If he wasn't doing the workouts, as evidenced by his wiry body, why did he have magazines with muscled men on the covers?

Xavier grabbed a pile of clothes and tossed it on top of the magazines.

Bentley saw everything, watching with those mercury eyes of his, but said nothing.

Liza danced her way over to the detective on tip-toe, braving the cold air valiantly. "Hi, Theo! What a nice surprise. Have you been here before? I would have had Xavier tidy up if we'd known you were coming." She wrinkled her nose. "He's such a messy boy," she said, emphasis on the word *boy*.

"It's fine," he said gruffly.

Liza reached out and stroked the lapel of the vampire detective's overcoat. "Is this wool? You have the best personal style. Do you have your clothes custom made? It's not off the rack. At least not in this small town."

Xavier's eye twitched. Could Liza be any more obvious about her crush if she tried? He actually felt embarrassed on her behalf.

"Hey, man," Xavier said with a chin lift. He was playing it *much* cooler than Liza, even though he also had a crush—a man crush—on the suave detective.

"Do you like bagels?" Liza asked. "They're a day old, but they're still good. I brought them over yesterday because Xavier is the sort of boy who lives on porkchops and ramen noodles."

"Thanks for the offer," Bentley said. "I'm not here to eat."

"Boo," Liza said, sticking her lips out in an exaggerated pout. In her rush to get dressed, she had "forgotten" to fasten the top three buttons on her shirt, and her lacy bra was showing.

"They're good bagels," Xavier said. "Poppy seed. No raisins." He was warming up to the idea of having the detective come in and break bread with them, even if it meant having to watch Liza fawning over the older man.

Bentley fixed Xavier with his glinting metallic eyes. "I need a word with you," he said. "Just you."

Liza sniffed dramatically, then turned with a head whip. "A girl can sense when she's not wanted," she said, channeling the spirit of a fussy dame from a black-and-white movie. She slowly gathered her things from around the room, including one of the takeout coffees. She gave Xavier a peck on the cheek, then left through the wide-open garage door.

As she walked away down the street, she pulled on her black hat with the ear flaps—the one that made her look, from a distance, like she had black hair.

Bentley, still standing outside the garage door's boundary line, glanced at the messy bed, then at Xavier. "I hope I didn't interrupt anything important."

"No, man. Well, yeah, sort of, but it's all good. Not my last chance. Liza's engine runs a little hot if you know what I mean."

The corner of Bentley's mouth moved up almost imperceptibly. "Sure," he said. "I know what you mean."

"Come on in," Xavier said. "Welcome to my lair."

Bentley arched an eyebrow. "It's not much of a lair." He glanced around. "But it has lair potential."

Xavier hit the button to close the garage door. The detective was wearing multiple layers of gray wool and didn't seem affected by the cold, but Xavier was dressed only in a pair of sweatpants. He apologized for the mess, yanked the duvet across the bed, and pulled on the nearest T-shirt. The shirt was, unfortunately, one of Liza's. It was small and pale blue. With a kitten graphic. And a pink bow.

Bentley cleared his throat. "You were involved in an altercation on Friday night, at the Roadhouse. You punched a young man named Nick Lafleur."

"Is that a question?"

"Should it be?"

"Is that what you're here about?"

"Would it be more believable that I came for the bagels?"

"Did Nick file a complaint against me?"

"Should he have?"

"Am I in some sort of trouble?"

"Should you be?"

"I dunno," Xavier said. "Can we start again, from the top?"

"Were you at Becky's Roadhouse Bar and Grill on Friday night?"

"Yes. I went there after bowling. Good game, by the way. The way you terrorize those pins, it's impressive."

"Were you involved in an altercation with Nick Lafleur?"

Xavier rubbed his knuckles. There was no getting out of this, so he might as well face the music.

"Yeah," Xavier said. "You could call it an altercation. His face ran into my hand."

Bentley pulled a small notepad from his breast pocket and made a note. "Nick Lafleur's face ran into Xavier Batista's hand," he repeated back as he wrote.

"When his face ran into my hand, it was entirely in self-defense."

"Self-defense." Another note. The pencil tip scratched on the paper. "That means he struck you first. Or that he threatened you or another party."

"Did I say self-defense? That might not be the exact right phrase. What's it called when a guy who used to hook up with your girlfriend is looking at her, and talking to her, while touching her arm and her shoulder and looking down her shirt, right in front of you?"

Bentley paused before saying, "Life. It's called life, son."

"Well, I felt threatened."

"Is that so?"

"He was *threatening* to take Liza away from me, so naturally I acted in self-defense by showing him my fist. Then his face ran into it. You could call it a misunderstanding."

"So you say." Bentley made another note on the pad. "The next morning, Saturday, at Nick's cabin, was it a similar misunderstanding?"

"Saturday morning?" Xavier rubbed his eyes. His whole face felt itchy. It must have been the vitamins in the banana bag that Ubaid gave him the day before. "I haven't been anywhere but here for the last," he did the mental calculations, "thirty-six hours. Except to get coffee, just now."

Bentley nodded. "I trust you have someone who will vouch for your whereabouts. Perhaps the owner of that kitten T-shirt you're wearing, whom I assume is Ms. Gilbert."

"Liza can vouch for me, sure."

"She stayed the whole weekend? Friday and Saturday night?"

"Not exactly," Xavier said. "She came over Saturday. But you can talk to my roommate, Ubaid. She'll tell you I was here Saturday morning. Did something happen on Saturday? Something with Nick Lafleur?"

Bentley ignored the questions and glanced at the stairwell. "Is your roommate here now?"

"She got called into work, at the hospital. She didn't say which one, and she works with Dr. Ankh at both of them." He couldn't take wearing Liza's tight kitten shirt anymore, so he peeled it off. He immediately regretted doing so. Standing half-naked in front of the mature, well-dressed detective didn't feel any more dignified.

"Ubaid," Bentley said, making another note. "Last name, O'Connor?"

"You know her?"

"I know who she is." He tapped the pad of paper and looked at Xavier.

Xavier couldn't take more than a few seconds of the detective looking directly at his bare chest before he broke and reached for a different shirt. This one was dirty, like most of the clothes in the room, but at least it fit.

The detective was still standing there, unmoving. He seemed to be contemplating something.

"Can I do anything else for you, sir?"

"You have no marks on your body. The fight with Nick Lafleur must have ended quickly. Who broke it up?"

"Oh, that's easy. It was your partner. Not Zara. The other one. Persephone."

The vampire's expression changed. It was almost imperceptible, but Xavier caught it, and it chilled him more than the cold air that had blown in from the open garage door.

"I see," Bentley said. "Tell me something."

"Sure! What do you want me to tell you?"

"Only the truth. Did Detective Rose leave the bar with Nick Lafleur?"

"I didn't see the two of them go. Liza took off with her friends, and then people started playing ukuleles and singing, and it got too weird for me, so I took off. But before I left, Nick and Persephone were..." Xavier's throat closed up. He felt like he was tattling on a friend, to her dad.

The vampire's stare intensified. "They were what?"

"Looking like two people about to hook up."

The vampire was suddenly directly in front of him, inches from his face.

Xavier's jaw dropped. He knew the man had speed, but knowing it and experiencing it were different things.

They were eye to eye. Bentley outweighed Xavier by thirty pounds of supernaturally strong muscle, but the man and the boy were the same height.

Xavier stammered, "Y-y-you can bite me if you want, but don't kill me." He was shocked to hear the words coming from his mouth, but not surprised. Wasn't this what he wanted? Wasn't this what everyone wanted? To be touched by the powerful, even if it left damage?

"I don't bite," Bentley said.

Xavier didn't believe it for a second. Especially not when the fangs flashed.

"Thank you for your time," the vampire said, and then he was gone.

The garage-bedroom was cold and empty.

Xavier's legs buckled. He let himself fall backward onto the messy bed.

CHAPTER 15

Sunday Afternoon
Detective Persephone Rose

Persephone rolled her chair back from her workstation computer. She remained seated, her palms on her knees, trying to calm her breathing.

At times like these, the new detective wished she could turn into her fox form and run away. But she wasn't a teenager anymore. She was an adult, twenty-six, with a serious job, and responsibilities. Kids got away with shenanigans, but adults didn't. She had screwed up royally, and now she had to face the music.

How bad would it be? The meeting had to be about the car. She'd all but ruined her department-issue sedan. It wasn't a new model, thankfully, but it hadn't been a clunker. How bad could the consequences be? People had accidents all the time. They were called accidents because they didn't happen on purpose.

She got to her feet and marched to the office of the new Chief of Police. It was the same office the old Chief had used, which was on the corner, with two nice windows. Rumor had it the room had a great view. She'd been summoned there once before, during her undercover assignment on the Krinkle case. At that time, she'd been too worried about screwing up to admire the view.

The whole Wisteria Police Department was quiet, even for a Sunday. She was grateful for that. If she was going to get chewed out, it was better to have fewer witnesses around.

She entered the office of Chief Ethan Fung. The newly-appointed chief, who'd been a detective before his accident and leave of absence, was seated behind the large desk. The office smelled of fresh paint. The walls were painted a strange green-yellow that reminded Persephone of overcooked peas. The color might have been ugly on its own, but it complemented the two wood bookcases. Fung was positioned between the bookcases, his head framed by a large painting of the sea.

Fung was an older guy, older than Bentley. Unlike many of the hairy cops at the station, Fung kept his face clean shaven and had his hair cut twice a month. Even his eyebrows looked like they might get waxed. He was cute, for an older guy. It helped that he smiled a lot. The guy was always in a light, easy mood, which made it easy to be around him. Unless, of course, he was sitting behind his big desk like he was now, not grinning.

He wasn't alone. Sitting in one of the visitor chairs was her partner, Detective Theodore Bentley. Why was he there? He hadn't been involved in the car accident.

Not good, Persephone thought. *Not good at all.*

She took a seat.

Nobody spoke.

Persephone broke the silence. "Whatever happens, whatever you decide to do to me, I completely understand," she said. "I'll take whatever punishment you deem appropriate. I can handle it."

Fung looked more amused than angry. He said, "What punishment do you think would be appropriate, Detective Rose?"

"I'll pay for the damage to the car," she said. "And also for the tow truck. You can take it out of my pay in installments."

The two men exchanged a look.

"The roads were really icy," she said. "I reached for my phone, but it wasn't where it was supposed to be." She quickly added, "Not that I would answer my phone while driving. I wouldn't. I was going to pull over."

The new Chief said, "I'm not concerned about the car."

Bentley was silent, as usual.

"If this isn't about the car, what's going on?"

Neither spoke.

She thought about the other thing she was feeling guilty about, realized she was there about *that* matter, and considered turning into a fox and running away.

Not this time, she told herself. This wasn't the type of danger her ability was to be used for.

Slowly, she asked, "Is it because I was seen acting in a manner unbecoming to the uniform?"

"You don't wear a uniform," Fung said. "But we could call it that."

She crossed her arms and asked, "When? When was I allegedly committing this offense?"

"Friday night," Fung said.

"That's not fair," she said. "I was off duty on Friday night. What I do in my free time is my business."

Fung raised an eyebrow.

She knew she was sticking her foot in her mouth, but she continued on anyway. "You're not my dad," she said defiantly. "Neither of you are. I can do what I want in my free time. I didn't do anything illegal."

Bentley leaned forward an inch, looking like he might say something, but didn't.

"This isn't fair," she said. "I didn't do anything wrong. Not really."

"You should have filed a report," Fung said.

"About who I sleep with?" She got to her feet. "Oh, that's unbelievable. Is it because I'm a woman? Does that make my romantic life everyone else's business? I'm not going to take this."

"Sit down," Fung said calmly. He was still seated, but she had the impression he could beat her to the door if he wanted to. His energy was tightly coiled, hard to miss.

She did sit down.

"You broke up a bar fight," Fung said. "There's no mention of the incident in the files. I realize it was a minor altercation, with only one solid punch landed, but you were involved. Rose, I called you in here because if you'd filed an incident report, it would have saved everyone a lot of time on the investigation."

"What investigation?" She looked from one man's face to the other for clues.

"Nick Lafleur is unconscious at the hospital," Fung said.

She gasped. "Oh, no! Is he hurt?" She'd thought about Nick plenty since the previous morning, but had been busy at her house, and hadn't heard the news.

"He's unconscious at the hospital," Fung repeated. "He's not getting a spa treatment."

Bentley leaned toward her and held out a closed fist over her lap. "Are these yours?"

"Are *what* mine?"

He dropped a pair of earrings into her open hand. They were emerald studs, in an ornate setting. She recognized them immediately. They were antiques, so the odds of them being someone else's were incredibly slim.

"They're mine," she said.

Bentley said, "I was surprised to find them at Nick Lafleur's cabin. On a table next to his bed."

She felt her face growing hot, but kept her chin up. "I must have left them at Nick's in my rush to get out."

"That's what I thought," Bentley said.

"And why were you in a rush?" Fung asked. "Was it because you'd just bashed Mr. Lafleur on the head with a hardwood lamp?"

She gasped again. Tears came to her eyes, humiliating her even further. She had to get control over her emotions before she ruined everything. She blinked down the tears and set her chin, composing herself.

"I left Nick Lafleur in excellent condition," she said neutrally. "I am sorry to hear he was injured. When did the incident happen?"

"Early Saturday morning," Fung said.

She held up both hands. "Well? Do you have any suspects?"

The men said nothing.

She dropped her hands to her lap and played with the earrings. "Let me save you some time," she said. "It's very simple. I didn't hurt Nick. You can take me off the suspect list. How bad was it?"

"He's stable," Bentley said. "Zara gave him first aid, and Dr. Ankh is treating him."

Persephone let out a sigh of relief.

Fung looked down at some papers on his desk.

Bentley avoided eye contact with his partner, focusing instead on the titles of the books on the Chief's bookshelves.

Persephone busied her hands, taking the backs off the emerald earrings and replacing them in her ears. The emeralds were one of her favorite pairs, and she wasn't surprised Bentley had noticed them at Nick's place and connected them to her. He was good at his job.

In the silence, a thought occurred to her. A pleasant one. She had been waiting for Nick to call her on Saturday. He'd promised he would, when he was rushing her out the door Saturday morning. But if he had been unconscious this whole time, then he couldn't have phoned anyone, could he?

She looked out the Chief's window. The view was nice, especially with the fresh snow on everything.

She wondered when Nick would be feeling better, and if he might take her ice skating.

Bentley broke the silence, asking, "Did anything unusual happen on Saturday morning between you and Nick Lafleur?"

Persephone had thought she was blushing at maximum capacity, but felt her cheeks flush again. Plenty happened between her and the night zookeeper, but nothing that she wanted to discuss with two men who were giving her a serious Disappointed Dad vibe.

"Nothing suspicious," she stated. "It's the truth. My word is my bond. I did not harm that man, or wish him harm." The magic of her word bond kicked in and she found herself adding, "Except for last night, and this morning, when he didn't call. But I only wished him mild harm, like a bad hangnail."

Both Fung and Bentley started talking at the same time.

Bentley said, "Go ahead, Chief."

Fung held up both hands and shook his head. "My mistake," he said to Bentley. "Sometimes I forget that you're *me* now."

Bentley tilted his head. "I'm you?"

"You're the detective," Fung said. "I'm not, sadly. As much as I'd love to dig into this case and find out who did what to Nick with the business end of a lamp, that's not my job anymore. Not since I was... promoted."

Persephone got the feeling Fung was less than thrilled about his promotion. She understood. Being the Chief came with its perks, but also a lot of responsibilities. Sitting behind a big desk couldn't be as fun as doing field work, no matter how good the view was.

Bentley said to both of them, "I was just going to ask about any other girlfriends or jealous boyfriends Nick might have..." He trailed off, looking over Persephone's head at the person who'd arrived at the doorway.

Persephone didn't turn her head. She knew by the headache-inducing perfume that it was Kelly.

Kelly said, "Sorry to interrupt, but I thought you'd like to know we got the report on the 9-1-1 call about the Lafleur case. Turns out the call originated from the log cabin after all. The whole phone system up there at the zoo is a real mess, and they have all the lines routed through the front ticket office, can you imagine? The line going up to the cabin is basically just a string and a couple of tin cans, but we're pretty sure that's where it came from. I had one of the tech guys look into it on-site. I had a recording of the call sent to your account. It should be available from your desktop under your regular login now."

"Thank you, Kelly," Fung and Bentley said in unison.

She left, along with her cloud of perfume.

Persephone resumed regular breathing.

Fung clicked on his mouse, and soon the 9-1-1 call was playing on his desktop speakers.

The voice was hoarse, the speaker gasping for air: "I'm an idiot. Come quick."

Fung played the short message a second time, then a third.

Neither detective spoke.

Chief Fung said, "I'm not a detective on this case, but it sounds to me like the Lafleur case may not be an attempted homicide after all."

"Not so fast," Persephone said. "He said he was an idiot. That could mean anything."

"Such as?"

"Maybe he picked a fight with someone tougher than him."

"He did," Bentley said. "A hardwood lamp. And gravity."

Fung snorted. "They didn't tell me you were so funny," he said to Bentley.

Persephone frowned. Bentley wasn't the funny one. *She* was the funny one.

Fung played the message again.

Persephone asked, "Are we sure that's even him?" She'd heard Nick breathing heavily while talking—never mind why—and it hadn't sounded like that. Not that she was an expert. But she did know the man more intimately than anyone else in the room.

"The call came from his cabin," Bentley said. "Why wouldn't it be him?"

"He'll wake up eventually," Fung said. "He can explain everything then."

Persephone didn't agree, but she bit her tongue.

Fung shuffled some papers on his otherwise spotless desk. "I'm glad that's settled. In the meantime, our resources might be better directed to other matters, such as your other open cases. Even excluding the reports by Old Man Wheelie about his garden gnomes being kidnapped, and the usual requests for information by Dorian Dabrowski, there's still a lot on your docket."

"Yes, Chief," Bentley said.

"Yes, Chief," Persephone said.

The two detectives left the Chief's office.

* * *

One Hour Later

"You had me worried," Bentley said, his metallic eyes glinting, hinting at emotions Persephone couldn't decipher.

They were in the break room, savoring the first two cups of coffee from a new pot. The downside of working on a Sunday was you had to make all the coffee. The upside was you got it fresh.

"I would have told you everything, but after I ditched my car on Saturday, I was cowering in my cave."

"You have a preferred cave? Nearby? Does it connect to the tunnels?"

"Not an actual cave," she said. "It's a metaphor. I was hiding at home. I didn't even check my email."

He nodded knowingly. "Because you were waiting by the phone for a fellow to call."

She snorted. He sounded so old-fashioned, calling Nick a "fellow." Bentley had the vibe of a man several generations older than he was. She wondered if it had come along with his vampire powers as a bonus gift, or if it had been a pre-existing condition.

"I was distracted by that," she admitted. "Plus I was doing that tidying up thing, where you take out all your clothes and roll up your socks while thanking them for their service to your feet."

"You were performing a ritual?"

"Sort of. You could call it a ritual. Everyone's doing it. There's a TV show about it."

"There are TV shows about everything," he said.

They sipped their coffee in unison.

Persephone opened a folder halfheartedly. Most of their cases were stored on the system in digital form, but Detective Theodore Bentley preferred printing things out on paper. He said he could think more clearly when he was looking over notes away from his computer. Yet another old-fashioned thing he did. Almost as eccentric as carrying peanuts in his pockets at all times.

She pretended to be interested in the file, but asked, "What's the deal with the Chief?"

"You tell me. We're both new here. You know him about as well as I do."

They both knew that she was referring to the Chief's supernatural powers, which neither of them had been briefed on.

Something had happened to Fung that year. Not just the accident that put him in the hospital, but something else. He'd suffered from several broken limbs.

Persephone's half-sister, Zara, had referred to him as being "broken apart like a Kit Kat bar." Horrifying as the simile was, it fit the case report. And now he showed no sign of the injuries, not even a limp.

Fung had disappeared from town for nearly a year, taking a much-deserved vacation, but even the most restful sojourn couldn't explain his perfect recovery, let alone the tight coil of energy Persephone had felt around the man.

"He smells like power," she said.

"I feel it," Bentley agreed.

"New power," she said.

"New power," he agreed.

CHAPTER 16

Sunday Evening
Zara Riddle

Persephone Rose arrived at the house for family dinner far ahead of the usual time.

"You're here early," I said.

"I can come back later," she said, but her body language said she didn't want to come back later. Her body language said she wanted to come inside and unwind with someone nice to talk to. A sister. Or even a half-sister, like me.

Persephone had inherited very few of my father's physical traits, so we didn't look like sisters to most people. She had dark hair, thick bangs, and eyes that could be joyful when she smiled, but, when resting, drooped down at the corners, giving her a melancholy appearance. She was lean and athletic in body, thanks to being young and having an interest in jogging and other sweaty sports, but her face was rounder than her body, with pale skin and rosy cheeks bordering on chubby. She had a baby-faced, youthful appearance that my aunt predicted would disappear in the next year or two, as she approached thirty.

Her eyes that day looked not just melancholy but exhausted.

I looked down at the substantial volume of wine she was carrying. Five bottles.

"Get in here," I said. "My mother didn't raise me to turn away any visitor with that amount of booze in their arms. If I did, she'd roll around in the coffin she sleeps in." My mother was a vampire, but she didn't actually sleep in a coffin—that I knew of.

"You're sure I'm not interrupting anything?"

"Get in here," I said again.

She stepped in, and handed me the wine while she took off her snowy winter boots.

I admired the rose logos on the wine labels. "This is a lot of wine. I hate to break it to you, but we're not having a big party. There are only going to be five of us for dinner."

"That's why I brought five bottles," Persephone Rose said.

"Of the five people, two of us are teenaged girls who will only be partaking... over my dead broomstick."

"Then we'd better get started now," she said, grinning.

"If I start drinking now, I'm liable to ruin dinner."

She wrinkled her nose. "Is that how it happens?"

My arms were full of wine, so I couldn't pinch her arm, except by magic. "Brat."

"Ow! You're as mean and vindictive as you are bad at not burning dinner. You are the worst."

"I'll take that as a compliment. It's always good to excel."

We stopped in the living room, where Persephone gave a curious look to Zoey and Ambrosia. "What's going on here?"

Both girls were sitting in comfortable spots, reading.

Zoey looked up and greeted her aunt.

Ambrosia's bleached-blonde head didn't move. She remained still, nodding over an open book. Seeing a pair of teen girls reading books would be ordinary enough, except Ambrosia's book was made of golden light. As we watched, the young witch flipped a shimmering page and continued reading, unaware that someone new had entered the room.

"She's lost in a good book," I explained.

Zoey went back to her reading, nearly as engrossed in her own book—a science textbook—as Ambrosia was in hers.

"I can see that much," Persephone said. "They didn't make me the station's youngest detective ever for no reason. What's the twist?"

"That glowing book isn't really a book. It's the spirit of Mrs. Minerva Pinkman."

"Pinkman," Persephone mused. "Am I supposed to know who that is? The name sounds vaguely familiar."

"She was one of our neighbors at our previous place, the apartment. Her budgie was the one who terrorized Zoey. The poor woman passed away last week, peacefully, with her dear old friend Hortense Hutchins praying at her bedside."

Persephone gave me an empathetic look. "I'm sorry to hear that. I'm sorry for your loss, Zara." Her down-turned eyes had a heartbreaking quality when she gave someone an empathetic look. I thought I'd gotten over the grief of Mrs. Pinkman's death, but it returned with double strength, thanks to a little tenderness from my half-sister.

"Thanks," I said, swallowing down the lump in my throat. "It was all very peaceful, from what Ambrosia has been able to learn. Mrs. Pinkman had been healthy and mobile, puttering around in her rubber clogs, then she started having dreams about suitcases and moving on, and sensed it might be time. She visited a lawyer, gave away a bunch of her antiques, and got all her affairs in order. After that, it was fairly quick."

"So why is she here? I thought most of your ghosts were victims of crimes."

"They're not *my* ghosts," I said, bristling at the suggestion.

"But it doesn't sound like the woman had any unfinished business." Persephone glanced around the living room. "Is she here now? Can she hear us?"

"She's contained in the glowing book," I said. "As for why she's here, a long way from her home, we don't know for sure, but we have a theory. She did tell everyone she was an atheist, so she might be here out of sheer stubbornness."

"No," Persephone said decisively. "There are a lot of atheists, and if they all stuck around as ghosts, you'd know about it." She rubbed her chin thoughtfully, then said, "What about poison? If she wasn't feeling well and sensed the end, it's possible someone was poisoning her slowly over time."

"We are definitely looking into that as a possibility. I made a few phone calls, using my charms over the phone, and everyone involved believes it was a natural death. There was no call for an autopsy, and the coroner reported nothing unusual."

Persephone asked, "Money?" She was looking for a motive, like any good detective.

"She had a modest savings account, all of which is going to a bird rescue charity," I said. "And her family knew about the will, so it wasn't a big surprise or anything."

"Enemies?" There was excitement in the young detective's voice.

"She was a sweet little old lady. The only person she fought with was Mrs. Hutchins, but the two of them only argued because, deep down, they were so close."

"Poor Mrs. Hutchins," Persephone said, giving me another heartbreaking look of empathy.

"She'll be fine," I said. "I talked to her on the phone, and she believes she prayed just enough to get her dear friend Minerva into heaven despite the whole atheism thing. She told me she can feel Minerva up there already, smiling down on us."

"It's a nice feeling for someone to have. You didn't tell her the truth, did you?"

"I'm not a monster."

Persephone smirked. "Of course not."

Ambrosia still hadn't looked up from the glowing book. Zoey was engrossed in her textbook.

We proceeded into the kitchen, where Persephone clawed the first bottle of wine open. She did the same trick I'd seen a wolf shifter named Chet Moore use, turning one fingernail into a claw to stab the cork.

"We *do* have a wine opener," I said. "Is that even hygienic?"

She blew cork bits off her long claw before retracting it. "Come on, Zara. You'd do it if you could."

"You're right. It must be fun to have a Swiss Army Hand." I got out two wine glasses. "So, what's bugging you? Did something bad happen at work today?"

Persephone turned away from my gaze, staring in the direction of the living room. "How long does it take to read a person's life like a book?"

I sensed she did want to talk about her problem, but not yet.

"Oh, you could never read the whole thing," I said. "Ambrosia's just skimming for highlights. She's been at it for hours now, parked right there in the living room. Can you believe she kicked me and Zoey out of the house? She wanted some privacy to get started. I'd just gotten home from a stressful outing with another witch, and I had to leave my comfy home again. I had to spend the whole afternoon walking in the park, then window shopping, then actual shopping."

"Poor you." She gave me a playful look. "Enjoying your Sunday afternoon while someone else does your job. How do I get one of these young people to work for me? I assume she's doing it for free."

"It's called 'having an intern.' You should look into it." I took my glass of wine, and we proceeded to the dining room, where we would have our privacy for at least an hour, assuming the pets stayed away. "Ambrosia was scared of using her powers with my modification, but I managed to convince her."

"Of course you did, Zara." Persephone's eyes twinkled. She'd inherited that from our father. "You do have a special way of convincing people to do what you want."

"Don't look at me like that. I didn't use any magic."

"Sure, you didn't." She sniffed. "Just your natural charm."

We sat in two dining room chairs across from each other. I'd had enough sisterly teasing, and was ready to hear about what was weighing on Persephone. I had some idea about what was bothering her, and wanted to hear her side of the story.

"A toast," I said, raising my glass. "What should we toast to? Your new relationship with a certain sexy zookeeper?"

Her full, rosy cheeks reddened. "You heard?"

"Through the grapevine." What I hadn't told Persephone yet was that Bentley had called me while I was out during the afternoon with Zoey. He'd phoned me shortly after speaking to the new Chief of Police, Ethan Fung. He would have talked to me first, but he respected work protocols.

Bentley had been upset about the idea of turning in his partner. I'd told him not to worry his gorgeous head about it, since the Persephone I knew wouldn't have hurt Nick, or anyone else for that matter, except possibly in self-defense.

He'd called me again after the meeting with Persephone and the new Chief, with the good news that she had been cleared of any suspicion based on her reaction in the interview.

At the time, I'd been shopping at Mia's, and had just found the perfect ugly Christmas sweater to wear during the holidays, so it was quite the upbeat afternoon for me.

"Bentley told me everything," I said. "He was genuinely worried about you."

Her eyes widened. "Worried he was partnered with some sort of crazed skull crusher."

"Which, obviously, you are not. I told him you don't have it in you."

She tossed her head nonchalantly. "I could crush some bones if I wanted to."

"With what?"

"My teeth." She grinned, baring her human teeth. She didn't mean those ones.

"I'm glad it's all settled," I said. "I knew something was up when he came out of the log cabin with that super intense look on his face, after he found your earrings in there." I pointed to her ears with my free hand. "They're lovely, by the way. I've always admired them." I lifted the wine glass higher and made the toast. "To Nick Lafleur waking up soon, and taking you in his big, strong arms."

"That'll be the day." She took a big gulp of wine, and then another. Her eyes turned down at the corners, looking even sadder. "It was a mistake for me to be with him, and I try not to make the same mistake twice."

"Where's the fun in that? You're so young. You should totally date the bad boy. Date all the boys. I wish I'd had the chance. When I was your age, I was raising a headstrong little girl who was ten going on whatever age it is when they think they know better than you about everything." I swirled my wine in the glass. "Date the bad boy."

Persephone sighed. "Nick Lafleur isn't the kind of guy who *dates*." She stared dazedly at the spot above my head. "The reason I got out of there so fast on Saturday morning was because I sensed he was expecting another girl to come over. Maybe more than one."

"More than one? I never thought of that. What if—" I was getting so excited, I had to catch my breath. "What if two girls found out he was seeing both of them at the same time, but didn't let on they knew about each other. What if they called up Nick, promised him an exciting time with all three of them, but then came over and beaned him on the noggin with a lamp? They could be each other's alibis, if anyone asked."

"Your imagination is getting the better of you," she said. "It was just an accident. Fung played the 9-1-1 call for us. Nick must have been doing exactly what you and Fatima thought he'd been doing, hanging from the ceiling, working on those washboard abs."

I reluctantly let go of my theory about the pair of girls seeking revenge. Bentley had mentioned the 9-1-1 call, though he hadn't sounded as certain about the injury being an accident as Persephone did.

"He really does have good abs," Persephone said.

"I noticed."

"When you were healing him?"

"Not at the time, but I got a good look at him in the hospital." I wrinkled my nose. "Dr. Ankh made me look."

Persephone narrowed her eyes at me over her wine glass. "Sure, she did."

I pulled the receipt from my pocket. "Speaking of which, here's the bar receipt for your case files," I said. She didn't know what the receipt was about because after the 9-1-1 call, Bentley hadn't thought it worth mentioning. I caught her up on where I'd been all morning, on my adventure with Fatima.

When Persephone heard about how Fatima had insulted my powers, she became offended and outraged on my behalf. "That girl has no right to talk to you like that," she said. "Talk about rude. It's completely out of line."

"Actually, she's not that far out of line," I said. "It's a coven thing for us witches to tell each other what we think, and always be honest. It's supposed to keep the air clear so that resentments don't build up."

"Does it work?"

"I don't know. There's a whole lot of air clearing at every coven meeting. I don't think witches are capable of keeping their opinions to themselves. I think they invented that rule after the fact."

"You should invite me sometime," she said. "I'd love to be a witness."

"First of all, it's pretty much witches only, so you can't come. Second of all, I would not inflict that on my worst enemy, let alone my sister, whom I love."

"Aww," she said, her eyes glistening. "I love you, too."

I lifted the bottle of wine and started pouring. "It's going to be a long night if we're already at the sloppy I-love-you's half a bottle in."

She raised her glass. "A toast! To Nick's abs."

"A toast to you telling me all the details," I said, clinking my glass to hers.

Being a good sister, she did tell me details.

Between the wine and the giggling, it was a miracle we managed to get some sort of dinner on the table before my aunt arrived.

And by *miracle*, I mean we ordered takeout and had Ribbons pick it up.

CHAPTER 17

Monday Morning

Ribbons gave me stink-eye, which was like his regular expression, but with his head whipping from side to side, propelling psychic stink from one eye and then the other.

He was perched on the ledge of my bedroom window, wearing an adorable leather backpack. In the pack was— if all had gone well on his second delivery run in two days —the bundle of premium spell ingredients I'd asked him to pick up from Maisy Nix.

"Good boy," I said, specifically because it annoyed him when I spoke to him like he was a dog. "Who's a good boy? Ribbons is a good boy." It was fair game for me to talk to him like he was a dog, since he usually talked to me like I was an idiot.

In his quirky Count Chocula accent, he spoke telepathically into my mind: "Terrible things have been done by wyverns to humans, as payback for much less than your daily insults."

I held out my hand. "Give me the delivery, like you said you would, or I'll stop buying maple syrup for this household."

"You would not dare to commit such a despicable act."

"Eliminating maple syrup from my shopping list would save me a lot on grocery bills." I wiggled my fingers. "Come on. I give you room and board, and I don't ask for much beyond the occasional errand."

"It is endless."

"And you did such a good job last night fetching our takeout dinner. I was a little tipsy when I unpacked everything, but I think you only ate about a third of it on your flight back here."

He removed the tiny backpack and flung it at me. He showered me in another blast of stink-eye before flitting off, flapping away in the dark, pre-dawn sky.

"You forgot your tip," I called after him. "I've got a twenty-dollar bill you can tuck into one of your secret little pockets!"

He sent me the telepathic version of radio static.

I yelled out, cupping my hand around my mouth, "I'll be sure to leave you a five-star review online!"

The static sound cut off with an indignant squelch.

The psychic stink-eye gradually cleared. It wasn't an actual smell but the *idea* that you were smelling something bad, yet not smelling it strongly enough to identify exactly what it was. The smell didn't correspond to the wyvern's body, which had no scent, or his breath, which was delightfully minty. I had a feeling it might be connected to some of his glands, but had not investigated that possibility, for obvious reasons.

I took the leather bag down to the basement, where I had a look.

Everything was there. Maisy had come through for me. For the two of us, keeping the air clear by constantly bickering with each other had its perks.

I mixed the newly delivered ingredients with some other items Zinnia had brought over the night before.

When it was time for the brewing, I took the cauldron upstairs, to the kitchen, and transferred the contents. I used the coffee maker, as I often did when brewing a small, not-deadly potion.

Zoey came in, looked at the coffee maker, which was filling with dark purple liquid, and said, "I'm not even going to ask."

"It's a wake-up potion for Sleeping Beauty," I volunteered.

"Sleeping Beauty? You don't mean me, I hope."

"Nick Lafleur," I said. "I'm going to pop by the hospital today and get him vertical before Dr. Ankh starts breaking him down for spare parts."

"You're going to revive him? Are you allowed to do that?"

"Who's going to stop me?"

Ambrosia, who'd stayed overnight after a marathon session reading the Book of Mrs. Pinkman, joined us and asked, "Who's going to stop you from doing*what*?"

I pointed to the coffee maker. "Wake-up potion. It's for Nick. I'm going to pay him a visit at the hospital. I got special beans, freshly roasted by Maisy Nix, delivered by wyvern this morning."

Ambrosia's heavily made-up eyes widened. "She gave you some of her wicked purple beans?"

"Seed of Purpureus, yes."

"That stuff would wake the dead."

"Exactly. And I combined it with a few other things that may or may not add some hair to his chest as a side effect." To Zoey, I said, "As for being allowed, or getting stopped by security, there's nothing wrong with bringing a hot beverage to visit a friend."

Zoey went over to the coffee maker and sniffed it. "Why does this smell so good? Is it vanilla?"

"The dominant smell is koodzuberry enzyme. Fun fact: The koodzuberry is not a berry, but a tuber. It's an excellent enhancer, because of the multiplying effect. Margaret Mills adds it to her blueberry bran muffins to increase the fiber content."

"That seems like a bad idea," Zoey said.

"Margaret Mills is full of bad ideas." The results of eating Margaret's fiber muffins could be startling, whether you were expecting it or not.

Zoey kept sniffing the brew.

"Don't inhale too deeply," I said. "Some of the organic compounds are volatile."

She backed away.

Ambrosia was perusing my base ingredients and the coffee grinder I'd used to mix the bean paste. Her bleached hair was straw-like, and her dark-lined eyes were red from staying up late, reading.

"How are your eyes?" I asked. "You look worn out."

She gave me a pained look. "I happen to like dark eyeshadow, and nothing you say is going to make me change my mind."

"They look red and sore. The eyeball part, not the eyelid. I like your makeup. It's grown on me. I'll talk to my aunt about the sleep sand she's always raving about. It rests and rejuvenates the eyes after late-night reading."

"Uh, okay," Ambrosia said. "I'd try some of that sleep sand. Thanks. Zoey sure is lucky to have you as a mom."

"Doesn't your mom look after you?" Before she could respond, I held up one hand. "Don't answer that. I don't want to know. How other people parent their teens is their own business. I'm not looking to be your other mother. You and I are coven members, which makes us more like cousins, or coworkers. I may be mentoring you from time to time, but we're still equals. I'm sure you could teach me a thing or two."

She continued sorting through my spell ingredients with interest.

"What do you think?" I asked.

"This all looks legit to me," she said. "If Nick is ever going to wake up, it'll happen after he gets some of this. Can I come with you and watch? For mentoring purposes?"

"You girls have school. I can't let you miss that, Ambrosia. You've already spent so much time reading the Book of Mrs. Pinkman. Speaking of which, did you get any insights while you were sleeping? Sometimes that's when various ideas and themes come together."

She yawned and tucked her bleached-platinum hair behind one ear. "I dreamed about suitcases, and going on long journeys, but mainly I dreamed about Henry."

"Henry!" I exclaimed. "That was the name Mrs. Pinkman used for her sourdough starter."

Ambrosia smiled shyly. "It was also the name of her first love."

Zoey and I exchanged a look.

"That actually explains a lot," Zoey said. "Mrs. Pinkman always spoke so tenderly to that lump of yeast and flour. No wonder. I just thought she was obsessed with making sourdough bread."

"Oh, she was," Ambrosia said. "I got lost yesterday reading multiple chapters that were entirely about making sourdough. It's profoundly complicated, and yet incredibly simple once you've got the knack. A bit like spellwork."

"I'm glad you're getting comfortable with spirit reading," I said. "Now that you're all trained up, I can subcontract all my investigative ghost work to you." I rubbed my hands. "I'm going to have so much free time from now on."

I expected Ambrosia to say something in protest, but all she said was, "Okay."

Both of the girls watched as I bottled the potion for Nick. Rather than using a jar or a bottle, I put it in a takeout coffee mug. It was always best to disguise one's potions as everyday materials—but not too well.

I used the takeout mug I didn't ordinarily drink from— the navy blue one with a cartoon man holding two smoking pistols. The mug was a promotional item from a gas station. Its mascot was a fellow who bore a striking resemblance to Looney Tunes' Yosemite Sam, if Yosemite Sam were to sport a thin, curly black mustache instead of a red bushy one. The cartoon fellow's name was Mountain Joe, as in Mountain Joe's Gas and Go. It was a small chain.

Zoey asked, "What would happen if you took a sip of that by accident?"

"You'd come home from school to a clean house."

"That's not so bad," she said.

"And I would shave the cat, so she didn't leave her white fur on everything."

Zoey narrowed her eyes. "Sounds like you've put a lot of thought into this scenario."

"Do you want to try some?" I held the mug out to Zoey. "A little slurp shouldn't do too much, except possibly rearrange your teeth."

She backed away, lips clenched.

I offered it to Ambrosia, who did the same.

Good parenting, I told myself. This would keep the girls from licking the coffee pot when I wasn't looking. *Zara is a clever witch who uses reverse psychology like only a mom can.*

"Fix yourselves some breakfast, then I'll drop you off at school," I said. "In a small town, everything's pretty much on the way to everything else."

"It's too early for school," Ambrosia said. "You can go ahead. We'll walk."

"Too early for school?" I raised my eyebrows at Zoey. "There's a phrase that's never been uttered in this house."

Zoey rolled her eyes.

I gathered my things and prepared to leave.

Ambrosia said, "Don't you need to get changed?"

"Why would I change? You need to get your eyes checked. I look casually chic." I was wearing a crisp white blouse and tan slacks. My closet had picked the outfit, which was similar to the one I'd worn at Halloween. I had a hunch I knew why, and I looked forward to finding out if I was right. Who *doesn't* like finding out they were right?

"I'm just surprised you're dressed like that," Ambrosia said. "I figured it was an accident, since this outfit is not as, uh, *vibrant* as your usual look."

"You look like Gigi," Zoey said, nailing it. Gigi was her nickname for her grandmother—my mother, Zirconia.

Ambrosia leaned toward me, inspecting my hair. "I could turn your hair dark with a spell I know," she said. "I use the spell to make my hair its natural color for things like family portrait days. Some people only have it done once a year, but my mom likes to get a picture for every season. My hair could never take that much dying back and forth."

"If you know a hair color spell, why don't you use it to make your hair platinum instead of bleaching it?"

She frowned. "Witches shouldn't use spells to change their appearance."

"I know, but it's just hair. It's not a magical nose job."

"The spell only lasts a few hours," she said. "Wanna try?"

"Go for it," I said. Like most women, I did love a makeover. I also wanted to observe Ambrosia's spellwork up close.

She cast the spell.

When she was done, I applauded her for a near-perfect job. The hair color had come out closer to a dark auburn than the onyx black that had been promised, but it had a great shine and lots of body.

I put my Mountain Joe mug full of purple brew into my purse, tossed my shiny dark auburn hair over my shoulder, and headed off to the hospital to see about waking Sleeping Beauty.

CHAPTER 18

Dear reader, I could keep you in suspense about the wake-up potion, but I can't see why.

It worked.

And why wouldn't it have?

The potion itself was a thing of beauty. I'd done everything right, starting with consulting the coven to attain the perfect ingredients. I'd taken my time to brew the purple liquid perfectly. I'd even gotten a peer review at the end by another witch.

The only snag in my morning—and it was a tiny snag —was that I neglected to brew regular coffee for myself. Several times on the drive to the hospital, I found myself reaching for the navy blue Mountain Joe mug. Reaching for, but not drinking. Phew. Though it had been a close one when I was stopped at a traffic light.

I got to the hospital for my second visit in two days. I bypassed the gift shop and didn't see anyone I knew.

After a few spells, I located Nick Lafleur, who'd been moved out of the ICU and into a smaller recovery room.

I wafted the potion under Nick's nose and told him to wake up. That didn't work—I hadn't thought it would— so I pulled open his mouth and poured some purple brew down the hatch.

As I did so, I was reminded of plumbing pipes, and about drain cleaner.

A shiver of doubt crept in. The brew was perfect, but was I doing the right thing?

I didn't have long to doubt myself.

Nick's fair eyelashes fluttered. Sleeping Beauty was waking up.

He yawned, stretched, rolled toward me, and then did something surprising. He sleepily reached for me, as casually as any man waking up might reach for his long-time girlfriend or wife.

"C'mere, you sexy thing," he said huskily.

I'd been leaning over his bed, close enough to grab. He easily hooked one of his strong arms around my waist and tugged me toward him.

I could have resisted. I could have blasted him with enough blue fireballs to wax the sparse golden hair on his chest. But I didn't.

I held the insulated Mountain Joe mug high, so it didn't splash on the sheets, and allowed myself to roll into the embrace. I stretched out next to him on the narrow hospital bed.

He nuzzled my shoulder, which wasn't the worst thing imaginable.

I cast a sticking spell on the door to the room to buy a little time in case someone came by to check on the patient. Not a locking spell, just a sticking one. I wanted to see where this was going, but I wasn't about to do anything regrettable.

"You were asleep a long time," I said softly.

"I feel so rested." He closed his eyes and stretched again. He was wearing a hospital gown, unlike the day before, when he'd been naked. The sleeves were very short—if you could even call them sleeves. I noticed that his armpits, filled with golden curls, smelled like hospital soap.

Nick made a smacking sound with his mouth, opened his eyes, and asked groggily, "Where are we?"

"We're in a hospital," I said. "What's the last thing you remember?"

"A hospital?" He jerked himself upright, took a more careful look at me, and recoiled. Before I could explain myself, he was falling off the other side of the bed. He got to his feet again, steadying himself with both hands on the bed. "You're not Zirconia," he said.

"I'm not?" I twisted a lock of dark auburn hair and gave him a coy look. "Is it the hair? Not dark enough. I asked for onyx, but you know how stylists can be."

He pointed at me. "I know you. You're her daughter, Zara. You work with my little sister at the library. You're a witch." He tilted his head to the side. "What's happening to your hair?"

The lock in my hand was transitioning from dark auburn to red. To speed it along, I cast a generic counter spell. My hair zapped back to my normal shade.

"You got me," I said, climbing off the hospital bed, still careful not to spill the potion. "You and I have not been formally introduced, only casually."

"You're a witch," he repeated.

"I am what you know me to be, and I won't insult you by denying it." That moment would have been the appropriate time for Nick to volunteer his powers, but he did not.

He rubbed his head, where the bandage was. "My head," he said. "What happened?"

"I was hoping you could tell me."

"Hang on. I gotta think." He groaned and rocked his head from side to side, cracking joints.

I crossed the recovery room to the small washroom, intending to dump the remainder of the potion. It was safe to dispose of, as it would neutralize when diluted with the same volume of water. I had only poured out a few dark drops before I changed my mind.

It was a good brew, too good to dump out. While it would lose some of its potency over time, I could bottle it, label it, and keep it in my basement in case someone in the coven had a need for it within the next few months. I screwed the lid on tight, and tucked it into my purse, which was enchanted to hold more than it appeared to hold. The purse hadn't become magical until recently, but it had always been handy. I'd used it for navigation when I was a ghost myself, and the handle had been a great leash when I'd pretended to walk a sheep shifter.

"I'm so confused," Nick said. "How can I tell you what happened if I don't even know what day it is?"

"Today is Monday," I said. "You've been unconscious for two days. On Saturday morning, I found you on the floor of your log cabin, bleeding out from that crack on your head. I managed to slow down the bleeding before the paramedics arrived."

"Where's Minerva?"

That was the last thing I'd expected Nick to say. "Minerva Pinkman? You know her?"

"Sort of. Maybe. I don't know." He took a seat in the chair next to the bed and yanked out his IV line. "Is she real? Minerva Pinkman? She was wearing rubber clogs."

"That's her, and she's real. What do you remember?"

"I remember her coming to me. I was on the floor, and then I was floating over myself. She was there. I'd never seen her before in my life. She introduced herself, and told me she was going to go get help from an old friend of hers who would save my life."

"That would be me," I said.

"She didn't say that, but she did say I could come with her, if I could figure out how to move through walls." He rubbed his arm where the IV had been and frowned at the red mark inside his elbow. "I think she was a ghost," he said. "I think *I* was a ghost."

"You were a disembodied spirit," I said. "An astral projection. It can happen when a person is near death, which you were."

He looked around the room. "Is she here now? I need to thank Minerva. She saved my life."

"She's not here, but even if she was, you probably wouldn't be able to see her now that you're fully alive."

He tsked, sounding disappointed.

"I will thank her for you the next time I see her." I washed and dried my hands to remove any stray potion, and then walked over to where Nick was sitting. There was no other chair in the hospital room, so I knelt on the floor so I could look into his eyes. "Nick, did someone hurt you, or was it an accident? The police say that someone called 9-1-1 from your cabin. Was it you?"

He blinked slowly and straightened up in the chair. All the color had returned to his cheeks. He looked alert and full of vitality. With the exception of the hospital gown, he could have been a model, posing for a sculptor's statue.

"9-1-1," he said slowly.

"Do you remember?"

"I remember," he said, his voice stony and flat. "I remember everything." He didn't volunteer any information, which I found odd.

"Was my mother there? Zirconia Riddle? Looks like me, but pointier? Especially around the teeth?"

"No," he said hollowly. "It would have been different if she had been there."

"Speaking of my mother, you're lucky she didn't scramble your pretty brains, Nick. She let you remember that you're seeing her. She didn't do that with one of her other... male friends. She had the guy so confused." I paused. I'd been talking about Bentley, and it gave me a suspicious idea.

"Wait. Maybe she did scramble your brains. Do you *really* remember what you were doing before you got hurt? Clearly?"

There was a rattle at the door. Someone wanted into the hospital room. I had only a few seconds before the sticking spell wore off.

"I was being stupid," Nick said ruefully. "An idiot. I should have known better."

"You can tell me what happened," I said, beginning to cast my bluffing spell. It felt more awkward than usual, with me in a kneeling position, one hand on Nick's bare knee. "Nick, listen. You want to tell me—"

The door burst open. Dr. Ankh stood in the doorway. "Zara Riddle," she said.

My spell fizzled out.

I stood up so quickly, I saw a flash of stars. "Good news," I said brightly. "Nick is awake."

"I can see that," she said, entering the room and closing the door quietly behind her. The strange woman's face looked extra smooth and line-free that day. She had her fair hair pulled back in a tight bun.

I checked that the mug of brew was safely hidden inside my purse.

Dr. Ankh said, "I knew it had to be you in here, bothering my patient. You must have jinxed the door using your sloppy magic."

Not well enough, I thought. "You know how we witches are," I said. "We don't *really* know how magic works."

Nick jumped in and said, "Hey there, Dr. A," shortening her name to an initial as a sign of familiarity. "Was I really out cold for two whole days?"

"You were unconscious," she said.

"Wow," he said. "I probably would be dead by now if you didn't do that thing to my blood, huh?"

My ears perked up. Nick knew Dr. Ankh, and she'd done something to his blood. How very interesting. I wanted to know more, so I didn't make any movement to leave the room.

Dr. Ankh gave me stink-eye. I didn't flinch. Ribbons' much stronger stink-eye had given me immunity.

"I did nothing to your blood," Dr. Ankh said to Nick, speaking as though testifying for my benefit. "It is a pre-existing condition."

"But that's not what you said, is it?" He rubbed his head. "Everything's fuzzy."

"You do have unusual vasculature," Dr. Ankh said. "This is related to your family's genetic history as feeders of the undead."

I raised my hand. "What?"

Dr. Ankh gave me a pained look. "Nick's ancestors have a long history of consorting with certain creatures."

"Certain creatures," I repeated. "Such as my mother, the vampire." I turned to Nick. "She's been visiting you up at your cabin, hasn't she?"

He nodded. "Whenever she's in town."

That explained the reports of a dark-haired, artificial-smelling woman that the small woodland creatures were afraid of. And also why he'd nuzzled me when he thought I was her. I'd had a hunch about my mother ever since that morning, when my closet had chosen my plain outfit.

Nick asked me, "She didn't tell you? Your mom never mentioned us?"

"She may have. I block my ears whenever she starts to brag to me about her romantic exploits."

Nick looked confused. "Why would you do that? She says she's very close to you. She says you two are like sisters, and you discuss everything."

"She said that? Wait. Are we both talking about the same Zirconia Riddle?"

He tilted his head and continued to look confused.

Dr. Ankh broke into the exchange. "Zara, you should be thanking Nick for your mother's good health," she said. "As well as for Theodore Bentley's. It is because of

Nick's *entirely voluntary* efforts that I was able to develop the serum they both rely upon."

Nick Lafleur was the inspiration for the fake blood serum? I'd always thought it was an ancient secret. Like Colonel Sanders' eleven herbs and spices.

I turned to Nick and did a formal bow. "Thank you for your service to vampirekind."

He rubbed his neck and blushed. "I don't mind."

Dr. Ankh busied herself picking up the IV line that Nick had tossed on the floor. Then she checked his pulse with her long fingers. Without looking at me, she asked, "How did you manage to rouse him?"

"Rouse him? I, uh, brought him some good, strong coffee."

She pursed her very large lips. "Coffee," she mused. "Interesting."

I might have told her exactly what was *in* the coffee, to give her accurate information about her patient's treatments, but Maisy had shared the potion recipe with me on the condition I did not. As a side bonus, it did give me some pleasure to keep it from the snooty doctor.

"You may go now," Dr. Ankh said to me.

"No need to dismiss me. I was leaving anyway." I hoisted my trusty purse onto my shoulder and headed for the door. "Feel better soon," I said to Nick on the way out.

I hadn't gotten far down the hallway when I realized one of my shoes was untied. I would have used a spell to tie it while walking, but there were people around, so I knelt down and did it the old-fashioned way.

"Dr. A," I heard Nick say, back in the room. "If everything checks out, can I get into the trials for Activator X?"

She answered quickly, sounding annoyed. "How did you find out about that?"

"Just a rumor going around," he said. "Is it true?"

"Never mind about Activator X," she said. "Those words should not come out of your mouth again, or..."

"Or what?"

"Or the next time you are injured through your own stupidity, you may not be so lucky."

"Come on," he said. "It's me, Dr. A. Your boy. Nicky. You can hook me up. I won't tell anyone. We can keep it between... Hey, what's that big needle for?"

"This is a sedative," she said. "It will balance out the poisoned coffee or whatever it was that witch gave you."

"But I feel fine. Great, even."

"You have a visible tremor in both hands."

"So what? Coffee usually gives me the shakes."

"Hold still."

"Ouch," he said, then, "I feel sleepy."

"You can take a nap while we prepare you for discharge."

There was no more conversation. I knew without seeing Nick that he was out cold again. All because he'd dared to ask Dr. Ankh about something called Activator X.

I finished tying my shoe and left the area quickly, keeping an eye out for Dr. Ankh and any big needles.

CHAPTER 19

Xavier Batista

When we last saw young Xavier, he was dying of embarrassment over having offered his neck to a certain vampire detective. Xavier survived the aftermath of humiliation and self-flagellation, but only because he thought there was a chance that news of the cringe-inducing incident wouldn't leave his bedroom. He was wrong, but didn't know that yet, so he wasn't feeling too terrible about himself or his reputation that Monday morning.

While Zara Riddle was at the hospital on Monday morning, eavesdropping on Dr. Ankh and Nick Lafleur, and various other Wisterians were doing various other Wisteria things, Xavier Batista was letting himself into the ground-floor offices of the WPD. The Permits one, not the Police one. He couldn't even get into the Academy, remember?

Xavier's coworkers wouldn't be in for another half hour, which would give him enough time to call the blood analysis company about his delayed DNA results.

His call was answered by a recorded message, and he was put on hold.

He was left on hold for twenty-three minutes, during which time he grew more and more agitated. He was so agitated, he resorted to doing some of his permit clerk job duties, even though he wasn't on the clock yet.

Finally, the saxophone music cut off, and an upbeat female voice said, "Thank you for calling BloodLines! This is Judy. How may I help you today?"

"I sent in my sample over—"

She cut him off abruptly but cheerfully. "Name and order number, please!"

"Xavier Batista," he said. "And my order number—"

"Is that spelled with a Z?"

"An X."

"Order number please!"

"I was going to tell you, but you cut me off—"

"Your thirteen digit order number can be found in your confirmation email, Mr. Batswan!"

"It's Batista. Mr. Batista." He heard his father's voice coming from his mouth. Had he ever referred to himself as Mr. Batista? In the moment, it gave him a flash of Impostor Syndrome.

"Yes," Judy said. "Xanadu Batswan. That is your name, sir. Order number please!"

He groaned and spelled out his entire name for Judy.

She eventually got it correct.

Then he gave her the 13-digit code. Multiple times. This was *exactly* why he hadn't phoned the company until now. Was there a big company that didn't have terrible phone support? He preferred to do these sorts of things by email, or not at all.

Judy managed to get all of his information typed into her computer. "That's funny," she said.

"Now what?"

"I don't know," she said in her perky voice. "There's a mysterious note on your file."

"Mysterious?" His heart sped up. He liked the sound of that.

"I'm supposed to transfer your call, but that's what's so funny. I don't know this extension number. I wonder what it could mean."

A mysterious note about an unknown extension number? His results had come in, and his DNA was full of magic! Xavier's heart fluttered and trilled in his chest like an aggressive robin during mating season.

"Judy, what do *you* think it means?"

"Well, I'm not supposed to tell customers about this, but I heard at the staff Christmas party that, not long ago, we located the lost heir of a vast fortune. He was the prince of some country he'd never even heard of. He'd been adopted overseas as a baby, and he had no idea! Can you believe it?"

"No," he said, his voice falling flat along with his mood. "That sounds like a scam. Are you hustling me, Judy?"

"Wha-a-at?"

"Judy, if that is your name, you need to hear something. If this act of yours, about the mysterious note on a customer's file, is your side hustle, your way of scamming customers into paying for extra service fees, you will regret it." Now he was definitely channeling his father, which was a good thing. The senior Batista usually got his way. Xavier was also no stranger to bluffing and bravado. He had once faced down an angry cougar with nothing more than a pocket knife.

Judy sounded upset and confused. "Side hustle? What are you talking about?"

"Judy," he said, because it felt powerful to use her name repeatedly. "I can tell you that I, Mr. Batista, did not fall out of a coconut tree yesterday. I know what a scam sounds like. What's next? News that I may be the missing heir to a wild fortune? Do I wire you a small amount of money so you can put together the documentation to bribe some foreign authorities in a distant land I've never heard of?" Xavier didn't know a lot about the world, so there were a good number of countries he'd never heard of, but that's beside the point. He was picking up steam, practically yelling into the phone receiver, "And then a larger amount of money? And another?"

"I-I-I don't know what you're talking about Mr. Batsworth. I mean, Mr. Botswana. Mr. Bosworth. I do have a side hustle, but it's sewing custom decorative covers for bird cages. I sell them online. They're quilted." She took in an audible breath. "I have a website."

"Give me the website," he said, cool as a cucumber.

She gave him the address. He typed it in on his desktop computer. A colorful intro screen for Judy's Custom Birdcage Cozies came up.

"You're not hustling me," he said, relaxing his muscles, powering down his bluffing and bravado.

"No, sir."

"I'm glad we cleared that up, Judy." His voice was back to business casual. "Now, if there is a note on my file to transfer my call to another extension, I suggest you do so."

"But I don't know this extension. It could be a mistake."

"Judy, what's the worst that could happen?"

"Just a moment, sir. I'm going to do a look-up on our backup system." There was the sound of a keyboard being typed. Judy was as fast at typing as she was bad at hearing names. All the better to screw up paperwork at top speed.

After a moment, she said, "Oh, dear."

"What's going on over there? Where are you located, anyway?"

"One moment, please!"

The hold music came back on.

The line crackled and went silent.

Then a voice came over the speakers. It was a male voice, and it was so crisp and clear, Xavier had to look around the office to see if someone was there in the room with him. He was still alone, but not for much longer.

"Mr. Batista," said the man, apparently having none of Judy's name amnesia or dyslexia or whatever it was. His voice was deep, and his accent was posh English, like that of a duke. "We have your laboratory results." He pronounced it la-*bor*-atory, which made it sound much more exciting than it already was.

"Great. What is it? Am I part Viking? Neanderthal?"

"Mr. Batista, you filled out Form 22X and paid the extra fee. Form 22X authorizes BloodLines to perform ancestral analysis for... mythical creatures. It is usually selected as a gag gift. We generate a random result... for entertainment purposes. It's all rather droll."

Xavier forced a dryly amused chuckle. "I know that," he said. "Just out of curiosity, what did it say?"

"It should not matter," the man said.

"It matters to me."

"The mythical ancestry portion is generated at random, by the computer." The man paused. "And even if it *were* an accurate analysis, and such things as supernatural creatures existed, and had theoretically populated your bloodline, your percentage would be so low that it would need to be activated." Crisply, he added, "Manually activated."

Xavier leaned back in his chair and stared at the ceiling. This was all coming together. The phone call had been a real roller coaster of emotions. He'd had his hopes soar twice, only to dip down twice as well. His body felt heavy. After this call, he might crawl under his desk for a five-minute nap, or to die.

"Go on," Xavier said to the man. His mouth was dry, his voice flat. "Let's hear your sales pitch. I hope your game is better than Judy's."

"My what?"

"Your sales pitch, man. Let's hear it. Judy didn't have what it takes to close the deal, so now's your chance."

"I beg your pardon?"

"You've got my results, and they're promising, right? You can see that I do have some powerful ancestry, but not quite enough to push me out of nothing-person territory. But it's in reach. Like the water, or the peaches, for that Tantalus guy in the Greek myths. All I need is a spell, or a potion, or a medical procedure to activate the ancient powers in my genes. And, surprise, surprise, you've got just the thing! But you need a bit of cash to know I'm serious. Am I on the right track?"

"As it happens, I do know of a means for activating such a thing, but it is strictly for... entertainment purposes only." There was another long pause, and Xavier imagined the man licking his lips, wolf-like. "There is, naturally, a fee."

"A big fee?" He'd already paid for the Form 22X testing, and it hadn't been cheap.

"A reasonable fee, considering the value."

"This is nonsense," Xavier said, though he used stronger words. "I want my money back. Transfer me over to Judy. I demand a full refund."

The man replied calmly, "Your fee shall be refunded." There was the sound of typing. "It is done."

"You refunded me? Does that mean I don't get anything?"

"Thank you for calling BloodLines. Is there anything else I can help you with?"

"I want what I paid for. I want my results!"

"BloodLines reserves the right to terminate any contract without notice. It's in the fine print."

"So that's it?"

"Your credit note will show on your next credit card statement. Please allow several hours for it to appear on your online statements. Thank you for your business, Mr. Batista."

Xavier told the man where to go and what to do with himself.

He slammed the phone onto its cradle just as the office door opened and the first of his coworkers arrived.

Margaret Mills came stomping in, her curly gray hair barely contained by a knit hat, muttering about children and snakes and a komodo dragon.

She looked at him with suspicion. "What are you doing here so early?"

"Stealing office supplies," he said grumpily.

"Who pooped in your cornflakes?"

He crossed his arms and didn't answer. He knew a rhetorical question when he heard one.

"Because I'll tell you who pooped in mine," Margaret said. "A hamster." She shook her fist. "A hamster who evaded my recent pet-reduction sweep. That Humphrey is not as savage or as thorough as his handler claims him to be."

"Humphrey?" Ordinarily, Xavier would not be interested in Margaret's household disasters, but this morning he was grateful for the distraction from his fuming rage at BloodLines. "Should I know who or what Humphrey is?"

"He's a komodo dragon."

"Enhanced or regular?" By *enhanced*, he meant by magic.

Margaret snorted. "I wouldn't let a *regular* komodo dragon loose in my house. Do I look crazy?" She yanked off her knit cap, causing frizzy gray curls to spray out in all directions.

"How is the dragon enhanced?" And, he wondered, more importantly, could a human being be enhanced?

Margaret saw right through his question. "Enough of that, Xavier. Let it go. So, you're a regular boy. What's the harm in that? I married a regular boy, the first time around. Mike had more than enough going for him. If he hadn't started up his nonsense all over town with every hussy who shook her tail feathers at him, I'd still be married to him, and he could have had his bowl of cornflakes pooped into this morning as well."

Xavier felt the sting of her non-comforting words, and let it sink into his core. "You shouldn't be eating cornflakes anyway," he said. "It's straight carbs. They feed it to pigs with low-fat milk to fatten them up."

The air tingled with magic. Margaret stamped the front of one foot, hoof-like. "How dare you," she said. "Are you comparing me to a barnyard animal? The insolence!"

Just then, the door opened and Gavin Gorman strode in, looking stylish and thin in his skinny trousers. Rumor had it he bought off-the-rack, then got the trousers tailored to have an even tighter leg.

"Hey, Gavin," Xavier said, enjoying Margaret's outrage so he could ignore his own. "Should people eat cornflakes?"

"Only if they want to fatten up," Gavin said. "Smart people have coffee for breakfast."

Xavier grinned and asked, "Has a hamster ever pooped in your coffee?"

Gavin shuddered. "I should hope not. I keep my beans in an airtight, vacuum-sealed container right up until the moment of brewing."

Margaret said to Gavin, using her tattle-tale voice, "Xavier is day dreaming about getting powers again."

Gavin, who was a gnome, shrugged as he sat at his workstation and turned on his monitor. "Nothing wrong with having a dream," he said. "I dream about the day Karl finally takes his retirement. How many days are left now?"

Dawna, who had just walked in, gave the answer. "One hundred and fifty-seven working days, if my math is correct." She waved her manicured hand with its long, brightly-colored nails that matched today's expensive designer handbag. "But don't start sizing up his office for yourselves just yet. He ain't goin' nowhere. That man's greatest joy in life is talking about retirement, not taking it." She dropped her purse on her desk and asked, "What are we talking about?"

Gavin answered, "Xavier dreams of being special." He flashed a mocking smile. "Isn't that adorable?"

"He *is* special," Dawna said. "If y'all would stop teasing him all the time, he might figure out what his true talents are."

"Thank you," Xavier said. He could usually count on Dawna to have his back. He couldn't say the same for his girlfriend, Liza Gilbert, who sat across from him and hadn't yet arrived.

"You know what you should do?" Dawna circled the air between them with one colorful fingernail. "You should get an internship."

Gavin snorted. "You mean work for free? For someone who does have powers?" He paused and rubbed his chin. "Now that you mention it, I could use someone to pick up my clothes at the cleaners."

"Not you," Dawna said. "Someone who could teach him something of value. All you can do is go *poof.*"

Gavin scoffed. "I can do other things."

"Fine," Margaret said, interrupting with a huff. "You can intern with me, Xavier. Just babysit my kids a few nights a week when they aren't at their father's place, and I'll teach you a thing or two about magic. We'll start with the rules and regulations."

Xavier held up one hand. "No, thanks," he said. He had met Margaret's children, and he knew a trap when he heard one.

He looked over at Dawna with hopeful eyes. She was a card mage. She could occasionally predict the future, but where she really excelled was selecting winning scratch-off tickets at convenience stores.

"Don't look at me with those puppy-dog eyes of yours," she said. "I don't even know *how* I read the cards. There's no way I could teach someone else."

"Thanks for the idea, anyway," he said. "I am going to look for an internship." He avoided eye contact with Margaret. "With someone outside the office. I wouldn't want things around here to get complicated."

Dawna raised her eyebrows. "It's a bit late for that." She glanced over at Liza's empty chair. "I could have told you dating the person you share a desk with was a bad idea."

Gavin, who was Dawna's deskmate as well as her on-again, off-again boyfriend, sniffed and said nothing.

"Everything's great with Liza," Xavier said. The high, squeaky tone of his voice betrayed him, but it wasn't a total lie. To some guys, what he had with Liza would be ideal. She came over to his place whenever she pleased, they had fun together, and she didn't expect any more of him. If he happened to be busy when she wanted to hang out, she didn't mind at all.

But it did bother Xavier that she wasn't more possessive of him.

He had to wonder, would she feel differently if he had powers? Of course she would. Girls always said they wanted a guy who made them laugh, but Xavier knew that deep down, every girl wanted to possess a man who was more than just a boy, and more than just a human.

And Xavier was going to find a way to become more than a nothing person.

Even if it killed him.

CHAPTER 20

Wisteria Public Library
First Coffee Break
Zara Riddle

Frank Wonder pulled a chunk of carrot cake from the pastry box and poked it tentatively with a fork.

"Still moist," reported the children's librarian.

His antics so far that day had been less zany than usual. The library had received some very smelly books by donation, and Frank had barely made any effort to trick me into smelling them.

He was almost as subdued as his new hair color.

When I'd met Frank, he'd been sporting bright pink hair. Apex Predator Pink. The kids loved it, and their parents did, too. But that morning, the older gentleman—he was in his fifties, but extremely fit—had showed up for work looking like his more conservative doppelganger. His hair wasn't pink anymore. It was a lovely silver, bordering on white, which was striking in its own way, but not like the pink. Even his wardrobe had toned down. He usually wore vintage cords and paisley shirts, but that day he wore a modern cut of corduroy trousers paired with a sleek pinstriped shirt. Instead of colorful sneakers, he wore some very snazzy wingtips.

I loved the new look, and we'd been talking about it all morning. Now, a few hours into our shift, the novelty had worn off, and I felt vaguely bereft.

"You're staring," Frank said, speaking out of the side of his mouth. At least that part of the man hadn't changed. He still had his charmingly crooked chin, which made his triangular face resemble a comma.

"It's a lot to get used to," I said. "You've had pink hair since the day we met. I used to call you Pinkie sometimes. Now what am I supposed to call you?"

He batted his eyelashes. "You can still call me Mr. Wonderful."

I closed my eyes, tried to clear my memory of the man, then opened them to get a new first impression.

I saw an attractive, energetic man in his fifties, with striking silver hair and stylish clothes. He wasn't the same Frank Wonder as before, but he did look good. He could have been on the cover of Gentleman Librarian's Quarterly, if such a publication existed.

"You do look wonderful, Mr. Wonderful," I said. "Any special reason for the change?"

He shrugged. "A new year is coming. You don't think I'm becoming a grownup, do you?"

"No. That can't be it."

"Good. Growing up is a trap." He shoveled more carrot cake into his mouth. "I wonder, is this the same cake you brought in last week for Fresh Pastry Friday?"

"What if it is?" I asked. "That's never stopped you before."

He counted on his fingers. "Friday, Saturday, Sunday, Monday. Four days." He shrugged and took a bite. "Heavenly," he reported.

We were in the staff lounge at the Wisteria Public Library. The head librarian, Kathy Carmichael, was running things out front while the newly-silver-haired

Frank and I took our first coffee break of the day. On Mondays, we usually ate stale pastry from Friday and discussed what we'd done all weekend. Today was no exception.

"I finally cleaned that chandelier," Frank said.

"You were busy this weekend. A full makeover, and home repair?"

"I have a lot of energy. Anyway, the stuff you gave me worked like magic. The crystals are sparkling. Honestly, it was the highlight of my weekend. What did you get up to?"

I held up two fingers. "I saw this many ghosts."

"A double feature! I suppose you were due, given how quiet November was." He took another bite of the leftover carrot cake. "Anyone we know?"

"Yes and no. One was a woman I knew before I moved here. Dead of natural causes, it seems, but I don't know why she's here. I have my intern looking into it."

Frank's eyes twinkled. "Your intern?"

"Marshmallow Salad," I said, using our not-so-clever codename for Ambrosia. "She's such a smart girl. And hard working."

He narrowed his eyes. "Zara Riddle, you always do like people a lot more once they become useful to you."

"Doesn't everyone?"

"True." He waved his hand. "Who's the other one?"

"Nick Lafleur."

Frank coughed, choking on his cake. "Poor Naomi," he said. Nick's sister, Naomi, worked with us part time, which was how I'd first met Nick. "Though I'm not surprised. That boy is way too popular with the ladies. What happened? Did he get caught in bed with someone's wife? And has your dashing beau rounded up the murderous husband, thanks to your help, for which you are never financially compensated, despite your tireless efforts?"

"Nick isn't dead," I said. "He's still alive. Or at least he was when I saw him at the hospital this morning. He had a head injury and was unconscious for a couple days, but he's awake now, and I think he'll make a strong recovery."

Frank rubbed his crooked chin. "So, he was just a temporary ghost. A tourist to the realms of the dark and deep." He nodded. "Is the jealous husband being charged with grievous injury?"

"There was no husband that I know of. No malice, either. Nick claims to have had an accident, then called 9-1-1 himself."

Frank touched his frosty silver hair, as though making sure it was still there. "But you believe there's more to the story. I can see it in your face, Zara Riddle. You've got that gleam in your eye that you only get when you're on a case."

"There may be more to the story," I said nonchalantly. "Would that be so bad? November was kind of boring."

"Spill it," he said. "Spill your tea."

"What do you know about Activator X?"

He paused. "Why do you ask?"

"I heard Nick asking Dr. Ankh about it."

"Dr. Monkey-Finger-Toes? The one who tried to vampirize poor Zinnia?"

"That's the one. And she didn't want to discuss it with him. Maybe she sensed I was listening." I pointed at him. "But you know something about it, Frank Wonder. You've got that gleam in your eye that you only get when you've got your own tea to spill."

He squirmed like a kid with a secret, then blurted out, "Activator X is a hypothetical substance. Like the fictional, extremely rare, impossible material that engineers call *unobtainium*."

"It's not real?"

"I said it's hypothetical. It could be real."

"What does it activate? Hypothetically?"

"If given to a *nothing person*, it would activate some latent powers."

I shook my head. "I don't like that term. Nobody is a *nothing person*."

Frank shrugged. "I was a nothing person for a long time. What you don't know that you don't have can't bother you."

That wasn't true. Before Frank discovered he was a shifter, he had always dreamed about flying, and felt something was missing in his life. Now that he was regularly flying around town in his flamingo shifter form, perhaps he no longer felt the need to dye his hair pink.

My own daughter had moped around incessantly before her powers had manifested. Being magicless in a world where other people had magic could be a blessing, but, if you let it drive you crazy, it could be a curse.

I didn't mention any of that to Frank. People didn't appreciate being reminded of their inconsistencies.

"If Dr. Monkey-Finger-Toes has created a working Activator X, that would be something," Frank mused. "It would change things around here."

"Around here? It would change the whole world," I said. "A lot."

"I truly hope she hasn't done it," he said. "And not just because I like being special."

I raised my eyebrows.

"Okay, *mainly* because I like being special," he said. "But, secondarily, I can't imagine it being good for the world if everyone was suddenly turning into rabbits." He paused and smiled. "Although, that would be adorable. Can you imagine? An entire city of rabbits. Picture dozens of rabbits going shopping with little baskets over their arms. Rabbits in business suits rushing to the courthouse. Rabbits driving trolley cars!"

Frank was our children's librarian, and his imagination did skew toward the adorable.

"They wouldn't be able to reach the pedals and see over the steering wheel," I said. "Not with their little rabbit feet."

"Adjustments would need to be made," Frank said. "The world can change, if it wants to."

"But the world wouldn't deal well with sudden change thrust upon it," I said. "And what are the odds that an entire city of people would secretly be rabbit shifters? I bet some of them would be witches, or sprites, or gnomes, or minor mages."

Frank sighed. "Boring."

"How would Activator X work? Would it activate whatever bloodline had the highest percentage in a person's DNA?"

"Probably not," he said. "Most of the time, powers don't work that way. Look at your family. You're half shifter by blood, and your daughter's only a quarter, but she went fox and you went witch."

"True," I said. "And once you go witch, you don't switch."

Frank rolled his eyes.

We still had a few minutes left on our break, so I grabbed some stale carrot cake and fresh coffee—the perfect combination for a Monday morning.

* * *

For the rest of the day, my mind was on the idea of Activator X.

I asked the head librarian, who was a sprite and knew a fair bit about magic, about Activator X. She told me the same as Frank had. It was an idea, a fantasy that had been around forever, probably as long as magic itself. There were many urban legends of transformation, with the activator taking any number of forms. Activator X could be in the form of a mushroom, a plasma transfusion, a trip through a particular type of portal, a spell, or even an enchanted object. We had endless books about transformations in our fiction genre shelves.

In my own experience as a witch, I'd encountered at least one object that fit the description. A woman named Temperance Krinkle had conned her way into getting her wrinkled hands on a million-dollar ancient amulet, using me as part of her scheme. She'd believed it would give her the ability to instantly transport herself around the world. She *thought* she was in for the holiday of a lifetime. What she *got* was a one-way ticket to rapid cremation.

Toward the end of my shift, I kept thinking of the words I'd said to my neighbor the day before. I'd been filling an awkward pause with small talk, and I'd said to Xavier, regarding his implied wish to have his own powers, "be careful what you wish for." I'd been as thoughtless as Frank, with his adage about people not missing what they didn't know about.

The thing is, Frank and I weren't wrong. Powers weren't for everyone.

Young Xavier could barely control his regular human impulses. He was cocky, headstrong, and constantly getting into trouble with other guys his age. Punching Nick Lafleur—or having Nick's face run into his fist—had only been the most recent incident in a long line of incidents. Xavier wasn't a bad kid, but he was undisciplined.

People could definitely regret getting their heart's desire. The tale of The Monkey's Paw by author W. W. Jacobs, first published in England in 1902, was all about the terrible consequences of having one's wishes granted.

If Activator X did exist, any good that might come of such a thing would be balanced by a big, huge, steaming pile of bad.

CHAPTER 21

I pulled up to the front of my house and started unloading the groceries I'd picked up on my way home from work. Talk about a full day of being a responsible adult. I'd revived an unconscious man, worked a full shift at the library, then gone to the grocery store to buy nutritious food for my family.

Well, maybe not everything I'd picked up was nutritious, but most of it was technically food.

Xavier Batista appeared at my side and took a bag from my hands. I'd been thinking about him during the day, and about his discomfort over not having powers, so I felt mildly embarrassed to be seeing him in person. Embarrassed, and suspicious. Could he know I'd been thinking about him? My mind was guarded most of the time, but it was no steel trap. Ribbons could get in whenever he wanted. Had the little wyvern been tattling on me? He couldn't speak to regular people, but he could communicate in other ways, such as writing notes. He had the most beautiful cursive handwriting.

Xavier held the grocery bag easily with his young, male arms. He was skinny, but he was tall, so he hid his muscles.

"Let me help you, Ms. Riddle," he said.

"It's just Zara." I took a step back and looked him over. His clothes were different. Everything looked ironed and fresh. "You always call me Zara," I said. "What's with the Ms. Riddle routine? And the clothes? Are you going somewhere?"

He peered into the bag, ignoring my questions. "There's a lot of ice cream in here."

"It's winter, so it doesn't melt in the car on the way home. Everyone buys more ice cream in the winter."

"They do?"

"Are you saying they don't?"

"My mother never buys ice cream. That's one of the reasons I finally moved out on my own."

"Stop breathing your hot breath on my ice cream. You're going to melt it."

He grinned. "I knew you'd say that."

Did he, really? "Make yourself useful and take it into the house." I twirled my finger to drop the defenses on the front door. "Door's unlocked."

He turned toward my porch, then paused. "If I walk in there before you do, is anything going to attack me?"

"Maybe," I said.

"Really?"

"Nothing you can't handle." I gave him a second bag to make the trip worthwhile.

He didn't move. "Home security systems can be very deadly these days. You should see the one my roommate installed at our place. We've got all these high tech cameras, trip switches, and two-way audio."

"Why do you need all that? Are you two growing some sort of high-priced magical crop in there?"

"No." He shrugged, making the grocery bags rustle. "Ubaid's into gadgets. Plus she's kinda paranoid."

"She's not wrong to be cautious. This town is a dream come true for many, but sometimes those dreams can be nightmares." I patted him on the shoulder and turned him toward the house. "Go ahead. I've disarmed the protections, so your main threat is Boa."

He tensed. "Snakes?"

"Boa is our cat. White and fluffy like a feather boa. Hence the name."

"Right." He relaxed. "I knew that."

He proceeded into the house with the groceries.

When I came inside with my own armload, I found him bent over Boa, cooing at her.

I did a quick ghost check. Mrs. Pinkman wasn't there. Ambrosia had taken the glowing book with her to school, so I didn't expect to see my old neighbor back anytime soon.

Xavier was still petting Boa. "You're a pretty kitty," he said.

"Ham," she said, swishing her fluffy white tail back and forth.

Xavier jerked his hand back and gave me a wide-eyed look. "Did that just happen?"

"You look like someone who's never seen a talking cat."

He crossed his arms and straightened up. "Oh, I've *seen* things. Things that would keep most people up at night."

"I know. I've heard the legends. You've seen sandworms from another world. And a giant, angry god made of volcanic lava." I waved my hand at the bags he'd left on the counter. "Put the ice cream in the freezer."

He opened the freezer compartment door and started loading it. With his back to me, he said, "Seeing a sandworm from the outside isn't so bad. Seeing it from the inside is like..." He trailed off and shuddered visibly as he put away the frozen treats.

"You've been through a lot for someone your age," I said. "It's given you character. Not many young men would offer to help a single mother bring in her groceries." I paused. "Not unless there was something they wanted from her."

He said nothing.

I said, "So, what is it, Mr. Batista? What's going on here? And don't say you came over to help me unload groceries because you wanted to learn more about my seasonal shopping tips."

With his back to me, he said. "I like helping people."

"Me, too. That's why I became a librarian. People who like helping people are the luckiest people in the world. Did you want to talk to me about a career in information services?"

"Not exactly."

"Then what are you after?" I paused and considered what I was about to say before I said it. I'd been thinking about Xavier that day, but also about something else. "Do you think I have a stash of Activator X in the attic?"

He whirled around. "Do you?"

"That seems unlikely," I said. "Everyone knows there's no such thing." I arched an eyebrow. "Right?"

He slouched and put his hands in his pockets. "Yeah," he said. "It's just something people say they have, so they can get more money out of us nothing people."

"Xavier Batista, you are *not* a nothing person."

He didn't look convinced.

I pointed at the freezer compartment of the fridge. "Pull the Rocky Road back out of there, and let's have a chat."

"Won't that spoil your dinner?"

"You can't spoil your dinner *with* your dinner."

"Ice cream for dinner?" He shook his head and looked up and down. "That supernatural metabolism of yours lets you get away with a lot. My mom can't even have a granola bar or she bloats up."

"Do you think I'm the same age as your mother?" I held up a hand. "Never mind. Don't answer that. I'll take the compliment as it stands."

"You're *way* hotter than my mom." He immediately dropped his gaze. "Please forget I said that," he muttered.

"Never. I'm making a note. *Hotter than Xavier's mom.*" I mimed writing it down on a piece of paper, folding it up, and putting it in my pocket.

He had the posture of someone wishing they were elsewhere, or possibly dead.

"Don't die on me," I said. "Get the Rocky Road."

He did.

I grabbed some bowls and spoons, and we started eating dinner.

I put a frozen pizza in the oven for our dessert. I used magic to turn on the oven and put in the pizza, so I didn't have to get up. It was nothing to me, just an everyday use of my levitation, but Xavier watched it all with big eyes.

"That is so cool," Xavier said. "You make it look so effortless."

"It takes great effort to make things look effortless. The key to doing simple things well is to do complicated things well. I can turn on the stove easily because it's just one little twist, which is nothing after you've spent hours peeling eggs."

"Peeling eggs doesn't sound so hard. I do that for my mom when she makes potato salad."

"It's tricky when they're uncooked."

He mouthed a *wow*. "You're amazing. Everything about you."

"I bet you say that to all the girls."

He rubbed his ears. "No," he said simply.

"You don't tell your girlfriend that everything about her is amazing?"

He shrugged. "Liza's, well, you know. Our relationship is, like, whatever. It is what it is."

"It's a relationship with no adjectives?"

He shrugged again.

"Xavier, you're making me really glad I didn't do any dating in my early twenties."

"I'm twenty-five."

"Exactly," I said. "At what age do you think you'll be ready to have a relationship worthy of adjectives?"

His expression grew deadly serious. "I'm ready now."

"That's sweet, but I have a boyfriend. Tall guy. Pointy teeth. You've met him."

Xavier rubbed the tops of his ears again and looked away. It was so easy to get a reaction from him. No wonder the guy was always getting into fights. He wore his emotions on his sleeve.

Xavier squirmed on his chair. "Speaking of Detective Bentley, did he, uh, tell you everything? About when he came to my house yesterday?"

"I heard you were cooperative," I said. "It sounded like you did or said something he found amusing, but he didn't say."

Xavier tugged at his collar, then pulled the front of his shirt back and forth, fanning himself.

From some unseen hiding place, Ribbons dropped a psychic line into my head. "Beware, Zed. The young human male is proliferating mating pheromones and sending them into the air."

I sent the wyvern a psychic thank you.

Ribbons asked, "When is the pizza ready, Zed?"

Without speaking out loud, I let him know the pizza would be ready in a minute, and that he could probably get a satisfying reaction from our guest if he made one of his grand entrances.

Xavier had stopped fanning his shirt and was watching me intently. "Where'd you go just now?"

"Nowhere. I'm right here."

"You were doing something." There was fiery accusation in his voice. "Did you cast a spell? On me?"

"Calm down. I didn't cast a spell on you. Why? Is that what you want? A spell? What does Mr. Batista want?" He bristled every time I called him Mr. Batista, so I kept doing it.

He leaned back, adopting a fake relaxed posture, and drummed his fingers on the top of the kitchen island. "What do I want? Well, I don't want to get bitten by a vampire, that's for sure."

"You don't?" We hadn't been talking about vampires, so the topic shift surprised me.

"No," Xavier said. "And if he told you that I asked him to bite me, then I'm afraid there was a miscommunication." He held my gaze steadily, unblinking. "I didn't really want him to bite me." Still no blinking. He was trying really hard to convince me.

I pressed my lips together to keep from smirking. So, *that* was the funny thing that happened when Bentley paid a visit to young Xavier.

I asked, "What *did* you want?"

"Nothing," he sputtered. "I wanted him to know that I understood that he *could* bite me, if he wanted to. Because he's a lot more powerful than me. I only said that so he knew that I knew where I stood."

"Did you tilt your head back and show him your neck?"

Xavier squirmed in his chair. "No," he said.

"Did you bat your eyelashes at him, and look at him with puppy dog eyes?"

Xavier's nostrils flared. "No," he said, then, "Ew. Yuck. I wouldn't do that."

In other words, that was *exactly* what he had done.

"Don't be embarrassed," I said. "So what if you have a crush on the guy?"

"Yeah," he said, then, "No!"

"So what if you exposed your neck and invited him to bite you? He has that effect on people. Or at least he does now, since becoming a creature of the grave. It's perfectly understandable that when the two of you were alone, your true feelings came out."

Xavier got to his feet quickly, knocking the chair over behind him in his haste.

At that exact moment, Ribbons made his entrance, flying in with his powerful wings cupped for maximum air disturbance. The wind blew all around us. He was a small beast, but powerful. When he wanted to whip the air, he was like a helicopter, except instead of the motor noise, there was a blood-curdling supernatural howl.

Xavier let out every swear word in existence in rapid succession, raised his fists in a fighter stance, and jumped between me and the wyvern.

Ribbons, loving every second of this, landed on the kitchen island. He continued to howl and blast us with wind.

Xavier was still between us, ready to strike. He was going to get himself killed if he took one shot at the tiny terror.

I snapped my fingers at the wyvern. "Stand down," I commanded.

Ribbons dialed it back to half the level of fury.

"All the way down," I said, snapping my fingers again. "You've made your entrance, now stop terrorizing Xavier. We don't want his hair to go white from shock. The poor boy's only twenty-five. And besides, you'd be more menacing if you didn't have one foot in a carton of ice cream."

Ribbons stopped flapping and howling. "I meant to do that," he said in my mind. Then he backed his way out of the open carton. He licked the Rocky Road ice cream off the talons of his foot with his long, purple tongue.

Xavier was still standing between us, ready to do battle to protect me. He stood absolutely no chance against the wyvern, but I was touched by his heroism. He was undisciplined and emotional, but the kid had heart.

I placed a hand on his shoulder. "You can stand down, too," I said. "Ribbons doesn't want to rip out your entrails. He's here for the pizza."

"He came out of nowhere," Xavier said. "It was a sneak attack."

"That's how he likes it."

Ribbon's nostrils flared. "This male human reeks of pheromones, Zed. You might be under his spell. I will get rid of him immediately, in exchange for half of the pizza."

"He's staying, and you only get a third of the pizza," I said.

Xavier was warily picking his chair up and returning to his seat. "He talks to you in your head, right?"

"Yes." Xavier worked with my aunt, plus it wasn't the supernatural community's best-kept secret that I had a wyvern in my house.

He asked, his voice cracking, "Can you get him to say something to me?"

Ribbons responded, only to me. I couldn't repeat what he'd said verbatim, so I gave Xavier a toned-down version. "No, he can't speak in your mind. But if you play your cards right, he might bite you on the neck."

Xavier scowled.

The timer for the pizza dinged.

CHAPTER 22

Zoey sat on the edge of the tub, brushing her teeth while I washed my face in preparation for bed. She'd just returned from the Abernathys, and I'd been telling her about my busy day.

She took the toothbrush out of her mouth and asked, "Then what?"

"Then the three of us ate pizza together," I said.

"You, Xavier, and Ribbons? That's a new combo. Did everyone use their best table manners?"

"Ribbons tried to terrorize Xavier a couple more times, but it didn't work as well as the grand entrance."

"He does know how to make an entrance."

"He really does."

"What did Xavier want?"

"He wasn't keen on tipping his hand early. It wasn't until the post-dinner round of adult beverages that he finally came out with his proposal."

"Proposal?" She resumed brushing.

"He asked to be my intern."

With her mouth full of toothbrush and suds, she said what I assumed was, "But what about Ambrosia?"

"That's what I told him. I already have an intern. Ambrosia. But then he got down on his knees and begged me to let him help me in some way, just so he could be

183

part of something magical. He said he would sweep floors, or mix potions, or run errands. Anything I needed. He volunteered to do sundry domestic chores."

She came over to share the sink and started rinsing. "And?"

"Of course I told him no. I already have Ambrosia as an intern. Plus I have *you* for sundry domestic chores."

"Plus all your spells." She opened the mirrored vanity. "Some of these lotions are multiplying," she said, changing the subject.

I leaned around her and looked in. "Multiplying?"

"They've been mating with each other and making babies. Look. There was a big bottle of cucumber body wash in here, and a tub of apricot cream. Now there's also a small jar of cucumber-apricot under-eye rejuvenator. They mated and made a baby toiletry."

"It does look that way. I don't remember buying any under-eye rejuvenator period, let alone cucumber-apricot. Do you think we should be worried?"

She picked up the petite jar. "I think that if we did happen to worry, and we gave ourselves worry lines, at least this would take them away."

"I love it. The classic problem that takes care of itself. Much better than problems that get worse when you ignore them."

She opened the new jar, sniffed it, then began applying a thin layer under her eyes, as instructed by the lettering on the jar. "What about Xavier? Is he a classic problem that takes care of itself, or one that gets worse when you ignore it?"

"Probably the latter. He kept begging me for a job. Any job at all. He was so desperate."

"Was he really on his knees?"

"Metaphorically, yes."

"I like Xavier, but I don't like him on his knees, metaphorical or not, making proposals to my mother."

"I think his crush on Bentley is far bigger than any feelings he might be harboring for your mother."

"If you say so," she said in a sing-song voice.

"During our second round of ciders, he pointed out that the ol' car could use some cleaning."

"How dare he? Foxy Pumpkin is spotless."

"Compared to Charlize's car, maybe. But it's got some sand in the floor mats, plus there's the weird smell in the back seat."

"That was from Ribbons. Remember when he didn't feel well last month, and asked to be driven around like a colicky baby?"

I pointed at her. "Yes. I do. And that's precisely the sort of thing we can get our new intern to do for us, assuming he does a good job detailing the car."

She went back to rummaging through the medicine cabinet. "Here's a turnip-flavored mouthwash," she said. "And something called Deeta's Dazzling Foot Powder with Friction Boost." She pulled out more bottles and jars, then plunged her arms deep into the dark cavity. "There's no back on this cabinet. It might go on forever."

"We'd better keep the door closed so Boa doesn't jump in there and get lost in the walls again."

My daughter returned to her seat on the edge of the tub and crossed one ankle over her knee. "I'm going to try the foot powder." She removed her sock and sprinkled the sole of her foot with the shimmering powder. "That's nice," she said, testing the friction boost on the tile floor.

"What about your day?" I asked. "Did the Abernathys feed you dinner?"

"Mrs. Abernathy made meatloaf from scratch. She didn't put any spaghetti noodles in it. She said when you add noodles to meatloaf, it becomes casserole. And, Mom?"

"Yes?"

"She wore an apron. A real apron, from a kitchenwares store. She got it at Bed, Bath and Beyond. Once a month, they drive up to an outlet mall up the coast. Everything in their house, they bought new, from a store. And the house is only five years old."

"It's just a baby house," I said. It went without saying that the Abernathys' house didn't have magic powers, although it did have a funeral parlor on the lower floor.

"Mrs. Abernathy doesn't like some of the light fixtures. They're basic builder grade, so she's thinking about upgrading to something trendier, but she doesn't want to be wasteful."

"How very normal."

"Mrs. Abernathy said I could come along on their next big shopping trip, but they're not sure if they'll go this month. The outlet malls get crowded around Christmas." She powdered her other foot. "She's really thoughtful. She's always offering to make me a fried egg sandwich if I'm hungry before dinner."

"Sounds like you have it pretty good over there."

"Ambrosia takes a lot of things for granted."

"You think? How so?"

"If Mr. Abernathy kisses Mrs. Abernathy in front of her, Ambrosia gags and tells them to stop being gross."

I nodded. I could imagine Ambrosia doing that. She was at a stage in her development where she was simultaneously fascinated and repulsed by the idea of intimacy.

Zoey jumped up from her seat on the tub, gave me a peck on the cheek, and said, "Good night, Mom."

"Do you want me to tuck you in?"

She laughed, thinking I was joking, and went off to bed.

I heard her calling for Boa, then the cat meowing as she also made her way to bed. Boa loved curling up on my daughter's bed, pretending to sleep while she waited for Zoey to nod off, at which point the cat would leave the room to begin her nightly rounds. Boa's job was protecting the house against the sort of threats a small white cat could deal with. Mostly spiders. She would return to Zoey's bed shortly before Zoey awoke, giving the impression she had been there all night. She was a good girl.

I collected the assorted bathroom products and their hybrid offspring, put them back in the cabinet, and closed the mirrored door.

I looked at myself in the mirror for what felt like the first time in a long time. I did an inventory. Hazel eyes, not as lined as Zinnia's. Red hair, not as bright as my daughter's. Freckles holding steady. Good cleavage, if I wore a fussy bra, which I had that day. Aesthetically pleasing waist to hip ratio. I could see some of what Bentley saw in me, most of what made Xavier so embarrassed, and a fraction of what I pretended to believe I had.

People would rather be around women who overrated their looks than women who went on and on about minor flaws, so I'd always erred on the side of being pleased with my appearance. Few of us truly see ourselves exactly as we are, so why not overshoot in the better direction?

I straightened up, turned to my best angle, and gave myself a nod of approval.

What had Xavier Batista said? That's right. *You're way hotter than my mom.*

It was never good to be compared to other moms, unless you could win a round. I could never be as "normal" as Mrs. Abernathy, but at least I was hotter than Mrs. Batista.

CHAPTER 23

Tuesday Morning

I came down to the kitchen, where I found my daughter and Mrs. Pinkman having breakfast together.

Neither of them seemed to be aware of each other.

Zoey nibbled her peanut butter toast while Mrs. Pinkman sipped tea from a chipped teacup. I puzzled over that one. If Mrs. Pinkman could manifest ghost tea and a ghost teacup, why would she manifest a chipped one? I would never know. Magic was quirky.

I'd noticed something amiss upstairs already, so I asked Zoey, "Is your bedroom getting smaller?"

"It did sound slightly different this morning," she said. "No echoes. I thought it was the new wall-to-wall carpet."

"You have carpet?"

"It sprung up overnight like moss." She munched thoughtfully.

Mrs. Pinkman continued to sip her ghost tea.

Zoey said, "Now that I think about it, the scale of everything was slightly off. I take it by your question that your room is smaller today?"

"Either that or all my furniture got bigger. No wall-to-wall carpet, though. How mossy is yours?"

"Very mossy. I like it. The carpet is a deep shade of green, and the walls are orange. It goes perfectly with your lamp. The one Auntie Z gave you as a housewarming gift."

I waved my hand. "Oh, no. It's not mine. That lamp is all yours."

She glanced up at the ceiling, in the direction of the bedrooms. "We must be getting a house guest," she said.

"That is what I'm afraid of."

I looked over at Mrs. Pinkman, who was calmly sipping her ghost tea. The teacup apparently held an endless supply. The woman offered no clues about who or what might be coming our way.

Zoey clapped her hands together. "It must be Gigi," she said. Gigi was her pet name for her maternal grandmother, or possibly her only grandmother. Her father was an immortal genie who didn't have parents in a conventional sense.

"It might be her," I said. "She did threaten to join us again, for the holidays."

"I hope she does, and she stays with us instead of Auntie Z. If our new guest room isn't nice enough for her, she can take my room."

"That's cute that you think you have any choice in the matter. Your grandmother will take whichever room suits her best."

Zoey rolled her eyes, then picked up her toast and took a big bite.

The doorbell rang.

"Doorbell," Zoey said, her mouth gummy with peanut butter.

"Doorbell," I agreed. "Who could it be? There's no door to the new guest room yet, so I don't think it's our house guest."

"It's probably Ambrosia," Zoey said. "That sounds to me like her ring."

The doorbell rang again.

"Doorbell," I said. It did have an Ambrosia Abernathy ring to it.

Zoey ran to answer the door.

A moment later, she returned to the kitchen with her best friend in tow.

Ambrosia was breathless. She spoke rapidly, like someone who'd just received Trinada's Confession Hex at full strength. "Minerva Pinkman got away from me, Zara. I'm really sorry. I don't know what happened. I was reading her last night, and this morning she was just gone."

"I know," I said.

"You know?" Ambrosia bit her lower lip. Her eyes glistened.

"She must be using me, or this house, as a homing beam." I waved at the ghost lady sipping tea from her chipped teacup. "She's having tea at the moment, and seems quite relaxed."

Ambrosia turned, saw the ghost, and shrieked. Even if you were aware of ghosts, and the fact that you could see them, it was still startling to encounter them around the house.

At this, Mrs. Pinkman smiled at each of the three of us in turn. Only two out of three of us were able to see this.

Zoey, who, unlike Fatima Nix, was good at drawing conclusions from clues, said, "Mrs. Pinkman is here with us in the kitchen? That explains why I felt like I was being watched when I was making breakfast. I thought it might be Ribbons, planning to swipe my toast."

"It's too early for him," I said. "He's either still out hunting, or getting his beauty sleep."

Ambrosia shook her finger at Mrs. Pinkman. "Naughty ghost. You're not supposed to run off like that." Ambrosia gave me a pleading look. "Can't you do a spell to bind her to me, so I don't have to go chasing her all over town?"

"I don't know if that's necessary," I said. "You've put in a lot of hours with her over the last couple of days. For now, why don't you leave her be?"

"But we don't know why she's here." Ambrosia frowned and twisted a strand of her bleached hair. "I haven't reviewed all her memories."

"And you never will," I said. "It's not possible, even on fast forward. Don't sweat it. I'm sure if there had been something important, you would have caught the scent by now."

Ambrosia put her hands on her hips. "What now? Are we supposed to let her roam around, doing whatever she wants?"

"We could," I said. "She's not hurting anything. Mrs. Pinkman might be the sort of problem that takes care of itself."

Zoey interjected, telling Ambrosia, "She was a very nice lady. I didn't know what I was feeling this morning, but it wasn't a bad thing. I could get used to having her around. In fact, some of the literature states that if a ghost is around long enough, even those without sight can start to perceive it." She squinted in the direction of the kitchen island. "Is that her, sitting on the chair at the end?"

Sounding surprised, Ambrosia said, "Yes. Can you really see her?"

"Not exactly," Zoey said. "But the light there is hazy, and the scent is different." She sniffed the air. "Maybe it's my mind playing tricks on me, but I swear I can smell her perfume."

"Perhaps you can," I said. "There are many ways of perception beyond sight." I sniffed. "Nose-wise, I've got nothing, but I don't have your nose."

"We can't leave her ghosting around forever," Ambrosia said.

"Why not?" I asked. "Does having a loose thread trigger your OCD?" In witch circles, OCD could mean

Obsessive Compulsive Disorder, as it did to the rest of the world, or it could mean Overly Cautious Disasterizing.

"No," Ambrosia said, scowling as only a teenager could. "If we leave her ghosting around, she could metastasize into a poltergeist."

"That's a possibility, but it's not going to happen overnight." I patted Ambrosia on the shoulder. "You did an excellent job reading her, and a fine job helping out as much as you could. I'm going to turn in a positive report to the coven."

"But—"

I cut her off with a hand wave. "Mrs. Pinkman doesn't seem like the sort of problem that gets worse when you ignore it, so why don't we try the other option? I suggest we leave her alone, and wait for her to sort herself out."

Ambrosia blinked at me three times, then turned to Zoey. "The skin under your eyes looks different," she said. "Fresher."

"Thanks," Zoey said. "It's a new under-eye rejuvenator. Want to try some? We have time before school."

"As long as it doesn't mess up my makeup," Ambrosia said.

Zoey grabbed the remains of her peanut butter toast, and the two girls clattered up the stairs to trade beauty tips.

I looked over at Mrs. Pinkman. "Teenagers," I said.

She smiled, then went over to the sink, where she washed her ghost teacup with ghost water.

CHAPTER 24

Wednesday Evening
Coven Meeting
Back Room of Dreamland Coffee, Downtown Location

As I'd promised Ambrosia, I gave the entire coven a glowing report of the job she'd done, reading Mrs. Pinkman under my guidance.

When I finished speaking, there was silence for several seconds—a rare occurrence at coven meetings.

Margaret Mills spoke first. "It's against the rules to get another witch to do work that fits under your own specialty."

My aunt, Zinnia Riddle, placed her hand on her best friend's arm. "Now, Margaret, we ought to be supportive of the refinement of our coven's skills. Ambrosia Abernathy is an asset to the coven and ought to be treated as such. Furthermore, reading ghosts falls into her skill set every bit as much as it does Zara's."

The owner of the coffee shop, Maisy Nix, eyed me with her scrutinizing gaze. The leggy, stylish, forty-five year old witch had been my friend when she'd helped me out with some special coffee beans for Nick's wake-up brew, but she was back in frenemy mode.

Maisy said, "The real question is, why does Zara feel the need to collect young people the way some people collect decorative spoons or classic cars?"

I held my hand to my chest. "Me? Collecting young people?" I looked over at Maisy's niece, Fatima, who was squirming in her seat. Fatima's gaze was fixed on something on the ceiling, all the better to avoid eye contact with me.

I scanned over at Ambrosia, who pointed her thumb at Fatima and mouthed the words *she's mad at you.*

I mouthed the words *you think?*

"Who'd want to collect young people?" Margaret asked. "But if you want any more, Zara, I've got a few kids who are getting old enough to be useful."

"I'm not collecting young people," I said.

Maisy asked, "Is it because your daughter is getting older and doesn't need you as much?"

"I'm not sure that kid ever needed me at all," I said. "From the moment she made her taxi seat debut, she's been calling most of the shots."

Maisy didn't look convinced. "She needs you less every day, and now you're overcompensating by finding other people you believe need your guidance. I know you have the Batista boy washing your car. He came in to get coffee today, and he was bragging about it."

Margaret said, "He's interning for you?" She crossed her arms and huffed. "Like that's going to work out. But I suppose he can get what he gets for not making a better choice in a mentor."

Zinnia said, "If it's any consolation, Margaret, he didn't ask me, either." She gave me an enigmatic look. "I suppose if we had as much flair as Zara, we might have been more... attractive." She blinked slowly. "As mentors."

Maisy turned on me, a malicious grin on her lips. "Is that what's going on, Zara? Bentley can be a little dull. It's no surprise you're hunting around for a younger model. And, since Nick Lafleur has his dance card full between your mother and your half-sister, I guess it's the Batista boy for you. The apple doesn't fall far from the tree, does it?"

I was too outraged about being compared to my mother to speak for a second, so I snorted.

The other witches cackled. Even Ambrosia.

I found my words and blustered at Maisy, "If anyone's been hunting around for young men in this town, it's you, Maisy. How many guys did you go on dates with this week alone?"

The other witches' cackles turned into a chorus of mild compliments for my "sick burn," as Ambrosia put it.

Maisy's otherwise lovely face twitched like a cat under a blanket. "That's none of your business."

Margaret Mills said, "Technically, it is coven business. We have rules. Witches are obligated to inform the coven of any romantic entanglements, since it could represent a security risk for all of us if one of us were to become compromised."

Ambrosia let out a squeak. I guessed it was the first the teenaged girl had heard of this rule.

Maisy crossed her arms. "I'm not going to be compromised, Margaret Mills. I'm not the one dating a mad scientist with two brains in one body."

Zinnia cut in with, "Barry has only one brain. He has two minds. The mind and the brain are not always the same."

Ambrosia raised her hand. "How does he think two minds' worth of thoughts with only one brain?"

"It's a type of pseudo-dimension overlay," Margaret said. "Like how the gorgons have snakes in their hair, but also no snakes in their hair."

Maisy snorted. "If you ask me, Barry Blackstone is a bigger security risk than anyone I choose to date."

Margaret raised her voice. "Nobody asked you about it, Maisy! Who we're dating is not even on the docket for discussion tonight!"

Maisy pointed at me. "Zara's the one who brought it up."

"I did not," I said, then quickly corrected myself. "Okay, maybe I did, but I was only..." All eyes were on me, except Fatima's. I sighed. "I was only trying to change the subject away from me and my pathological need to be useful to people, especially the younger ones, it seems."

The coven said nothing. Funny how the truth cut through even the deepest manure.

Everyone stayed quiet. Even Humphrey the komodo dragon stopped pacing in his cage.

"Not that my efforts to help people always work out," I said, looking directly at our second-youngest witch. "Fatima, are you really that angry with me? Just because I took you on an adventure that included a stop at Becky's Roadhouse for a free soda? I'd hate to see how you treat someone who buys you dinner."

Fatima's mouth dropped open.

Margaret said, "Popcorn, anyone?" She'd brought popcorn, and started handing around self-popping bowls.

I looked over at the one person I could expect to support me. "A little help, Aunt Zinnia?"

My aunt shook her bowl of magically popping popcorn. "We have two ears to every mouth for a reason, Zara. If one of us has a grievance with another, we ought to have the matter aired out, regardless of familial relationships."

"Fine," I said. "Let's keep clearing the air, if that's what this is."

The others turned to Fatima. Her aunt prompted her to go ahead and speak of her issues.

Fatima stared at the ceiling for a long time, her eyes brimming with tears that she kept blinking back, before she spoke. "It's just that some of the more powerful witches like to take advantage of the weaker ones."

Margaret suddenly blew out the popcorn she'd been eating. "What's that supposed to mean? Is every one of us either a bully or a victim? Are those the only two choices?" She turned to Zinnia. "Which one am I?"

Zinnia shook her head slowly. "That's not the point."

"Isn't it?" More popcorn sprayed from Margaret's mouth. She'd quickly reloaded while Zinnia had been speaking. "If everyone at the bottom is oppressed, and everyone at the top is an oppressor, how big is the middle?"

Ambrosia raised her hand. "If there is a middle, how do you know you're in it, and you're not one of the others?" She shrank in her chair and rubbed her forearms. "Sometimes I feel like what I think doesn't matter to anyone." Very softly, she added, "Even to myself."

Maisy rose to her feet. She wasn't the leader of the coven, but she owned the venue, which gave her a bit more sway. "We will not be indulging in the game of victimhood bingo tonight. Not a single witch here is, by anyone's definition, weak. Now, can anyone tell me the purpose of the coven?"

The chairs squeaked as the whole coven squirmed. Margaret reloaded her popcorn cannon. My aunt gazed past me, giving away nothing. Fatima was still crying, but quietly. Ambrosia was frowning like a sulky teen. Maisy stood, looking hopeful and patient, like a good teacher.

"The purpose of this coven," Maisy said. "Anyone?"

Meekly, Ambrosia answered, "Is it like a book club, except we share spells and magic books?"

Maisy raised her arms like a preacher. "We lift each other up." Her voice filled the space, increasing in volume as she spoke. "In a world of constant peril, with beings of every kind scrabbling for power and dominance, it is our sacred duty as witches, and as daughters of the Four Eves to—"

She was interrupted by Margaret jumping up. "Look at the time," she exclaimed, spraying her final mouthful of popcorn over the table. "I have to pick up my kids from their hockey lessons." She trotted over to the door. "Good pep talk, Maisy. I'll get my notes tomorrow from Zinnia."

Zinnia, who was also getting to her feet, said, "I'm afraid I must duck out early as well. An old friend has requested my company for a glass of wine so that he may 'pick my brain' regarding a redhead he would like to pursue romantically."

Maisy, who'd dropped her arms to her sides, looked exhausted from the effort of an incomplete pep talk. She said to Zinnia, "Don't do anything I wouldn't do."

The others stirred as well, preparing to leave.

Ambrosia muttered something about helping her father put a spit-shine on the new caskets for the showroom.

A moment later, the only ones left at the table were me and the two Nix witches.

The table itself, which was extremely jinxed and had been wobbling all evening, gave up and fell over on its side abruptly, as though it were a dog playing dead for treats.

"I guess that's it," I said. "Another successful coven meeting."

Maisy said to me, "You could always cap off the evening by insulting my niece further." She smiled, baring the maximum number of teeth. "Or you could apologize for what you put her through."

"What I put her through? *Your niece* let a hairy goat thing knock me over, on purpose. If anyone was put through anything over the weekend, it was me." I rubbed my backside. "My tailbone is still sore." It wasn't.

Fatima got to her feet and pulled on her shaggy jacket. Glaring right at me, she said, "I'm the one who's sorry, Zara." Her tone was more than sarcastic. It was contemptuous. "I'm sorry I invited you to participate in a time-honored Christmas ritual when I should have known you wouldn't appreciate it. You don't care about any customs. You only care about yourself, and getting what you want." She turned on her heel and left.

I looked to Maisy, prepared to receive a second blast.

All Maisy said was, "Huh."

"Huh?"

"Fatima has never expressed herself so well. Whatever you've been doing to her, keep it up. She seems to be building some true character."

"Are you serious? You think it's good that I've made your niece so angry?"

"Yes. She's one of those young people who doesn't know what she wants, or even who she is. She latches onto ideas that sound right in the moment, but without any understanding of the big picture. I believe you have been forcing some growth upon her."

"It's possible I have. Accidentally, of course, so I'm not sure I deserve any credit."

"Even so, credit is due." Maisy righted the playing-dead table. "Please continue the work you have started. I'll try not to stand in your way." She cast a spell on a nearby broom so that it began sweeping up the popcorn mess.

I headed toward the door, where I paused. "Maisy, I didn't mean what I implied, about you dating all those guys to overcompensate for something."

"Don't be silly. You said it because you meant it, and also because it is true." Her tone was soft and friendly, which surprised me. "Let the witch who is perfect cast the first spell from a castle of glass," she said.

We stared at each other for a moment.

I broke the silence. "It's darn hard work trying to mold young people," I said.

Maisy smirked and raised one eyebrow. "It's darn hard work juggling as many men as I do."

I shrugged. "We gotta do something to keep ourselves busy."

"The devil finds jobs for idle hands." She pointed at the door. "Turn the knob to the left, and it will lock automatically after you go."

"Will do," I said, and I did.

CHAPTER 25

Thursday Morning

Boa looked up at me with innocence in her green eyes.

Ribbons, perched on top of the refrigerator, gave me a dirty look with his beady little eyes.

"We are not guilty," the wyvern said. "Why must you blame us for everything, Zed?"

I pointed to the broken dishes on the kitchen floor. "Not for everything. Just these broken dishes."

Boa walked over to the dishes, sniffed them, and backed away in the scaredy-cat stance, back high and tail extra fluffy. She let out a guttural moan, swishing her tail back and forth.

"I know Miss Whiskers didn't do it," I said to Ribbons. "She's not sophisticated enough to put on an act like this. If Zoey had dropped them, she would have also cleaned up." I pointed at myself. "And I know *I* didn't break those dishes, so who did?"

"It is obvious, Zed."

"Are you saying it's connected to that new room upstairs that the house has been making, mostly using square footage from my bedroom? I've been banging my shin on furniture every day this week. The nightstand is so close to my bed, it's practically in bed with me."

"I do not know the nature of the new space, except that it is interior, and I have not found an entrance."

"Then what's so obvious? Do you know who broke these dishes, or not?"

"A ghost did it."

"A ghost," I said. "Did you happen to see this ghost?"

"I do not see ghosts. I saw a ball of light. The light had a type of energy."

"As in, the energy of someone specific? Did you catch a name, Ribbons? Help me out, buddy. I can't read your mind unless you let me."

"I believe it was the ghost whose human name at the time of her passing was Minerva Pinkman."

"Mrs. Pinkman did this?" The idea checked out, so I took the wyvern's word. He had broken plenty of things before, and he'd never bothered to lie about it. If anything, he seemed proud of his chaos and destruction.

Ribbons blinked at me and said nothing. He didn't like answering the same question twice, unless the answer titillated him on a personal level.

"She must be leveling up fast," I said. "That's got to be..." I used levitation to lift the broken shards "...five pounds of dishware she knocked out of the cupboard." I looked from the cat to the wyvern and back again. "Did either of you see it happen?"

Boa had backed herself into the far corner of the kitchen, where she continued moaning her unpleasant refrain.

"I have seen Minerva Pinkman move other objects, Zed. She is, as you say, *leveling up*." He used his long, purple tongue to clean one eye and then the other. "As she grows in strength, the time of her becoming a poltergeist draws nearer."

"I realize that."

"You do know what a poltergeist is, yes?"

"Yes. I know what a poltergeist is. But, as evidenced by a *certain beast's* continued reign of terror in this household, I'm not very good at booting out destructive forces."

"Boa has her good qualities," the wyvern said, pretending he didn't know I meant him.

I tossed the broken dishware into the garbage with a noisy clatter. The plates had been a thrift store find, fine china with an attractive green motif featuring a pheasant. My sadness over the loss was mitigated by the anticipation of shopping at Mia's Kit and Kaboodle for replacements.

I asked the ancient creature perching like a gargoyle atop my fridge, "Do you think I should try to banish Mrs. Pinkman?" I felt awful saying the idea out loud, let alone thinking about doing it.

"Such magic exists, Zed. In many circles, it is done."

"Not in this circle," I said. "Not yet, anyway. Those spells are for bad spirits. Malignant ones. There's nothing evil about Mrs. Pinkman."

"Then why is she hiding from you, Zed? She is not here now, though she frequently haunts this kitchen. She knows that she has done wrong."

"Bah." I waved a hand. "She's probably wandered off and gotten lost in the folds of time. I bet she's walking through a psychic hallway full of doors leading to rooms holding the key memories that formed her personality."

"If you say so, Zed." He turned his seahorse-like head toward the kitchen clock. In a lighter tone, he transmitted into my mind, "Because I have been awoken early, I will partake in the morning coffee ritual."

"Oh, will you? Can you say the magic words?"

He hissed a little, then spat out, "Please and thank you."

I grabbed the coffee pot, which—thank my lucky stars —hadn't been broken by Mrs. Pinkman, and began brewing for the morning ritual.

CHAPTER 26

Friday

Frank and I took lunch together, leaving the library for a shopping trip to Mia's Kit and Kaboodle. I needed more plates to replace the ones Mrs. Pinkman broke, plus we hadn't been there in ages. Frank loved the vintage clothes, whereas I loved the... everything.

We took my car, and silver-haired, dapper-dressed Frank whistled over how clean Foxy Pumpkin was.

"If I didn't know better, I'd say it was brand new," Frank said. "It even smells new. How is that possible? One of your spells?"

"My new intern has detailed it three times this week," I said. "The wyvern funk is finally out of the back area."

"I thought a squirrel had died back there." Frank leaned back and sniffed the Nissan 300ZX's very small back seat area. "That is quite the improvement. Which intern do you have detailing your car three times a week?"

"The boy. Xavier Batista."

"He's going to get bored of cleaning your car and expect to do something more hands-on."

"I know." I put Foxy Pumpkin in gear, and started driving toward Mia's. There was some snow piled up between the street and the sidewalks, but the streets were clear and dry.

Frank said, "In fact, the boy probably won't be satisfied until you've put his life in danger."

"I would never do that."

"Then he'll never be satisfied."

"Xavier says he's perfectly happy doing sundry chores, as long as it's for a witch."

Frank scoffed. "The boy might *say* he's perfectly happy doing sundry chores, but people don't always mean what they say. Especially not when they use the phrase 'perfectly happy,' as in, 'Oh, go on ahead without me, dear. I'm *perfectly happy* to stay home with my sore foot, all alone, rearranging the linen closet.' See?"

"Xavier didn't say it with so much passive aggression."

"My mother did. She always said she was 'perfectly happy,' and my father always took her at her word." He gazed out the window. Frank's parents were both deceased, and he didn't talk about them much.

I kept quiet while Frank remembered his parents.

We got to Mia's and parked. As Frank was stepping out of the car, he asked, "What's this?" He pulled something from the crack of the passenger seat. It was a pair of in-ear headphones. "Are these your daughter's?"

"I don't think so. I've seen Xavier wearing them. He must have dropped them in the seat crack the last time he was detailing the car." I circled around the back of the car, took the headphones, and put them in my purse, next to the Mountain Joe mug that was still in there. "I'll be sure he gets them the next time I see him."

"Be sure to fire him, as well," Frank said. "If you don't terminate this ill-advised internship, there's only one way for your little arrangement to end."

"Oh? You mean with him thanking me for my wise mentorship?"

Frank managed to give me the look of a librarian peering over a pair of reading glasses, despite not wearing any glasses. "Bloodshed," he said. "That's where your internship is headed. Deep down, that's what the boy wants. If you're lucky, it will just be his blood being shed, not yours."

I made an expression of disgust. "You can be kind of dark for a children's librarian."

Frank beamed. "That's what makes me so good at my job."

"What if I keep asking him to clean my car, and nothing more interesting than that? He'll eventually get bored and quit. That would be much better than firing him. I don't want to break his heart. He's a good kid."

"And what happens to the 'good kid' in every single war movie?"

"I don't watch a lot of war movies."

"But you know what happens to the good kid," Frank said. "The sweet farm boy who's never left Iowa, or Ohio, or one of those places with all the wheat fields."

I pulled open the door to Mia's, hoping it would end the conversation.

Inside, Frank followed me to the housewares, and the display of mismatched china.

"The sweet farm boy gets shot in the guts, and dies slowly," Frank said. "He asks the other soldiers to look in on his folks back home, and to tell his mama he loves her."

I tried to peruse the dishware. "Now you're being morbid for the sake of morbidity."

Frank picked up a delicate teacup with a rose pattern. "How about these?"

I was relieved by the topic change, but not his choice. "I need plates, not tiny teacups."

"These come with matching saucers. They're a decent size."

"You can't serve food on a saucer," I said, then quickly clapped my hand over my mouth.

Frank, looking alarmed, asked, "What's wrong? Do you see something? Is the deceased owner of this rose tea set standing behind me?"

I whispered, "I just told you that *you can't serve food on a saucer*. Have you ever heard me say anything like that? I fear I am becoming my mother."

"Don't sweat it." He put the teacup down and lifted a gravy boat for closer inspection. "We all become our parents eventually. Just the other day, I caught myself telling someone I was *perfectly happy* about something when I was not."

"That's a nice gravy boat."

"You can't have it." He held it to his chest. "It's mine. You know the rules."

I pretended to be disappointed over not having grabbed it first.

Just then, the owner, Mia Gianna, came over with an armload of dinner plates in a variety of colors. She looked at me carefully, then said, "Should I even put these on the shelf, Zara, or shall I go back to the counter and wrap them up for you?"

I asked, "How did you know I needed plates?"

She shrugged, chattering the stack of plates she was cradling. "You might say it's my special talent. I get a feeling about what people might need." She glanced around and lowered her voice. "Don't tell anyone I said that. Whenever people hear that someone thinks they're a little psychic, they treat them differently. I wouldn't want people to think I believed in such woo-woo nonsense."

Frank said, "Your secret is safe with us."

"Phew," she said.

"You may be a Belongings Mage," he said.

She blinked rapidly. "I may be a what? A Belongings Mage?"

I tapped Frank on the shin with my foot. Okay, I kicked him. Telling a regular person they might have supernatural powers was not something to be taken lightly. Not only did it expose the teller, but it set up the person being told for colossal disappointment if they found out they weren't.

"Frank is the librarian in charge of our children's storybooks," I said. "He has quite the colorful imagination."

He grinned. "Indeed."

Mia stood there, as though someone had pressed her pause button.

The three of us stared at each other as an awkward moment passed.

"I will take the plates," I said.

Mia let out a sigh of relief. "They'll be waiting at the front when you're done browsing," she said. "Take your time." She nodded toward the women's clothing section. "Some cocktail dresses came in this morning."

I cocked my head. "Do you think I need a new cocktail dress for... some reason?"

"It's December," she said. "There are always plenty of Christmas parties and work events this month."

"I'll have a look at the dresses," I told her. "Thanks for the idea."

Mia looked at Frank. "And how are you set for housewares?"

Frank said, "I believe this gravy boat has my name on it."

"I believe it does." She nodded for him to add it on top of her stack, then smiled and left with all the dishes.

Frank leaned in close to me and whispered, "You don't suppose...?"

"If she is a Belongings Mage, she doesn't know it." I gave him a pointed look. "And you, Frank Wonder, could be more discreet."

"Where's the fun in that?"

"You and your double standards," I said, taking a step back. "It's all fine and dandy for you to drop clues in front of people you barely know, but I can't have a helpful neighbor do a few chores for me?"

"Oh, you *can* do whatever you want, Zara Riddle, and I'm certain you will."

"That's right," I said.

He rubbed his hands together. "Now, let's see you in some cocktail dresses." Talking a little louder, so the ladies in pearl necklaces shopping nearby could hear, he said gruffly, "Get your clothes off, woman. We don't have all day."

Both of the nearby ladies gave us a shocked jaw drop as they clutched their pearls.

This was exactly why shopping at Mia's was more fun with Frank.

CHAPTER 27

At three o'clock on Friday afternoon, I opened the F drawer of the vintage card catalog cabinet we kept in the library atrium. Our collection had been digitized for decades, but we kept the old cabinet around for its decorative appeal. We stashed various odds and sods in the drawers. The F drawer contained plant fertilizer. I took it out and put a few drops into the potted tropical plants we kept on top of the antique piece.

As I was putting the fertilizer away, I heard something behind me that made my blood run cold.

"Zarabella, what on earth is that you're wearing? Is it a belt or a scarf?"

I whipped around to find a pointy-toothed creature of the grave standing behind me. Not the handsome one I was dating. The other one.

Zirconia Riddle was dressed in an outfit similar to the one I'd worn to visit Nick Lafleur in the hospital—a crisp white blouse and tan slacks, topped with a long, camel-colored wool overcoat. Her boots were more pointy and cute than they were practical for the winter weather.

My mother's hair had been red when she was living, but for the past five years that she'd been a vampire, it had been black. Flashes of red still shone through in bright light, as though her true nature was always trying to peek through the artifice. Since the transformation, her freckles had entirely disappeared, giving her skin a pale, almost translucent quality. She looked the same as the last time I'd seen her. Fifty-something, but holding steady, and mistakable for thirty-nine. Vampires aged, just like regular people, but the woman who birthed and raised me refused to.

"Hello, Mother," I said.

She was squinting at my midsection, awaiting my answer.

"It's a scarf that I'm wearing as a belt," I explained. My closet hadn't been specific about how to wear the items it had selected that morning.

"Do you not own a decent belt? Of course you don't. Why else would you be wearing that rag?" She stepped up to me and air-kissed both cheeks. She'd become more European lately, thanks to her glamorous world travels. "I'll be in town a while, all through the holidays. We must find time to go shopping. I shall buy you a belt, dear."

"And I shall *let you* buy me a belt."

"Good. Has your quirky little house made space for me?"

"Yes. There's a deep hole in the backyard, and a fresh coffin."

She blinked at me.

"The coffin was cheap," I said. "The Abernathys gave me their family discount."

More blinks.

"That's a joke," I said.

"If you say so."

At that moment, Frank came trotting up to join us. He was breathless. "Zirconia Cristata Riddle, you have become even more beautiful since our introduction." He took her hand and kissed it, while bowing, as though she were royalty. "Always a pleasure," he said.

"Fred Williamson, is it?"

"Frank Wonder," he said, showing no sign of offense she'd forgotten.

"You are no longer pink on top," she said. "The hair. It's different. I like it."

"It was time for an update," he said.

"Your shoes are spectacular. I always notice good footwear. It's a shame my taste didn't spread to other members of the family."

I knew she meant me, but I let it go. I'd save up until there was another opportunity for a coffin joke.

"Frank, you are a man of impeccable taste," she said, leading to something as she pressed one pale, skinny finger to her lips thoughtfully. "Would you like to join us for dinner tonight? We have a reservation at a place called Grazie. I have been told it is the finest restaurant in town."

Frank pressed his lips together and shot me a knowing look. "The finest? Well, I don't know about that, but Grazie is the most *Italian* restaurant in town," he said.

"Oh, dear," she said. "That doesn't sound promising."

I waved my hand. "What do you mean, *we* have a reservation? Do you have worms, or are you taking my presence for granted?"

She pulled her head back and blinked rapidly. "I spoke to Zolanda. Your daughter is busy tonight but she said you would be available. Zinnia is bowling with her little rag-tag bowling team after she gets off work, so she's not coming. I understand that Teddy B is working this evening, leaving you without any other plans."

Teddy B. I clenched my jaw. Why was it she referred to everyone by their full name, except my boyfriend, whom she referred to by the most embarrassing nickname possible?

I loosened my jaw enough to squeak out, "You already talked to Zoey?"

"I dropped by the high school to see my precious granddaughter. She told me you were free this evening. Was she mistaken?"

"Of course not," I said. "Zoey's rarely mistaken. I'll go to dinner, but only if you keep the reservation for Grazie. I'm dying to see what you think of the decor."

"I would also love to go," Frank said. "Thank you for the invitation. I do allow myself to eat freshly prepared pasta once a month." He patted his svelte torso.

"Good for you, Frank," she said. "Live a little, laugh a little. That's what I always say."

I stared at the black-haired stranger who wore my mother's face. *Live a little, laugh a little?* That was what painted rocks in gift shops said. It was not something Zirconia Riddle said.

She frowned at my scarf-belt. "Zarabella, you should have enough time to go home and change into something more appropriate for fine dining."

Frank put one arm around my shoulders. "*Zarabella* has just the thing," he said, hitting the full version of my name with gusto.

"Please feel free to invite one more friend," my mother said. "The reservation is for four. The more the merrier! That's what I always say."

The more the merrier? Also not a thing I heard growing up.

She glanced around, as though just noticing we were in a library. "So many books in one place," she said. "What a tragedy. So many dead words by dead people. It's like a graveyard of ideas."

"That's... not how we market the place," I said.

Frank, who looked more surprised than offended, said, "I've never heard anyone put it quite like that." He looked at me. "She's not wrong."

"Books come alive when you read them," I said. "There's nothing dead about them. Unlike *some people*."

Ignoring my dig, she leaned out and touched the spine of an old hardcover, then pulled her hand back as though burned. "Dreadful," she said.

I waved at the magazine display. "We have some glossy ones with pictures that are more your speed." I knew she enjoyed decorating magazines.

She wrinkled her nose. I recalled that she couldn't enjoy decorating magazines if they'd already been dog-eared by other people.

"I'm not here to linger," she said. "I'll see you tonight at dinner. Seven o'clock."

She dispensed more air kisses, then breezed out as swiftly as she'd arrived,

Still staring after her, Frank said to me, "That royal purple cocktail dress you picked up today is going to look smashing against the decor at Grazie."

"You mean in front of the fake rock walls made of manufactured stone?"

"You're being too generous," Frank said. "I happen to know half of those fake rocks are plaster and paint. One wall was created for a high school production of Romeo and Juliet. The boy who played Romeo moved to Hollywood, and he got some work playing small roles in crime dramas. And the rock wall went on Grazie, to continue playing a rock wall."

"At least the food is decent. Not decent enough for my mother, but we won't starve."

Frank pulled out his phone and started scrolling. "Who else should we invite? Kathy's got her knitting club tonight."

"Good question. It's Friday, so most of the people I know will be bowling."

"Zoey's got plans with her friends?"

"The Abernathys are having a make-your-own-pizza party."

"They're very normal for a family of undertakers. Seems suspicious to me, like a cover. Are you sure Ambrosia is the only Abernathy with powers?"

"As far as we know. It must have skipped a number of generations."

"They're not from around here," he said. "When they moved to town, it might have triggered something in the girl."

"Are you saying that the town of Wisteria itself could be Activator X?"

Frank didn't look up from his phone. "It would explain a lot of what goes on around here," he said. "But, as for the town being Activator X, the idea is not as exciting as, say, a specialized laser gun that activates DNA on a epigenetic level."

"Or the bite of a radioactive spider," I said.

"Now we're talking."

The air around us swirled with magical foreshadowing. It was a subtle spell, usually triggered by the impending entrance of a fellow witch.

Frank must have sensed it, because he put his phone away and turned to look at the front door at the same time I did.

In walked Fatima Nix, dressed in her fuzzy teddy bear jacket. She had a giant book bag over one shoulder. She made eye contact with me, then lifted her chin and pretended to not see me as she passed by on her way to the romance novels.

"Brr," Frank said. "It's shady over here all of a sudden. Maybe I shouldn't stand so close to you in case she comes by again."

"She's still mad at me," I said. "Even after all the air clearing at our last meeting."

"Do you ladies ever do anything besides bicker?"

"Not really. Which is probably why we haven't been shut down by more powerful organizations," I said.

We watched as the short veterinarian assistant stood on her tiptoes to reach the top shelf of romance novels. As her head tilted back, her long, dark hair extended down past the hem of her fuzzy coat. The image reminded me of a little girl in one of Frank's storybooks.

"You could bring her the step stool," Frank said. "A small gesture might melt away those icicle daggers she's got for you."

"Actually, I have a better idea."

Frank raised an eyebrow. "Better than a step stool?"

"Having Fatima drop by this afternoon is perfect timing," I said. "I've been thinking about the possibility of two problems canceling each other out, and I believe that such magic may be about to happen."

"I'm intrigued," he said.

"Fatima!" I called out warmly. "How would you like to join us for a fancy dinner tonight, on my family?"

She turned to us, dropped her book bag from her shoulder to the floor with a plop, and gave me a wary look. "That depends. Where?"

"Grazie," I said. "The Italian place."

Her eyes widened and her mouth made an O shape. "I love that place," she cooed. "It's like a theme park."

"Perfect," I said.

Her smile fell away. "I'm still mad at you, about you-know-what." She narrowed her eyes at Frank, probably wondering if he knew what you-know-what meant.

"I'm okay with that," I said. "I do owe you an apology for hurting your feelings last weekend. I am sorry. I should have said so at the meeting instead of getting defensive. If I have to repeat my apology again tonight for good measure, I will. But we both know it's hard to hold a grudge over candle light, wine, and bread dipped in balsamic vinegar and olive oil."

Fatima smacked her lips. "It's true," she said. "And I'm sorry I said you were cursed."

"Apology accepted," I said.

Her eyes said, *but you are cursed.*

My eyes said, *I'll pretend I didn't see your eyes say that.*

Frank said, "Did you see the new arrivals, Ms. Nix? We had some wonderful Christmas romances come in."

She hadn't, and thanked him. The two chatted about holiday-themed novels while I went back to my usual Friday afternoon routine.

CHAPTER 28

Fatima Nix and my mother. What an amazing combination for an entertaining dinner out on the town. Possibly the best idea I'd ever had.

Fatima couldn't detect sarcasm or passive aggression, both of which were my mother's primary modes of communication. Thus, my mother's powers had been rendered inert. Neutralized.

It started when Fatima draped her jacket over the back of her chair, and my mother said, "The fur on that jacket certainly is unique. The first time I saw it, I thought my vision was experiencing technical difficulties."

Fatima beamed. "It's one of a kind!"

"Was the poor creature you had skinned molting at the time?"

"Oh, it's not real fur."

"That explains why I've never seen anything like it."

"Thanks," Fatima said, rolling her shoulders back with pride. "And thanks for letting me come to dinner." She glanced around. "This place is real classy, just like you, Ms. Riddle."

My mother did her impression of someone eating a lemon. "This establishment is *nothing* like me."

Fatima stared at her blankly. "Huh? Because you're not Italian?"

My mother didn't answer. She gave me an exasperated look.

I shrugged. "We might be a little Italian. I do like pasta."

"We are *not* Italian," my mother said. She had nothing against Italians, as far as I knew, but she was rattled by Fatima's imperviousness.

I couldn't have been happier. Witnessing my mother's exchanges with Fatima was like watching a trained marksman shoot blanks, over and over.

Frank was snickering, but very quietly and discreetly. He'd also gotten dressed up for the occasion. In a full tuxedo. With tails.

The four of us discussed the menu and placed our orders, then moved on to various conversational topics.

When Fatima's career choice as a veterinarian assistant came up over our first round of wine, my mother said, "But you only *assist* the veterinarian. Surely that doesn't require specialized training."

"You'd be surprised," Fatima said. "When you're squeezing out a Standard Poodle's rear glands, you'd better know what direction to twist, if you don't want to get splattered in the face!"

My mother did her impression of someone eating a dozen lemons.

Seated next to me, Frank began shaking and crying. He was trying so hard not to laugh out loud that tears were streaming down both cheeks.

Fatima slurped some wine, then asked my mother, "So, Ms. Riddle, why did you kill yourself, anyway? And why didn't you want to be a witch anymore?"

"That's hardly an appropriate topic for dinner," Zirconia Riddle said icily.

"Okay, Mother," I said. "Let's go back to the Standard Poodle's glands. Fatima, tell us. In which direction should one twist?"

Frank lost control of his giggles.

My mother straightened in her chair, commanded our attention with a fierce glare, and said to Fatima, gravely, "It was a curse. If you must know, curious young lady, I renounced my powers because of an old family curse."

The four of us were inside a privacy sound bubble that muted the sounds of the restaurant around us and vice versa. Now, sensing the unsealing of secrets, the bubble tripled in strength. The space around our table for four was as quiet as the inside of a tomb.

Frank got himself under control and dabbed the laughter tears from his cheeks. "Don't stop now," he said encouragingly. "Tell us the whole story. I love hearing about old family curses."

Tilting her nose up at me, my mother said, "I was planning to tell you eventually, Zarabella. Would you like me to tell you now, in front of your friends?"

"Sure," I said. "These two know most of my secrets anyway. If it's really bad, and I don't want them to remember, I can always send them to the DWM for a memory wipe."

Frank fake-howled in outrage and smacked me on the shoulder. Fatima gave me a horrified look.

I smiled at her maliciously. "This month, they're running a two-for-one special on memory wipes."

Frank cut in and told Fatima, "Zara's joking. There's no two-for-one special. Memory wipes are always free at the DWM."

My mother tsk-tsked impatiently. "Everything's a joke with you people. Would you like me to tell you about the Riddle curse, or not?"

"Go ahead," I said. "I'll be quiet and let you talk." I stuffed my mouth with half a crusty bread roll and waved for her to go on. My friends did the same, dipping their pieces in the plate of balsamic vinegar and olive oil.

My mother rearranged all the cutlery before her, stalling. Then she checked her lipstick using the reflection of a butter knife, which she knew was poor manners but always did anyway. I watched the black-haired, former-witch, current-vampire with great interest. I'd always assumed she'd renounced her witch powers out of sheer disagreeableness. My aunt had hinted there was more to the story, but she'd refused to betray her older sister's trust and tell me.

"It's more of a prophecy than a curse," my mother said.

Frank hit the table with his open hand. "I knew it! There's always a prophecy!" Crumbs of bread flew from his mouth. He apologized and swept the crumbs from the table, then off his tuxedo pants. My mother picked one crumb off the shoulder of her dress. She had changed for dinner, and wore a low-cut gown that was nearly the same shade of royal purple as my new-to-me cocktail dress.

She looked at me and said, "Are you absolutely sure you want to know?"

"What the heck," I said. "Hit me."

"The prophecy states that a Riddle woman is destined to rule in hell, as Queen of the Underworld." She looked down and flicked at the area of her gown where Frank's crumb had been. "There are more details, but that's the crux of the translation, anyway."

"A Riddle woman," I said. "Destined to rule in hell, as Queen of the Underworld."

"Yes," she said.

"Sounds like a great job," I said, smiling. "For a *vampiress.*"

"Don't use that word," she said.

"You can try and stop me, but I don't think you can anymore. I'm immune. I can say vampire, or vampiress, or Vampirella. By the way, that's who you look like tonight, in that low-cut gown. Vampirella from Drakulon."

"And *you* look like a *call girl,*" she said. "Not a high-priced one, either."

"Thanks. It's exactly what I was going for. I like matching you when we dine out together."

Her nostrils flared.

Frank rubbed his hands eagerly. "I'd love to get a copy of this prophecy," he said.

I shot him a dirty look. I liked it when Frank took an interest in my life, but not this much.

"The book was destroyed," she said. "My father saw to it."

My grandfather had died when I was too young to know him well, but that did sound like him. In our family, the love of books had skipped a few generations.

Fatima said, "Excuse me, Ms. Riddle. It doesn't matter that your dad burned the book. Burning or burying a prophecy doesn't cancel it. You have to do a lot more than that."

"There were rituals," my mother said. "And steps were taken." More flicking at invisible crumbs. "For one, I renounced my powers. That should have been the end of it."

I asked, "How do you know the prophecy wasn't about Aunt Zinnia? She's a Riddle woman."

"The prophecy specified a first-born daughter."

"I'm a first-born daughter," I said. "And so is Zoey." I snapped my fingers and pointed at her. "Hey, is this prophecy related to the one Chessa Wakeful was translating? I don't even know if it's real, or a fake scroll Chet Moore concocted as part of his scam to get me to help him, but there was a lot of chatter in it about Zoey being a Soul Eater." I held both hands wide. "Obviously she isn't. She's just a fox shifter. But it was worrying for a while."

My mother was quiet for a long time. "There were rituals," she said again. "Steps were taken."

Frank leaned in. "Such as?"

My mother slowly raised her hand and pointed at me. "*Zarabella* was supposed to be a shifter."

"Instead, I was a disappointment," I said.

"That is why I mated with the matchmaker. That is the *only* reason I mated with the matchmaker." She crossed her arms. "Though he was very persistent, so, eventually, seeing the value in doing so, I relented and said yes."

I snorted. "That's not what the matchmaker told me. He said you seduced him."

"Whatever gave him that impression?"

"It must have been the way you got him drunk and threw yourself at him."

"I did no such thing."

"You did *exactly* such a thing. Multiple times."

"It was only once," she said.

"That's not what I heard."

"Regardless, you should have been powerless, or a shifter of some type, or perhaps a minor mage." She listed those three options as though they all had equal value.

"And yet I am not," I said. "I may be a late bloomer, but my powers are anything but minor."

Frank nodded, following along easily.

Fatima said, "Huh? Matchmaker?"

My mother said to her, "A lady does not say *huh.*" She waved her hand at Fatima's dropped chin. "Close your mouth, dear. It's unbecoming to gape."

I explained to Fatima, "My father has had a lot of jobs, and for a while he was a matchmaker."

My mother said, tiredly—as though she was exhausted from constantly explaining it to people, "Rhys Quarry was hired by the Riddle family to find me a mate with powers that would cancel out the witchcraft in our bloodline, so that my offspring might avoid the curse."

Fatima tilted her head to the side. "Like an arranged marriage?"

"Not exactly, but something like that," my mother said. Heaven forbid she might just say yes to a simple question and be agreeable for once.

"So, what happened to the family's original plan?" I asked. "Didn't you like any of the potential victims, uh, husbands he rounded up?"

She sipped her wine. "Rhys Quarry's choices were... uninspired."

Frank nodded knowingly. "Compared to the foxy gentleman matchmaker himself." He waggled his eyebrows.

She narrowed her eyes at him. "Rhys Quarry does have some positive qualities. Zinnia seemed to like him. And the other one. The one who's the mother of that other girl."

"You mean Persephone Rose's mother," I said. "Yes, my father does have a way with the ladies."

My mother drew herself up taller in her seat, her cantilevered chest threatening to pop out of the low-cut cocktail gown. "I stood by my choice at the time," she said to Frank and Fatima. My mother did love a captive audience. "It seemed to have worked. My daughter appeared to be, for most of her formative years, perfectly normal."

Frank waggled his eyebrows at me. "No way. Zara? Normal?"

"Until she was driven astray by a bad element," my mother said. "She was only fifteen when she met *that boy*, and it all went wrong." She sighed dramatically, as though some great offense had been committed, and she'd been the sole victim. "The Riddle family performed the rituals to liquidize the genie before the two could run away together, but the damage to Zarabella had already been done." She dabbed her napkin to the corner of one bone-dry eye dramatically. "I was heartbroken."

By damage, she meant my pregnancy with Zoey, who was now her "precious" granddaughter.

Frank asked, "When it comes to the first step in reincarnating genies, is it *liquidize* or *liquidate*? I've always wondered."

Despite the decent wine we were drinking, I had a bitter taste in my mouth. I knew some of this story, and had pieced together the rest, so I wasn't that shocked. However, hearing it in her words, with herself as the heartbroken one, brought up some feelings that hadn't become any less raw with the seasoning of time.

When she paused, I said, "You made Archer Caine disappear." My voice sounded as raw as I felt.

He hadn't been Archer Caine at the time. The name he'd gone by then was difficult for me to remember, so I always called him by his current name. Archer Caine had been my first love, Zoey's father, and just a boy at the time. He hadn't known what either of us were.

"The *family* made him disappear," she said. "I only played a small role. I had already renounced my powers years earlier, remember?"

"I'm sure your role was anything but small," I said.

Fatima and Frank watched quietly, eyes round.

My mother rearranged her cutlery again.

I went on. "I might have been happy with Archer, but we never even had a chance, because you took him away from me. What kind of a mother does that to her daughter?"

She answered quickly, automatically. "The kind of mother who knows what's best for her daughter."

I felt the heat inside me. I was reaching the maximum level of outrage acceptable for a restaurant meal, even with a magical sound bubble of privacy. I pushed the ugly feelings down and held both hands up in surrender.

"If you say so," I said.

"Oh, Zarabella, don't be tiresome. Look at your life. You have everything you've ever wanted, and more. You get to work around those grungy old books all day. What about me? I gave up all my powers. I made the ultimate sacrifices, time and time again, for the good of my offspring, and what did I get?"

"Poor you," I said. "Your life is a real tragedy."

Her head twitched. She didn't like what I'd said, and was switching course. "I wouldn't say that. I have made the most of opportunities. In fact, people have been known to envy what I have." She quickly switched back again from heroic martyr to victim. "Only because they don't understand the full story."

"Right," I said. "It must have been so awful, faking your own death so you could go traipsing around the world with your famous friends."

She gave me an injured look.

An awkward silence passed, into which Frank interjected, "Is it true you were staying in Venice with a certain deceased rock legend?"

My mother didn't answer, except with a sly smile.

Fatima, who'd been listening raptly, said, "I hear Venice is crazy expensive."

I picked up the nearest bottle and poured more wine for all of us. The three of them chattered about Venice and tourism.

When the conversation petered out, I asked my vampire mother, speaking carefully and precisely, "Were you ever ill?"

She shrugged one exposed shoulder. "Of course I was ill." She shrugged again, in an overcompensating way. "Why would you ask?"

I shrugged one shoulder as well, mimicking her. "I was just wondering if you were actually sick, or if you got tired of not having your old witch powers and decided to become a vampire."

"Of course I was sick," she said, not moving her head or body at all. "I did not feel well."

"With what? What was the name of the illness?"

She blinked rapidly. "Dr. Ankh didn't know. She believed it was a side effect of the renunciation ritual. The symptoms began almost immediately. You wouldn't remember. You were only twelve at the time it began, and you were too busy following the Partridge boy around to notice the pain I was suffering."

"Were you dying?"

You could have heard a bread crumb fall within our sound bubble.

I asked again. "Were you dying?"

"Zarabella, we are all dying," she said. "From the moment we are born."

I sat back in my chair. "I knew it. You didn't have to fake your death and abandon me for all those years. You chose to, so that you could have powers again. How do we know that what you did wasn't precisely the thing needed to trigger the curse? If your old witch powers are still inside you, and I have a feeling they are, by taking an additional set of powers you effectively doubled your powers." I paused for drama, then said, "You doubled up. Doesn't that sound like something the future Queen of the Underworld would do?"

Her hand fluttered to her throat. "I was ill," she said. "I did not feel well."

Frank leaned over and said to me under his breath, "Go easy on her, Zara. We can't ever know another person's full experiences."

Fatima slurped some wine, then took the last bread roll. "Do you guys know if it's non-stop bread here? Can we just ask for another basket, or will they charge it to the bill?"

My mother raised her hand and did something magic. I felt a pulse of compulsion wash over me. I had my guards up—I always did around her—but she was powerful, doubled up on powers or not.

Two waiters appeared at the table, coming from opposite directions and bumping into each other.

"More bread, please," she said. "And see to it that our first course is on the way."

I hadn't reduced our sound barrier, but her command got through to them perfectly. Both waiters ran off to fetch more rolls and check on our food.

Frank clapped his hands together repeatedly, applauding my mother. "Great technique on the waitstaff," he said. "Also, thanks for the wonderful story about the Riddle family's curse. It certainly is colorful. My own family has its legends as well, but nothing like the possibility one of us might become Queen of the Damned."

"Queen of the Underworld," my mother corrected.

A second and third basket of bread arrived.

Fatima ripped a roll apart as she asked, "Does that mean Zara is going to hell when she dies?"

"*Before* she dies," my mother said. "That is, if the prophecy is about her. Who knows? It could pertain to me, or to Zoey, or to some child many generations away."

"It's too bad you burned the book," I said. "It might have been nice to get an alternate interpretation."

"Something will turn up," Fatima said. "My aunt always says that if a prophecy is important enough, it will keep inserting itself into other books, until the party it concerns has seen it."

I asked my mother, "Is that why you don't like books?"

She pursed her lips and stared at me. "What do *you* think? Don't tell me I raised a fool."

I nodded. I'd already figured it out before asking her.

The waiters returned, this time with our first and second courses.

"Oh, good," my mother said. "Some of this actually resembles the dishes we ordered."

Frank said, "The food is much better than the decor."

"Well, it can't possibly be worse," she said. "I bumped my elbow against the fireplace by the entryway, and it left a dent. I believe the material was a type of rigid foam."

To my absolute surprise, I felt one of my smart comments bubble up. I let it fly.

"Are you sure it wasn't actual granite?" I asked. "Your elbows are quite pointy."

She laughed at my joke for what felt like the first time ever. "My elbows *are* pointy. Good one, Zarabella."

Live a little, laugh a little? Was that not just her new motto, but a philosophy she embraced?

Fatima said, "I don't get it. Nobody's elbows are that pointy."

Frank patted the young witch on the shoulder. "You are an absolute delight, Fatima. Don't ever change."

She gave him a confused look, then picked up her utensils and started eating her salad.

The rest of us began eating as well.

CHAPTER 29

The rest of our dinner at Grazie went surprisingly well, once we'd broken the ice with the whole Riddle family prophecy thing. It was hard to hold a grudge over a table of good food and wine.

We shared more of our family histories.

Fatima told us about the Nix family, and their knack for powers that involved communicating with animals. When I mentioned that her aunt, Maisy, must have broken the line with her Flame Touched specialty, I learned that Fatima and Maisy were not that closely related after all. They were technically fourth cousins from different generations. Fatima didn't have any true aunts, but she'd called Maisy and other adult women by that term growing up, as was common in her mother's culture. The title had stuck, and the two enjoyed having each other. There were no other Nix relatives in Wisteria—long story, according to Fatima—but they had more than enough family with each other, plus the coven.

Frank regaled us with tales of the Wonder clan, mostly about his uncle, Felix. I'd heard most of the stories, but enjoyed hearing them again, especially the story about how his swan shifter sister, Bellatrix, discovered her powers during a forest encounter with a bear. The tale had been improving with each telling, and nobody could tell a story quite like Frank.

It was eleven o'clock by the time my mother and I returned to the house.

"Your friends are such characters," she said as she came through the front door behind me. "What they lack in some areas, they make up for in colorfulness."

"They're good friends," I said. "I'm lucky to have everyone I need, right here in Wisteria."

She gave me a sweet smile. "When your mother is in town, anyway."

I smiled back and let her have that one. I'd been so angry at her at the start of dinner, but then I'd realized the effort of holding onto the grudge wasn't worth it. She couldn't help how she was. She was probably doing the best she could. I'd learned to see the most challenging people that way, thanks to Bentley. So what if her best wasn't as pleasant as other people's bests? She was still alive—sort of. Still around, anyway. Her book's final chapter hadn't been written yet. Perhaps she would surprise everyone and stop being a COW—an acronym so rude, I can't say it, so you'll have to figure out something with your imagination. Here's a hint: The last two words are Old and Witch.

She parked her designer suitcase at the foot of the stairs and looked around. "You've done something with the place. It's less dreary."

"Is it? You know how this house is. It's always changing things around."

"Doesn't that bother you? Wouldn't you prefer to be in charge of the renovations? That's the only way you can be sure everything is up to date with the trends."

"Being up to date with the trends is your thing, not mine."

"But trends are for everyone to enjoy." She walked over to a wall sconce and inspected it. "I do approve of this fixture. Is it new?" She rubbed the top of the glass shade. "There's no dust. It must be new."

"It might be new," I said lightly, dodging her implication that I didn't dust my wall sconces. I didn't, but it was none of her business. "I stopped trying to keep track of things, and I just enjoy the changes. It's like when you go to your favorite store and they've switched up all the displays for a new season."

"I suppose," she said.

A door upstairs squeaked.

"That will be your room," I said, pointing up the stairs. "As you just heard, it's ready for you, right on time."

She picked up the rolling suitcase easily, as though it were empty, and headed up the stairs.

I followed her, and Boa followed me on her quiet white paws, curious but wary of my mother, as usual.

I found my mother inside the new room, clasping her hands girlishly. "I have my own washroom! What a wonderful surprise."

She did have her own washroom. That explained why my bedroom was claustrophobically small, and why I'd heard the pipes rattling more than usual all week.

"Come in and relax," she said. "Have a seat on the sofa. I'll pour us a drink using this bar trolley. Wait. It's not a trolley. It's a built-in bar, with a working sink, and an ice cube dispenser. Oh, Zarabella. This is extremely on-trend. Your house knows how to treat a guest."

I took a seat on the cream-colored sofa, then accepted the cocktail napkin and drink.

"The house has pulled out all the stops," I said. "The house must think you'll be staying a long, long time. But you won't be, will you? You must have more exotic destinations in mind."

She sat across from me, perching on the edge of the bed, which was covered in a cream-colored duvet and a dozen matching pillows.

"Don't worry," she said. "I've cleared my schedule so that I can spend plenty of time catching up with my daughter and precious granddaughter." She wriggled her fingers at Boa, who was standing in the doorway. "Here, kitty, kitty." She patted the bed next to her.

Boa turned and ran away, tail high in the air.

"She must be nervous about the new room," my mother said.

"I'm sure that's it." I took a sip of the drink. "Do you mind if I cast a threat detection spell on the room? It can't hurt to be too careful."

"Go ahead."

I cast the spell. I had been thinking about something for a while, and now I wanted to test my theory. The room was threat-free. The only thing that glowed was my mother, but no more than would be expected, given the nature of her powers.

"That color," I said. "I knew it!"

"Do I have an aura?"

I had definitely seen that shade before. It had been all over Nick Lafleur's cabin.

Carefully, I asked, "Did you really just arrive in town today?"

"This afternoon. Why?"

"You weren't here a week ago? Last Saturday?"

"Zarabella, that had better not be a crack about my age and my memory. I may be older than you, and I may have been through some life changes, but I am quite in control of my faculties. I was on the Champs-Élysées on Saturday. That is in Paris, which is in France, which is very far from here."

"Then why was your glow all over Nick Lafleur's cabin on Saturday morning?"

She reached for her purse, for the cigarettes she hadn't smoked in decades, but that she still reached for in times of distress. She tossed the purse aside and slumped her shoulders.

"My glow," she said, looking down. "It might have lingered behind me after my last visit. I'm so ashamed. Must you make me tell you?"

"I'm not going to make you do anything, but I don't see what your sudden modesty is all about. I know you've been seeing a young zookeeper named Nick Lafleur. Fatima talked to a snowball vole, who said there was a scary lady with dark hair who'd been coming 'round the mountain." I pointed at her. "It was you. I knew you'd been comin 'round the mountain. When I saw Nick at the hospital this week, he told me you've been seeing him."

"So, you know."

"When did it start? Was it in November, when you were supposed to be helping Zinnia get back to her regular size?"

"It's complicated. I've known Nick for a while. It started before then, but yes. I did see him in November." She gazed off in the distance dreamily and bit a fingernail. "Several times."

"Since when are you secretive about your romantic exploits? Did you think I'd be jealous or something?"

She dropped her hand and reached for her phantom cigarettes again. Frustrated a second time, she tossed her purse onto the in-room bar counter, out of reach.

Time out, I thought. Her imaginary smokes were on a time out. I was surprised I hadn't been banned from her room and put on time out as well. My vampire mother loved *talking* about her romantic exploits, yet she didn't appreciate being *questioned* about them.

"The only reason I didn't tell you sooner was because of the age difference," she said. "I knew you wouldn't approve. Judging by the look on your face right now, it's very clear I was right to keep it from you."

I pointed to my face. "This look? It's not about the age difference. It's because—" I was too worked up to continue. I took a sip of my drink, then a gulp. As I swallowed the amber liquid, I felt Ribbons touch my mind. Without words, he let me know he was nearby, in contact and listening, should I need him to eviscerate anyone.

I set the drink down and continued. "The look of horror on my face is because shortly after I came upon the cabin, which was glowing with your color, I entered the cabin, where I found Nick Lafleur unconscious on the floor, staining the hardwood with a puddle of blood. What exactly did you do to him?"

Her lips scrunched together. She glared at me a moment before saying, "I was not there. I was in Paris. And I do not appreciate your tone, young lady."

"Just because you were in Paris doesn't mean you didn't do something to him. Your glow was there. Did you do it by remote?"

Her eyelashes fluttered, then her eyes widened. "I did," she said, sounding surprised and no longer angry. "Nothing that would have harmed him, but I did have one of my bird agents in the area."

"One of your blue jays? You were spying on him?" I remembered seeing the blue-feathered bird. A blue jay had flitted onto Fatima's shoulder briefly. I hadn't thought much of it at the time, but it must have stuck in my subconscious, leading me to suspect my mother when the next clue came along.

"Nothing as vulgar as spying," she said. "I do a flyover from time to time. If nothing interesting is happening wherever I am, I check on things back here. I can cover the whole town in an hour or two." She held up one hand. "Before you ask, the answer is no. I do not, and would never, invade your privacy by peering in windows. I only survey public spaces."

"Let's back it up a sec. What did your blue jay see? I mean, what did you see, when you were looking through the blue jay as your familiar?"

"On Saturday?" She tapped her fingers on her chin and looked up at the ceiling a moment, then said, "I saw you getting knocked over by a goat!"

"You were spying on me and Fatima?" That did explain why my mother had commented on Fatima's jacket, saying that the first time she'd seen it, she thought her vision was experiencing *technical difficulties*. So far, the story checked out against the facts.

"I was looking in on you, as a good mother does," she said. "The blue jay flew up and down the mountain a few times. I also saw your father's other daughter, leaving Nick's cabin." She chuckled. "The little fox was lucky she got out of there when she did. A few minutes later, Nick had yet another girl show up."

"You're not jealous that Nick's been seeing other women?"

"Not at all. If I wanted him to be faithful, he would be." She rubbed her ring finger and looked wistful. "Wouldn't that be something."

I twirled my finger. "Back it up again. Are you saying that on Saturday morning, after Persephone Rose left the cabin, but before I got there and found him bleeding out, someone else was at the cabin?"

"A girl. She must have left before he had his accident."

"Or maybe she *was* his accident. Do you know her name?"

She shrugged.

"How about a description?"

"She was between twenty and forty. Kind of plain. Not a very pleasant face."

That wasn't helpful. My mother described most other women as being kind of plain with unpleasant faces.

"Hair color?"

"I don't recall," she said. "She might have been wearing a hat. Blue jays look down from above."

"I wonder who it was."

"She was wearing a spectacular pair of boots. I had my bird fly down for a better look."

"*The suspect had spectacular boots*," I said. "You'd make an excellent detective."

"Me? A detective? Oh, I wouldn't want to step on your toes."

"What do you know about Activator X?"

"Is that a designer boot label?"

"Never mind," I said.

"Now I'm dying to know why you're asking. What is Activator X?"

"It's a theoretical treatment that would activate powers in regular people."

"Oh. Just a silly fantasy," she said with a hand wave.

"Is it? Bentley was a regular person before he drank whatever was in that vial around his neck. You could say that was Activator X. It was your blood, and something else, wasn't it?"

She sidestepped the question. "It wouldn't have had any effect if he hadn't been at death's door. You could put it in the town's drinking water supply, and it would do nothing but improve the taste."

"Let's hope nobody gets that bright idea. Especially not..." I trailed off, distracted by a thought. The town's secret supernatural agents worked under the cover of the Department of Water. If anyone had the means to distribute a compound town-wide instantly, it was them. Were they already doing so? People always joked about there being "something in the water" in certain small towns. What if, in our case, it were true?

"You seem distracted," my mother said. "Are you keeping secrets from your mother?"

"No." There was an instinctive tinge of guilt in my voice, long-trained by decades of it being true. I swallowed hard.

"I heard about your Halloween costume," she said. "You were dressed as me, and making all sorts of jokes at my expense. Don't try to deny it. I've seen the photos."

"Oh, that? If I'd been trying to keep it a secret, I wouldn't have posed for any pictures."

"Hmm," she said.

"Hmm," I said.

She yawned. "Oh, look at the time. It is getting late." She stood, hoisted her suitcase onto the suitcase stand, and began unpacking.

I yawned as well. It was getting late.

This new development about another girl being at Nick's cabin on Saturday was intriguing, but it also might have been nothing.

Why would I give it another thought? Nick's injury wasn't even an active case. He'd admitted to calling 9-1-1 himself. It wasn't my business. I had enough job duties, between being a mother, a librarian, a ghost wrangler, and the mentor to various young people.

Whatever Nick had been up to at his cabin, now that he was no longer a ghost, was his private business. That didn't mean I wasn't curious, but I wasn't curious enough to keep my mother up past her preferred bedtime.

She took her nightgown into the adjoining bathroom, where she cooed about the array of fanciful bathroom products set out on the small marble counter.

"Use as much of that stuff as you'd like," I told her. "There's plenty more where that came from."

"Are you off to bed?"

"Shortly." I was still sitting on the sofa with my thoughts and my drink.

"This is nice," she said. "You and me, alone in a house together. It kind of takes you back in time, doesn't it?"

"It does," I admitted. As much as she drove me nuts, there was also something comforting about having my mother around.

"Would you like to bring your toothbrush in here so we can fight over the sink and you can *accidentally* spit on the back of my head, for old times' sake?"

"Maybe tomorrow night," I said. "It is late."

"Good night, darling." She blew me a kiss.

"Good night, Mom." I got up and blew one back at her.

CHAPTER 30

Xavier Batista

While Zirconia and Zara Riddle were saying goodnight, across the street, Xavier Batista was brushing his teeth and dribbling onto his favorite Kiss Me I'm Irish T-shirt, which he often wore on Fridays. He enjoyed the attention he got wearing it, which happened because he didn't look Irish. And also, on very rare occasions, someone would take him up on the offer. Usually a dude, but not always.

While he brushed and dribbled, he looked out his bathroom's tiny window at the Riddle house. His home was not directly across from where Zara and Zoey Riddle lived, but the converted garage was positioned so that he could spy on them a little.

Xavier was fascinated by all things supernatural, so he was transfixed by what the neighborhood kids called the Red Witch House. Tonight, there was something different going on within its walls. From the outside, it looked the same as it had last week. The windows and doors were in their usual location.

However, the light coming from one of the upstairs windows was more diffuse on one side than the other. The house had grown a guest room. He was sure of it. Xavier knew the house rearranged its interior as needed, plus he had seen Zara's elegant, dark-haired mother arrive with a suitcase.

Earlier that week, on Monday night, when he'd enjoyed ice cream, pizza, and cider with Zara and her macho wyvern, the house had seemed normal enough, but he'd seen its powers at peak supernatural.

Back in October, Xavier had not received an invitation to the ball at Castle Wyvern. Most of his coworkers did, but not him, because he was a nothing person. He'd been moody and belligerent while the others in the office talked about their costume plans.

Then, things had looked up for the young man when he'd received an invitation to the alternative house party at the Red Witch House. The costume instructions, as he interpreted them, were to dress up as something both terrifying and tasteless. He took the costume instructions seriously. He would do anything to fit in, to be part of the magical scene.

The scariest costume Xavier could think of was the old man version of himself as a nothing person. But this idea was too abstract, and likely to be insulting to others. People were always taking offense to attempts at humor. Instead, Xavier played it safe. He had dressed as Dr. Frankenstein's Monster. However, he'd mistakenly referred to himself *as* Frankenstein, rather than as Frankenstein's *Monster*, so he had offended lots of people anyway.

When he arrived at the party, a green-faced Xavier was disappointed to find that all the cool, powerful people were only interested in each other. Then, when he followed a group of minor mages into the kitchen, he alone had been sucked into a vortex. It was a tunnel that unceremoniously deposited him in a room full of plastic balls that acted like quicksand. By the time he'd climbed his way out of the ball pit and found his way back to the party, everyone was running around in a panic, yelling about the lack of exits. Chaos ensued. An adventure was being had—by others. Without him.

The house eventually opened up its doors again. He heard the news of what had happened at the Monster Mash. An actual monster had been vanquished. A big, gross one. Ordinarily, this would have been cause for celebration by the supernatural community. But by then it was getting late, and everyone's mood had soured from being stampeded over in the search for exits. Also, the food ran out.

A green-faced Xavier had collected his coat from the Capuchin monkeys, then stomped his way home in his thick-soled boots. He'd never felt so empty handed and directionless.

But things were looking up for Xavier now that he lived across the street from the Red Witch House and its supernatural inhabitants. He could feel it in his bones. He sensed that this weekend, things were going to change for the better.

He hadn't been formally introduced to Zara's mother, the former-witch, current-vampire, but he knew of her. If he played his cards right, he could spend some time with the raven-haired, eldest Riddle. There was a rumor she enjoyed the company of younger men. Xavier was willing to do whatever he had to do to be near someone with power. It didn't hurt that she was smokin' hot, in a Vampirella-from-Drakulon kind of way.

Xavier finished brushing his teeth, went to bed, and enjoyed pleasant dreams about a dark-haired vampiress.

CHAPTER 31

Detective Persephone Rose

Persephone was sitting up in bed, reviewing phone messages when Nick Lafleur returned from the washroom.

"Yeah," he said, lazily rubbing his bare chest. "So, uh, that happened." Nick wasn't a dumb guy, but he sure acted like one sometimes.

They were at Nick's log cabin, on Mount Woolbird.

Persephone had come by earlier that Friday night to drop off an area rug she didn't need at her house. The two had been text messaging all week, but it had been the first time they'd seen each other since Nick's accident. He'd made a full recovery, with only a light scar on his head from where he'd "fallen on his lamp like an idiot."

Nick had not taken Zara Riddle's suggestion to hire Ruth's Cleaning Service. He'd done the cleanup job himself, and so the bloodstain hadn't come out of the hardwood floor. It had been a good excuse for Persephone to come by, "just to drop off the rug and leave."

She hadn't left yet.

"Listen," Nick said, crawling back into bed beside her. "I'm really into you, Officer, but you should know I've got a few things going on in my life right now."

Persephone set her phone aside and said, flirting, "If you keep calling me Officer, I might have to handcuff you." She grinned. "Again."

"So, we're cool?"

"You're free to date other girls," she said.

"I don't want to date other girls," he said. "I only want you." He used two fingers as legs and walked his hand across the bed linens toward her. "Why would I want burgers when I can have steak?"

"Are you saying I'm steak?"

He kept walking his hand up until he was at her face. He stroked her cheek tenderly. "You're better than steak."

"Thanks. I guess." She caught his hand and gave it a kiss. She'd never done that before, but it seemed like something lovers did, and she'd seen it in movies. "What are all these other things you have going on? Is work busy? I thought winter would be a slow time at the zoo."

"It's complicated," he said. "I'm not sure if it's going to happen or not, but I might have to go out of town for a bit over the Christmas holiday."

"Family stuff?"

He pulled his hand away. "I'd rather not say."

"Something illegal?"

He coughed, then grinned. "What if it was, Officer? Would you arrest me?"

"I'd lock you up and throw away the key."

He rolled toward her and playfully bit her shoulder.

She bit him back.

He yelped and rolled away. He rubbed his shoulder. "Were those your fox teeth? Did you shift your face and bite me?"

"Don't be a wimp. I didn't even leave a mark."

He stopped frowning. "You really are something, Officer Rose."

"It's *Detective* Rose," she said.

"Detective Rose, can you detect what I want to do to you?"

She could.

* * *

At two o'clock in the morning, Persephone was staring up at the ceiling above Nick's bed, unable to sleep. He was snoring away peacefully.

She realized what was wrong. She hadn't shifted, or gone for a jog, all week. If she didn't get out and exercise a few times a week, in either form, she got restless legs.

She climbed out of the warm bed and pulled on her clothes. She didn't have her running shoes with her, let alone a pair that would be appropriate for hiking on a snowy mountainside, so she used her human hand to turn the door handle to let herself outside, then shifted into her fox form.

As she stretched her furry limbs and picked up speed, entering the treed area, her thoughts crystallized and simplified. She felt good about where she was, and why.

Zara had encouraged Persephone to go ahead and date a bad boy. "Date all the bad boys," she'd said. Zara had a few years of life experience on Persephone, which, in theory, made it wise advice. Never mind that Zara had only briefly dated a genie and a vampire, with a sixteen year stretch in between. It was good advice because it aligned with what Persephone wanted to do anyway, and you couldn't get advice better than that.

Persephone-Fox reached the peak of the Mount Woolbird. She threw her head back and yipped at the night sky. It felt good.

Her yips echoed back to her, but they came with another creature's sound. A low growl. It was coming from the woods behind her. She'd seen a few mischievous woolbirds on her run, and snowball voles, but none of those local creatures growled like that.

Persephone-Fox ducked for cover behind a fallen log and hunkered down. First of all, who or what was that? Secondly, would she be a better match for it in fox form, or as a human? She did have her gun, assuming she could find it in the holster where she'd left it before shifting.

Something was definitely coming through the woods toward her, crashing through the underbrush.

It sounded big, which wasn't necessarily a bad thing. Big critters didn't move as quickly as foxes. Whatever it was, she guessed she could easily outrun it in fox form.

The crashing got closer.

Her fox eyes saw well in the dark, especially with the contrasting white snow on the ground.

She watched as an enormous beast emerged from the woods. It was a bear. Ursus arctos. A big, scary grizzly bear.

The bear sniffed the ground, then lumbered over to where she'd been yipping at the sky a moment earlier.

The bear looked up at the night sky and growled ferociously.

Persephone peed a little. But she was in fox form, so that was okay.

And then, much to her surprise—but not really—the bear shifted into human form. A male human form.

He walked over to a stump and took a seat.

He said, "I know you're up here, Rose."

She knew that voice. It was the Chief, Ethan Fung. Even if she hadn't identified him by voice, she could see his profile clearly with her keen fox eyes. He wasn't dressed for hiking. He was wearing one of his usual light-gray wool suits with a white shirt, no tie.

"I'm new to this," he said, conversationally. "I'm not sure about all the protocols. Am I supposed to pretend I don't know you're hiding behind that log? Do we go back to work tomorrow and act like we didn't run into each other up here?"

She shifted to human form and stood. All her clothes and belongings had manifested right back to where she'd left them, including her gun, which she no longer needed.

"Why are you here?" She didn't move from her spot. "Am I in trouble?"

He let out a chuckle. "For going on a run through the woods? Of course not."

"For seeing Nick Lafleur again," she said. "That's why I'm up here."

"I don't care what you do with Nick Lafleur. I don't care what you do in your free time, as long as it's legal. But I'd appreciate it if you didn't tell too many people about this place. Not too many of the local shifters come around here, and I'd like to keep it that way. It's hard for a big bear like me to get some privacy. I don't need some well-meaning conservationist shooting a dart in my hide because they think I should be hibernating."

She felt relaxed enough to make a little joke. "Shouldn't you be hibernating?"

"Ha ha," he said. "Bentley's sense of humor must be rubbing off on you."

She snorted, then came over to where Fung was seated. She brushed the snow off a large rock, and took a seat. The stone was chilly, with only her jeans to protect her from the elements.

She asked, "This is new to you? Being a bear?"

He took a flask from his jacket pocket and took a sip before offering it her way. "Want some? It's not booze. It's green tea with ginseng." The flask glinted in the starlight. "I got into health foods a few years back. You reach a certain point and realize you're off warranty, and you're on your own, as far as your health goes. Or at least that's what I thought back then." He extended the flask.

"Sure. Why not." She rubbed the rim and took a sip. It was bitter. It went well with the night air and the forest around them.

"I've known about magic for a long time," Fung said. "I always wondered if I had a little of it in me. They say it comes out when you need it. But mine didn't. I almost died, but Zinnia Riddle saved me. She saved this badly broken human man."

"How did it happen?"

"Oh, that's a long story."

"I mean..." She took another sip, then handed the flask back. "The whole bear thing."

"When I was in the hospital back in January, the doctor wanted to give me something he said would help my recovery." He looked down at his hands. "It was Dr. Bhamidipati. He's not around anymore. This was before your time here."

"I've heard of him." He was a terrible man who'd reached a terrible end but had deserved much worse.

"I got the feeling he wanted me to be a guinea pig for something experimental. It turned out he did, but I got off lucky. What he did to me wasn't the worst thing he was doing to people."

"Seems like it worked out for you," Persephone said. "As far as strength goes, it's hard to beat a bear."

He grinned, his teeth flashing in the dark. "If I'd had any choice in the matter, I would have chosen something stealthier."

"Like a fox?"

"Honestly? No offense intended—foxes are great—but if I had any choice in the matter, I'd pick Golden Retriever."

"I get it," she said. "Because they can blend in any environment. You could put on one of those service dog vests and go anywhere."

"Plus Golden Retrievers are the best dogs," he said. "The best. They're big, but not too big to sit on your lap for a minute or two. A bear can't do that."

Persephone was quiet. She didn't know if she should tell the Chief she was sorry he had to be a bear, or try to talk it up. She wouldn't want to be a bear herself. She loved being a fox and couldn't imagine herself any other way.

After a moment, Fung picked up the conversation again. He told her how Dr. Aliyah Ankh had taken over Dr. Bhamidipati's research, and that Fung's experiences had furthered their understanding of how powers manifested.

He'd healed perfectly from his injuries, and for that he was grateful. As for being part of a medical discovery that had the potential to change the world, he wasn't so sure how he felt about that.

"Some powers should not be in the hands of mortals," he said.

"Or even immortals," she said. "I don't trust that genie, Archer Caine. He's the father of my niece, but I don't like him."

"I don't like him, either." He put the flask away. "You know what, Rose? I don't even know why I'm back here, or why I took the job as Chief. I could have had a great life somewhere else. I could have moved somewhere boring, and settled down. I could have gone back to medical school and become a doctor, like my mother always wanted."

"Where's the fun in that? I've been to those places. They're not that great."

"You're young," he said.

"You're not exactly old," she said. "What are you? Fifty-five?"

"Oof," he said. "I'm only forty-eight."

"I knew that," she said. She had not. "Just giving you a hard time."

"And after I was so nice to you. I didn't say a word about your taste in men." He got to his feet and stretched. "Nick Lafleur? Really?"

"He's actually pretty sweet," she said. "But thanks. Thank you for implying that I could do better. My dad isn't around much, and I appreciate the feedback from an older man."

"Even if he's only forty-eight, and nowhere near fifty-five? Which I am. I am only forty-eight, Persephone."

"And you're still single? Maybe I shouldn't take dating advice from you," she teased.

"You probably shouldn't. I am a disappointment to my mother, who tries so hard. Every time I go to a dinner party, there's a young woman who just happens to be single, too." He looked down at his dress shoes and kicked some snow. "Or at least they used to be young." He quickly added, "Not that there's anything wrong with an older woman. I'm not one of those guys who reaches middle age and goes for the girls half his age. Not at all."

Persephone did nothing but listen.

"I guess that's my problem," Fung said. "I don't go for them at all. I'm sure they're everywhere, but it's almost like I don't see them as anything but friends, or as whatever job they do."

"Then you need to open your eyes."

"Oh? It's that simple? That's the same thing one of my friends told me recently."

"Yes. It's that simple. Your friend is right."

"Detective Rose, you're pretty wise for a young person. You must have an old soul."

"I might."

She stood and stretched. The cold was getting to her, and she was itching to run some more. She didn't shift yet, but said, "What do you say, Chief? Race you down the mountain? Last one to reach the cabin is a rotten egg?"

"I could never beat you in a race," he said. "Not unless there was a path cleared, and I had a really big toboggan."

There was a pleasant interlude as they both imagined an enormous grizzly bear riding a toboggan down the mountain.

"I'll give you a head start," she said.

"Done." The Chief shifted into bear form and lumbered away at top speed.

CHAPTER 32

Saturday Morning

Xavier Batista

Xavier had only enjoyed three glasses of beer at bowling the night before, so he woke up Saturday morning with practically no hangover.

He still felt *something*, though. A light headache lurking behind one eye. It sucked being a nothing person. It sucked having normal human genes and enzymes governing his methylation processes.

As he had done exactly a week earlier, he went upstairs to hustle his doctor roommate into giving him another banana bag.

Ubaid was in the shower. Judging by the amount of steam coming out around the door, she was yet again testing the capacity of the home's hot water tank.

Xavier's headache moved from its spot behind his eye to the center of his head, where it hunkered down and sprawled out like a family on holidays. He went from wanting hydrating fluids to needing them.

He opened the fridge and got the water pitcher. It was empty, thanks to Ubaid. If he'd been a macho wyvern, he might have fantasized about eviscerating his roommate.

Instead, Xavier scowled at the closed bathroom door then went to her room to grab her medical bag. If she didn't have the decency to refill the water pitcher, he had the right to fix his headache using her stuff.

He took the bag to the kitchen and unzipped it. He didn't see the supplies on top, so he started digging, dumping the bag's contents onto the kitchen counter.

There was a lot of stuff in the bag. What *didn't* Ubaid keep in there? He pulled out five vegan granola bars, two packs of gum, a stuffed teddy bear, a pair of novelty handcuffs, and a silver object he wrongly assumed to be a flashlight. Next was a rolled-up change of clothes, a sizable wad of cash in various denominations, and two passports, one with a name he'd never heard of. Both passports had Ubaid's photograph, but taken with different haircuts.

Where were all the medical supplies? This was a *go kit*, or a *bug out bag*—a stash of emergency supplies for getting out of town in a hurry. It was the sort of thing kept by the likes of spies, criminals, and survivalists.

He reached the bottom of the bag, where he found a small, black zippered bag that looked more medicinal than the rest of the contents. He knew it was too small to contain a bag of IV fluids, so he had no excuse whatsoever to unzip the bag, but he wanted to know what was inside.

Xavier did *not* hear the shower turn off in the other room.

Deep down, he knew he had no excuse to violate Ubaid's privacy. Leaving the water pitcher empty was a crime, but not a crime that justified the search of his cousin's personal property.

Let's make one thing clear now:

The events that unfolded that Saturday morning would have been much different if Xavier had respected his roommate's privacy.

But Xavier Batista did *not* respect his roommate's privacy. And the hangover was getting worse.

He unzipped the bag.

Inside were a trio of vials.

The vials were labeled Activator X, Activator Y, and Activator Z.

This was something! This was It! The big It with a capital I. He became so excited that he immediately dropped the bag.

That was when Ubaid emerged from the bathroom, swathed in a towel, and demanded to know what he was doing in her things.

"I have a terrible headache," he said. "I was looking for Aspirin."

She stood there, dripping wet. "You mean the big bottle of Aspirin we keep in the bathroom?"

Her heap of possessions, strewn about the counter between them, looked more personal and private than ever. Underwear was visible.

Without looking down, he toed the little zippered bag under the edge of the cabinet. "You were in the bathroom, having one of your long showers. I didn't want to disturb you."

"Why not? The curtain is opaque, and it's never stopped you before." Her eyes bore into him.

He didn't like the attitude she was giving him. Nobody liked getting caught doing something dishonorable. Rather than be a man, and own up to what he'd done, he decided to turn the tables instead. It was a tactic he'd picked up from his father, and not an honorable one.

He demanded, "What's all this stuff for, anyway? Are you planning to bail out of here with no notice and leave me paying the next rent check?"

In a low, deep tone, she said, "You're an idiot."

"I'm an idiot with only one job. How am I supposed to pay the bills if you take off? What's with all this stuff?"

"That stuff is..." Her face reddened. "It's none of your business what I have in my bag. Now put it all back."

He put most of it back. The zippered bag containing the three vials was still where he'd dropped it, by his feet. The kitchen island was between them, so Ubaid couldn't see it there.

She grabbed the bag and rummaged through the contents. She grabbed the silver, cylindrical object he had wrongly assumed was a flashlight, and brandished it at him.

"Stop messing around," she growled. "I know you have it."

"Have what?" He held up both hands, which were empty, except for sweat. He'd begun sweating when he'd read the labels on the vials, and his sweat glands hadn't let up yet.

She pressed a button on the cylinder, and a glowing blade, three inches long, emerged. It reminded him so much of a Star Wars light saber, except shorter, that he might have laughed, if the look on Ubaid's face hadn't been so deadly serious.

"Don't mess with me," she said, a growl to her voice. "I don't want to have to hurt you."

He took a half step back, surprised. "Easy now. Why would you hurt me? It's me. Your cousin. We've known each other since we were kids. What is that thing, anyway?"

"Give me the vials. Now. And you won't have to find out what this is."

"They're on the floor. I dropped them."

Her eyes widened. "You idiot. You horrible, stupid, nothing person! Pick it up now!"

Xavier didn't appreciate her words, her tone, or the fact she was brandishing a weapon at him, but now was not the time to register his dissatisfaction with their cohabitation situation. He bent down and picked up the zippered case. The vials appeared to be, to his relief, unharmed by the fall.

Slowly placing the case on the counter between them, he asked, "Is this what I think it is?"

"That's none of your business." Her face was red and contorted with emotion. He'd seen his cousin like this on other occasions, typically when the two of them were younger and being busted by their parents for getting into some sort of trouble.

He knew Ubaid well enough to guess what she was feeling. He raised a hand and pointed at her. "You're not supposed to have this," he said. "You stole it, didn't you?"

Her nostrils flared. He could hear her breathing. Her chest, visible above the towel, was flushed as red as her face.

"You stole Activator X," Xavier said. The trace of fear he had over the glowing blade was replaced by excitement over the discovery. "And Activator Y, and Activator Z. I didn't even know there was a Y and a Z. Why so many? Do they do different things?"

"The three have to be given in sequence."

"And what are you going to do with them? Who are they for?"

She shook her head. "You shouldn't have gone into my personal property." The hand holding the glowing blade wavered.

"Answer my questions, and I won't tell anyone you have this stuff. Did you steal it from the lab?" Now he shook his head. "Never mind. Of course you did. What are you doing with it?"

"I'm not a thief," she said.

"That's not what I asked."

"I had to take it," she said. "I'm not a thief. I didn't have any choice. I'm being blackmailed."

"Why didn't you tell me? I've got resources. I know people. If you're being blackmailed, we can get you out of this. It's not too late."

She jabbed the air with her glowing weapon. "I knew you wouldn't understand. I knew if I told you about the Activators, you would never let it go."

"Who's blackmailing you? Who else knows about this?"

"Nick Lafleur."

"That guy? He's a wimp. He doesn't scare me. What does he have on you?"

She said nothing.

In the silence, Xavier almost pieced it together. Almost, but not quite.

"Screw that guy," Xavier said. "He's just a zookeeper." He picked up the zippered bag and held it high. "Nick Lafleur isn't getting his hands on this. No way. There's got to be another way out of this."

Ubaid started walking toward him slowly, holding the weapon steadily. "I don't want to hurt you." Tears were streaming down her cheeks.

Xavier heard something outside. Someone was walking up the steps to the entrance. A female, wearing boots, by the sound of it.

"Someone's coming up the stairs," he said.

"Give me the bag." She'd stopped crying, and now her eyes were a different color. They'd turned from blue to black. Xavier was so startled by the change, he nearly dropped the bag.

Instead of handing over the bag as requested, he did something so colossally stupid that he almost couldn't believe what he was doing.

That fateful morning, Xavier Batista said to his cousin, who was clearly very angry and turning into something terrifying, "Make me."

CHAPTER 33

Saturday Morning
Zara Riddle

I woke up Saturday morning to the sound of my mother having a conversation with someone. I could only hear one side of the chat, so I assumed she was on the phone, but I would soon find out she was communicating with Ribbons. Mild spoiler alert: It wouldn't be the biggest surprise of the day.

I left my tiny bedroom, moving sideways so I didn't hit my knees on the furniture, and walked into the new luxury guest suite. I found my mother sitting on the room's sofa, cradling a certain wyvern in her arms like a baby. Ribbons shot me a glassy-eyed look that was equal parts guilt and delight—a typical Ribbons expression.

"That's a new one," I said. "I should take a picture for the family Christmas card."

"You really do have the most colorful friends," my mother said.

The wyvern wriggled with happiness as she tickled him under his chin.

"Now I've seen everything," I said. "From here on, nothing can surprise me." Yeah, I was tempting fate yet again.

Ribbons spoke privately into my mind. "This creature who holds me has the correct levels of ferocity and tenderness for a strong mother. Any being would be fortunate to have been raised by her. What happened to you, Zed?"

"She wasn't always like this," I said to Ribbons.

My mother asked, "What did he say about me?"

"That you're ferocious and tender."

"Yes, I am." She leaned over and cooed directly into the wyvern's scaly face. "Aren't you a clever boy? And so handsome."

He made a delighted chittering sound with his throat.

"I'd say you two should get a room, but you already have one." I looked around. "Is it bigger than last night? I swear it's bigger."

"My daughter has a vivid imagination," Zirconia said to the beast playing baby in her arms.

Ribbons must have said something amusing into her mind, because she said, "Now, now. Be nice. Zarabella does let you live here rent-free."

"Not for much longer," I said, then, "How's he communicating with you if you're no longer a witch? We know he can talk to Zoey, but just barely, and it took some time for them to develop a connection."

"How should I know? Does it really matter?"

"It matters if you believe you're not a witch when you still are."

"I might have retained some of the hardware," she said with a shrug.

"We're people, not computers," I said.

She gave me a blank look. "Who do I speak to about ordering breakfast?"

So that was how it was going to be. No discussion about her powers. I wasn't surprised. Some things were out of bounds, such as whether or not she supplemented her intake of synthetic-blood serum with actual blood, such as that from the bountiful Nick Lafleur.

"Breakfast," I said with an air of formality. "Would you prefer room service, Your Majesty? I could probably rustle up a serving tray. It may not be silver. How do you feel about eating off a Frisbee?"

"No need to make a fuss over me," she said. "I can take my morning meal in the dining room. Is the orange juice organic?"

"I don't know. Is Tang organic? I can check the packet."

She wrinkled her nose.

"I should be able to find something suitable," I said. "For Her Royal Highness."

"More juice, less attitude," she said.

I bowed, then curtsied for good measure.

* * *

My mother and I took our breakfast in the dining room, with Ribbons, who'd gotten up early to enjoy more time with my mother. Zoey had stayed overnight with the Abernathys. Boa was staying well clear of my mother.

As we ate, all three of us noticed the dining room window was doing something interesting. It was boosting the winter sunshine, tripling the warmth and light.

"Fascinating," my mother commented, reminding me of her preferred necromancer, Dr. Ankh. Neither of them liked it when I referred to Dr. Ankh as a necromancer, which was why I kept doing it. Technically, I was correct. A necromancer raised the dead. That's what Dr. Ankh had done for my mother, as well as for Bentley, though it had been indirectly for him. He'd had to chomp into the glass vial around his neck with the last bit of strength he had as he lay dying in the DWM cafeteria. Poor guy.

My mother asked, "What are your plans for today? I did promise to buy you a belt."

Across the table from us, Ribbons choked and spat out half a croissant.

"Never mind him," I said. "He gets sensitive when people say the B-word."

"Belt?"

"Apparently, people have bullied wyverns over the years, threatening to turn them into leather belts. It can be a touchy topic. Me, I think he'd make a great pair of boots, but everyone's different."

Ribbons said, "You are not funny, Zed. And this orange juice is not organic. It is not even orange juice."

"It's mango lemonade, and you've never cared about organic before today," I said. "He eats cat food," I said to my mother.

"That explains the breath," she said.

He snorted his indignation, blowing ribbons of colored flame over the table. Then he gathered up the remaining croissants and flapped out of the room.

My mother arched an eyebrow. "Someone's in a mood."

"He's not much of a morning monster," I said to her. "His attitude doesn't improve much over the course of the day, but it's worse if he gets up early."

"Sounds like a certain daughter I raised."

I let the comment go. If the size of her room was any indication, she was going to be at the house for a while. I had to pace myself.

"So, shopping?" Her hands twitched with eagerness. Shopping was one of the few things we both enjoyed equally.

"Sounds like a plan," I said. "And just in time. It's been nearly twenty-four hours since I last shopped."

"I'd like to freshen up and change clothes. Give me about fifteen minutes, then we can go."

"No problem," I said. "I can find something to do. I'm sure I can kill a whole fifteen minutes until you're ready." I anticipated waiting far longer than fifteen minutes. My mother's day wear outfits all looked the same, yet it could take up to an hour for her to select the right tan slacks and white blouse for the occasion.

How would I kill the time? I vaguely remembered there was some small errand I'd been meaning to do. What was it? I reached for my purse and unzipped it. Lying on top of the other stuff was the pair of earphones that Xavier had left in my car.

"I'm going to pop across the street to see a neighbor," I said. "His name is Xavier. He works with Zinnia, and he's been helping out..."

My mother had already left the room. She had vampire speed when she wanted to. It had not translated into any improvement in the time it took her to get ready to go out.

I would have plenty of time for my quick errand, unless something surprising were to happen.

* * *

I crossed Beacon Street, walked around the converted two-story garage that Xavier and his cousin rented, then walked up the steps.

Walking up brought back a memory.

These were the same steps I'd walked up behind the ghost of Ishmael Greyson, dead at twenty-six, murdered as revenge for killing someone's family member for sport. I'd never known Ishmael when he'd been alive, so I didn't know much about his personality, but he couldn't have deserved decapitation. Few, if any, deserved an ending like that.

The owner of the property, Ishmael's great-uncle, Arden Greyson, lived in the main house. He was a friendly guy who loved going out on his boat with his dog, looking for sea monsters. Arden had renovated the rented garage since the tragedy. The place looked fresh, but there was no amount of fresh paint that could wipe the memory of the blood-soaked apartment from my mind.

As I lifted my finger to ring the doorbell, I noticed a slight hesitation. There was a shivery feeling in my bones. The skin on the back of my neck was taut. My teeth were clenched. There was a winter chill in the air, but I felt much colder than I should have been for the weather.

What was I feeling? Was it leftover residue from Ishmael's death, or was something else happening?

As I waited for Xavier to come to the door, I drew my jacket tighter. I considered draping the headphones over the door handle and bolting out of there as fast as my legs could take me.

I could hear the sounds of movement through the door. Someone was home. I rang the doorbell again.

The doorbell was shiny and new-looking, set in a polished nickel setting. The door was freshly painted, and above the entry way was not just one security camera but two. Beside me was an enormous panel with a button for a two-way speaker. What an over-the-top system for a simple carriage house. These kids were serious about security. You'd think I was trying to get in through a back door of the DWM.

There were more indistinct sounds of movement inside.

Was the doorbell not working? I hadn't heard the chimes on the other side.

I pressed the button below the speaker. "Hello? Xavier? It's Zara, from across the street. I'm dropping off some headphones you left in my car."

I released the button and waited.

The house was quiet.

I pressed the button again. "If you're busy, that's fine. I'll leave it on the door handle."

A female voice came over the speaker. "Hang on a sec."

"Ubaid?"

She didn't answer. I'd forgotten to press the button to speak.

I pressed it. "Ubaid? If you're busy, don't worry. It's just headphones. I can come back another time."

The door opened.

Ubaid was flushed. Her blonde hair was wet. She wore a sweatshirt and jeans, and smelled of shower products. Her eyes were strangely dark in a way I'd never noticed before. The pupils were four times the normal size, giving her an unsettling appearance.

"Zara," she said. "Xavier's not here."

"His car is parked on the street." I stood my ground instinctively. I might have taken her at her word, but my senses—the human ones, as well as the witch powers—told me something strange was happening.

"He might be sleeping," she said. "I don't know. I'm not his keeper."

"Is he sleeping with the lights on? I walked past the garage door on my way in."

The blacks of her eyes grew larger, and a deep frown line appeared between her eyebrows. She narrowed her darkening eyes. "What do you want?" She shifted her body, blocking the doorway.

I leaned to the side, looking past her. There was a medical bag open on the kitchen island, and a pile of clothes and snacks next to it, along with two small booklets. Passports.

"Planning a trip?" I asked.

"Maybe. Why are you here?"

I looked down at the young woman's bare feet. Next to where she stood, on a rubber mat, were several pairs of shoes and one pair of boots. Very attractive boots. Like the kind my mother would have admired as the wearer made her way to Nick Lafleur's cabin.

Everything clicked into place.

"It's okay that Xavier isn't available," I said, choosing my words carefully. "I actually wanted to talk to you about something. How well do you know Nick Lafleur?"

Her eyes grew blacker, covering most of the whites. I couldn't believe my luck. Who needed a bluffing spell when a person's body language gave everything away? If Ubaid had powers, which it seemed she did, she hadn't been well trained in controlling them.

"Nick? He's a friend," she said.

"Did you happen to see your friend Nick last Saturday?" I still didn't cast any spells to boost my words, or compel her to speak. A witch would have to be blind to not recognize that Ubaid was not entirely human. Those black eyes! Was Ubaid an elf, or something else? I'd read in the magical reference books that those with elf blood had eyes that turned black when they slipped into a rage state.

She answered tersely. "What happened between myself and Nick is private business. It doesn't involve you. It's no business for a witch."

"Oh, but it is," I said. "When you bashed poor Nick on the head with a lamp, he came to me for help." I surreptitiously powered up my blue lightning balls, palming them behind my back. "He came to me, Ubaid, which makes it my business. Why did you hit him?"

"I caught him with one of his whores."

My right eye twitched. "I'd go easy on the name-calling," I said. She was referring to my half-sister. Persephone didn't have the best taste in men, but she didn't deserve that. "Even if he was carrying on with other women, he didn't deserve what he got."

"Why do you care? He's fine now. He's better than ever," Ubaid said. "I barely left a dent."

"You're right that he seems fine. And, if he's not pressing charges, then you've got nothing to worry about from a legal standpoint. But I'm wondering about something. Why did he lie for you? I don't think he's in love with you, or he wouldn't have been seeing other women. So, what is it, Ubaid? Is Nick an incredibly forgiving person, or do you have something on him?"

She glared at me with those black eyes. There was a scuffling sound. Movement on the other side of the kitchen island. Someone was there. Someone who was groaning.

"Xavier!" I took a step forward instinctively.

Ubaid stepped back with surprising speed. She slammed the door closed. In my face.

"Open this door," I said. I was no elf, but my own dark rage was rising. Xavier was in danger, and that wasn't right. Nobody put my interns in danger except me.

She did not open the door.

I almost laughed. Elf or not, Ubaid was a fool to think a slammed door would keep me out. To a witch, there was no such thing as a locked door. I reached inside with my magic to twist the handle.

The door still didn't open.

I tried again, but it was impervious to my efforts. It must have had some anti-witchcraft mechanism—something I'd heard of, but never encountered.

I turned to the two-way speaker and pressed the button. "Open this door immediately."

There was no response. Nothing verbal, anyway. A mist started seeping out the panel. A thick, dense mist, with a distinctive, chemical smell.

I'd encountered something like this once before, coming from what appeared to be an air freshener.

The fog enveloped me rapidly. I held my breath, but it didn't help. The chemical agent was seeping through my skin.

I felt my consciousness fading.

I became both heavy and light at the same time, as though I was being pulled apart, soul from body.

Not again.

CHAPTER 34

Xavier Batista

Xavier was struggling to sit up when he heard the front door slam shut.

Ubaid returned to where he was slumped on the floor and helped him upright. She seemed a lot nicer now than she had been a few minutes earlier, when she'd punched him in the face.

Groggily, he asked, "Who was at the door?"

"Nobody," she said.

He was still on the floor, but at least he was sitting upright. He lifted his chin and met her gaze. Ubaid's usually pale eyes were entirely black. It scared him so much he pulled away, banging his head on the kitchen cabinet.

He groaned and pressed his hand to the back of his head, and then to his eye. His eye was puffy, and he was losing the ability to see out of it, due to the rapid swelling.

"You punched me," he said. His head was foggy, dazed from having been knocked down. His memory of the last ten minutes didn't stretch out in a linear narrative the way it should have. He remembered, but in flashes, like still frames from a film, out of sequence. There'd been Ubaid, wearing a towel, her eyes growing black.

271

Then she was in the shower, using up the hot water. It wasn't enough that she never refilled the cold water pitcher, she had to hog the hot water as well. Then her fist was coming at his face. Also, Xavier had a clear mental image of a black zippered case with three vials inside. And a pair of passports. These images mixed with the steam coming out of the bathroom. Then he saw her face, contorted with rage before she struck him. Then back to his hands, showing no hesitation as he dug into his cousin's medical bag.

He reorganized the fleeting images into cause and effect. Action and reaction. Shower steam, his hands in the medical bag, three vials, and a fist in the eye.

He had brought this upon himself. Why did he have to go snooping in her things?

"I barely touched you," she said.

"You punched me. In the eye."

"You'll be fine. Don't be a baby. Get up."

He didn't move. "Someone was at the door," he said dazedly. Cause and effect were mixing up again.

"Don't worry about it. We have a good security system."

"You punched me," he said for the third time, sounding even more hurt and confused.

"Because you're an idiot, and you asked me to punch you."

"I did?" It all came back to him, and this time it stayed in sequence. Ubaid, telling him the vials were for Nick Lafleur, who was blackmailing her. Xavier, refusing to hand them over, then taunting his cousin with those foolish words: *make me*.

She had made him, all right.

He looked around. The zippered bag was nowhere in sight. Also, Ubaid was no longer in a towel. She'd pulled on some clothes. How long had he been out? Her hair was still sopping wet from the shower. He hadn't been out for long, which meant the vials hadn't traveled far. He kept talking about the punching, but he only cared about the vials.

"You might need to help me," Ubaid said. The blackness in her eyes was closing in on itself, returning her pupils to normal. "Can you help me?"

"I dunno. What do I get?"

She smiled. "Everything," she said.

He rubbed his swelling eye. "Don't punch me again."

"Xavier, you do have a supernatural bloodline," she said. "I ran my own DNA report. You're special, Xavier."

"Shut up." He wanted to believe her, but she *had* punched him in the face.

"Listen," she said, still smiling, but not in a way that was reassuring. It was the smile of a shark. "I may have made a few errors in judgment recently. I took some calculated risks, and not everything has worked in my favor."

"You're a thief," he said. "You've been stealing from Dr. Ankh."

She didn't deny it. "I'm going to need your help straightening out a few loose ends."

"Such as?" He was no longer seeing stars, so he got to his feet, steadying himself with his hands on the counter. "Who was at the door?"

"That's what I need your help with. You've got to help me convince her to keep her mouth shut." Ubaid frowned. "If it's even possible for someone like her to keep her mouth shut. She'll tell her whole nasty coven, and her creepy vampire boyfriend." She eyed the door. "We could kill her," she said, as casually as one might discuss killing a rat who'd been getting into the cupboards.

"Are you talking about Zara? Is that who was at the door? We're not killing Zara. Are you insane? We're not killing anyone."

"I should have known you'd be more loyal to her than to a member of your own family."

"This isn't about loyalty. This is about, you know, not murdering people."

"That witch's blood would be worth quite a lot on the black market. Especially if we drained every drop of it."

Xavier's jaw dropped. He stared at his cousin, whom he'd known his entire life, and realized that he didn't know her at all. She wasn't just bad or corrupt. She was evil.

There was a sound at the door. It was muffled, but someone or something on the other side was moving. He knew it was Zara. He knew it was, because that was the worst possible explanation for the sound he was hearing, and it was that sort of day.

Xavier gave his cousin an angry look of his own and demanded, "What did you do to Zara?"

"She's taking a nap," Ubaid said. "She should be immobilized for a while. As harmless as a kitten." She thrummed her fingers on her chin thoughtfully. "We could do it in the tub, so we don't waste anything."

He was speechless.

"Don't act like you didn't want this all along," Ubaid said. "How many times have I heard you whine about how you'd give anything to have powers? This is your chance, stupid. It's now or never. Do or die. Would you be willing to give anything or not? Are you a liar, Xavier?"

"We don't——" His voice caught in his throat. "We can't—" He swallowed hard. "No," he said.

She pouted, adopting a relaxed posture, even as her eyes turned dark again.

"No," he said again. "I want it, but not like this. It's wrong." He pointed at her. "There's something wrong with you. You're wrong."

She narrowed her eyes. They were entirely black now. "Come on, Xavier," she hissed. "Don't you want this power? Take my hand. I'll let you feel it."

She extended her palm toward him. The air between them was crackling.

"Take it," she hissed. "Feel what could be yours."

He yanked his hand to his chest, then behind his back, as far away from hers as it could get. "There has to be another way," he said.

There was a scratching at the door again.

"Zara," he said, and he moved toward the door.

Ubaid grabbed him with one hand while she punched the other into his stomach. He found it odd that he didn't feel much from the impact. She must not have punched him very hard, if at all. Because she hadn't punched him. She'd stabbed him.

He looked down at the blood that was now flowing from his stomach and spreading across his white t-shirt like a poppy blossom.

Ubaid had the silver weapon with the glowing blade in her hand.

She took a step back. "Oops," she said, then cursed. "That was supposed to be the stun setting. It was only supposed to shock you."

He was shocked, all right.

"Xavier? Are you okay?"

"You stabbed me," he said. He fell to his knees. Now the blood was gushing, and his hands were slipping on the floor. He crawled toward the door.

And then Xavier's day, which hadn't been going well, got worse.

That was when his cousin, Ubaid O'Connor, stabbed him a second time. Between the shoulder blades.

He felt it this time. The glowing blade was hot and cold at the same time.

He slumped to the floor.

Slowly, gradually, he felt something good. Relief. This was how it ended. It was sooner than expected, but at least all the torment of being a nothing person was over.

He did have his regrets. All the things he thought he'd do, like telling Liza Gilbert she had to show him more respect than she did. He wouldn't get to see her princess attitude fall away with his refusal to worship at her feet, and that was sad.

But at least now he would never live to be an old man, with an old man's regrets.

Better to die with untapped potential than as a failure. As a nothing person, through and through.

He relaxed and let the nothingness, the darkness, take him.

CHAPTER 35

Zara Riddle

When you last heard from me, things were bleak. My spirit was trying to break up with my body. The mist from Xavier and Ubaid's home security system was doing its best to knock me out. And it would have succeeded, except for two things.

First, when I'd been rendered helpless a few months earlier thanks to a similar substance, I hadn't merely filed the experience away as yet another interesting memory. I had wisely prepared some spells that might help me against such an attack. And by *some*, I mean three. And by *prepared*, I mean I had looked into it, but I wasn't entirely comfortable with my casting. *Zara tries to be a prepared witch, but even a prepared witch can only prepare so much.*

Long story short, the first two defensive spells did not work very well against the knock-out mist. They only managed to keep me conscious enough to cast my last chance spell, number three, which turned out to be lucky number three.

However, even that spell didn't completely reverse the effects of the mist.

Even though I remained conscious, all I could do in the home's front entryway was my impression of a worm. A worm who had been poisoned by mist from a nightmarish security system.

I kept trying to reassure Xavier that I would be busting in there to save him. Any minute now. I let him know by rubbing my nose on the door ferociously.

I was wriggling like a worm for what felt like an eternity. I couldn't cast anything. I could rub my nose on the door, but I couldn't locate my tongue, let alone use it to form the Witch Tongue necessary for most of the good spells.

After a while, I took a break from ferociously rubbing my nose on the door and rested with my face on something pillow-like.

Who kept a pillow on their front step?

It wasn't a pillow after all, but my purse. Ziggity!

Slowly, clumsily, I used my teeth to drag the zipper open, then wormed my hand inside.

The purse was full. Not as full as the wall vanity in my washroom, but I did have a number of lotions and potions stored in there for emergency use, as well as granola bars and clean socks.

I kept digging. What I needed was the other thing I'd been meaning to deal with all week but hadn't. Ten points for procrastination!

Finally, I pulled out the Mountain Joe mug, which you'll remember from my trip to the hospital to wake up Nick Lafleur.

I unscrewed the top, wished myself luck, and brought to my lips the same purple brew that had resuscitated a man from his coma.

Did I have confidence that using the brew on myself would work out perfectly, reversing the effects of the mist rather than amplifying them?

No. I did not. I didn't know *what* would happen. But I had to try something, and rubbing my nose on the door wasn't doing much.

As the liquid passed my lips and into my mouth, I had one thought: Not half bad.

Considering the smells and tastes of the raw ingredients that I'd used to make the concoction, the resulting fluid was not half bad. Not bad at all. Even cold and five days old, the purple brew was refreshing and brisk.

I practically jumped to my feet.

And that, my friends who are keeping track of the numbers, was the second thing that saved my bacon that day.

Now I had to get through the door.

Rather than fumbling with the witch-proof tumbler locks that must have secured the door, I used an old cop trick I'd learned from Bentley. I kicked it with my foot. Hard.

Thanks to the boost of the purple brew in my system, plus the witch equivalent of adrenaline in my veins, a substance we called witchatonium, the door blew off its hinges in one kick.

I walked in on strong legs, feeling about ten feet tall. Ah, the power of a good cuppa brew.

Just inside the door, Xavier Batista lay face down in a pool of blood.

Ubaid wasn't there, which was lucky for her. Her bag and belongings, which had been on the counter, were gone, along with the attractive boots that my mother and I had both admired.

A drafty breeze passed over me. It didn't chill me. I was beyond the point of feeling such things, but it did tell me the big garage door was open downstairs, and that Ubaid must have fled in that direction.

I knelt over Xavier and checked his wounds. He was still breathing, but it was ragged. He wouldn't last long.

I had no time to remember warnings, but I did anyway. I recalled Frank's words about war movies, and the sweet farm boy who always dies with his guts in his hands. Frank had been right. And I didn't care. I'd admit it to him first thing Monday, and I'd take the razzing. I just wanted Xavier to live.

I had been studying my medical magic all week, some nights getting through a lot more than three pages. In the week following my encounter with Nick in his cabin, I had learned a dozen modern techniques for assessing and treating violent injuries.

On the other hand, I'd also studied the handwritten margin notes from other witches, criticizing the traditional medical magic techniques. One witch in particular, who wished to be anonymous, wrote an in-depth appendix note about how the old ways were often better than the new ways. She believed strongly that few of the new methods for stopping blood flow worked as well as an old-fashioned pipe-mending spell.

And so, trusting some anonymous witch plus my own personal experience, I cast the pipe-mending spell on Xavier. I cast it once from the back and once from the front.

I rolled the boy onto his back and held him in my arms. "You'll be okay," I said, rocking him as the magic took hold. "Hang in there."

He gurgled, blood coming from his mouth. "I'm dying," he said.

"We're all dying," I said. "But neither of us is dying today."

Blood dripped down his cheek. His eyes filled with tears. Gruffly, he said, "Tell my mother I love her."

"Tell her yourself," I said.

His eyelashes fluttered. "That's what they always say in the movies," he said. "That's what the hero says to the nothing person."

I could feel that the blood had stopped flowing out of him. What remained was circulating within his system. I could see, through the hole in his stained T-shirt, that the wound on his stomach was closing.

And then the instinctive part of my healing magic took over, and I felt my power pouring into him. The raw stuff, no spells required. He would be healed.

But he didn't have the confidence I did, so he went on, getting even more dramatic. "Thanks for trying to save me," he said. "I'm sorry I'm not worth it."

"You sure talk a lot for someone who's supposedly dying," I said.

"Do I?" He started to laugh, coughed, swallowed, then looked up at me. "It doesn't hurt," he said. "Why doesn't it hurt?"

"Because I fixed you. I fixed your leaky pipes, after your horrible cousin..." I shook my head. "What did she use to do this to you? A flaming knife? You were cut, and burned."

"She didn't mean it," he said. "It was an accident."

"Stabbing someone once might be an accident. You were stabbed twice, and, unless I'm mistaken, your back was the second wound. Stabbing someone in the back, while they're crawling away, is no accident."

"But you came to save me, Zara," he said. "You knew I was in trouble. That means we have a special connection. I'm special to you."

"I came over here to..." I stopped myself. I wouldn't tell him I'd only come over to return his headphones. He'd just declared that we had a special connection. If I told him it was mere coincidence—was it?—the poor boy would probably go ahead and die—of embarrassment.

"Yes," I said. "Xavier, you are special to me. And you're special to my aunt, and your family, and a number of people. You are special Xavier, and you *do* matter. All of us are connected to each other for a reason. We might not be able to see the whole picture, but that's only because we're inside it. A piece of yarn doesn't know it's part of a beautiful tapestry."

His eyes fluttered closed. "That's a nice image," he said. "Can I sleep for a while? Everything feels weird, like I'm itchy, but on the inside." He licked his lips. "Why does my mouth taste like duct tape?"

"Sleep now," I said, casting a spell to help him slip under.

The house was quiet. The draft kept coming through, blowing between the two wide-open doors, and I started to feel the chill.

The floor squeaked.

I jerked my head up, worried Ubaid had come back, but it was just a ghost.

Mrs. Pinkman stood on the other side of Xavier's feet.

She was nodding, giving me approval.

"Is this what you're here for?" I asked. "Does this close off a chapter for you, Mrs. Pinkman?"

She clapped her hands together silently, once, and smiled.

"Did you do something?" I asked. "Did you make me forget about the headphones all week, until the perfect time?"

Her smile remained enigmatic.

"Either way, I appreciate you being here," I said. "It's been nice seeing your face around." My eyes threatened to leak. "I guess I must have missed you. I'm sorry I moved away and abandoned you."

Minerva Pinkman gave a little bow, stepped back, and then faded away.

CHAPTER 36

Bentley and Persephone arrived at the scene, along with Dr. Ankh and an emergency medical crew.

As I handed over the unconscious patient, I explained everything that had happened that morning, and what I'd figured out.

Dr. Ankh gave me a begrudging thank you, then said to the detectives, "This explains the recent thefts in my lab. I am beyond disappointed in the careless actions of Ms. O'Connor, but this means you can close the investigation file."

Persephone said to Bentley, "We had it all wrong, going after the janitorial staff. What a waste of time and police resources."

"It was a good hunch," he said to her.

She rolled her eyes. "Not as good as my sister, the witch, and her magical hunches. I wish I had some of her knack for showing up at the right place at the right time."

"More like the wrong time," I said. "If I'd gotten here a few minutes earlier, Xavier might not be sporting quite so many holes."

Bentley said, "And Ubaid O'Connor might have hurt you, instead."

I snorted. "I'd like to see her try." I waved the idea away. Never mind the pesky detail that the young doctor had gotten the better of me. Details, schmetails. I hadn't been a helpless worm for long.

Bentley pulled me toward him and hugged me to his side for almost two seconds before pushing me away. The Saturday morning emergency had really brought out his softer side. What a generous public display of affection.

Dr. Ankh had walked away, so I said to Bentley and Persephone, "Did I hear that right? You two were investigating internal thefts at Dr. Ankh's lab?"

"We were," Persephone said. "She suspected someone was stealing a compound that..." She and Bentley exchanged a look. "Well, it's classified."

"You mean Activator X," I said.

Persephone's eyebrows shot up. "You knew?"

"Yup." I hadn't known for sure, until that moment, but pretended I had.

"Thanks for helping out," Persephone said. "It's a good thing someone in this town can solve cases."

"I never meant to step on your turf," I said. "I literally walked into this one."

The medics who had loaded Xavier on a gurney began rolling him toward the door.

Xavier hadn't yet regained consciousness, so we hadn't talked about what Ubaid had done. In the coming days, before Christmas, I would see him again and we'd talk things through. He would tell me how Ubaid had been jumpy last Saturday, and how she'd accused Xavier of having snuck out during a specific time period that she claimed to have been home. She probably hadn't meant to hurt Nick, but the uncontrollable rage from her new elf powers must have taken her by surprise. Technical analysis would confirm she was the one who'd called 9-1-1 from Nick's cabin, not Nick. The fact that she'd called for help led me to believe she wasn't entirely evil. She might have hoped for a good outcome, but she'd also been preparing for a bad one, using Xavier to set up an alibi for herself.

The medics rolling Xavier away and then carrying him down the stairs were calm and quiet. They were agents from the DWM, not our town's usual crew. Nobody told me the medics were from the underground organization. I could tell by how none of them yelled "first!" as they'd arrived at the blood-soaked scene.

Dr. Ankh rejoined us. "Zara, you were helpful," she said.

I waited for more, but there was none. "You're welcome," I said. "Since you're here, can I ask you something? How does Activator X work?"

Bentley and Persephone turned toward the doctor. They must have been wondering the same thing.

She looked me dead in the eyes. "The name indicates its action."

"It activates?"

"That is correct." Her lavender eyes gave away nothing extra.

"What does the X stand for?"

"The unknown," she said. "There is no way to solve for X until it has been activated."

"Did Ubaid use it on herself to activate elf powers? When we were talking, her eyes went black. Like, totally black."

Dr. Ankh said, "You already know the answer to your question." Her large lips twitched. She turned to Bentley and said, "It is imperative that you track down Ms. O'Connor, with the samples intact."

"What about Xavier?" I asked. "He's Ubaid's cousin. Does he have elf blood, too?"

She turned slowly, looked me in the eyes, and said, "Not much. Not even a tenth of what I have."

Both Bentley and Persephone stole a knowing glance at each other.

"You're an elf?" I asked.

She gave me an exasperated look. "What else would I be?"

"My money was on alien," I said.

"The two are not exclusive," she said. "Elfkind originates elsewhere, though we did not arrive on this planet by space ship, no matter what you may have heard." She leaned down and picked up the medical bag she'd used for examining Xavier. "I trust the three of you will pass along the news to all the appropriate parties. It is no longer my secret. It is no secret at all, now that one witch knows." She gave me a pointed look. "In a short time, all shall know."

I held up my hands. "Hey, that's not fair, lady." I was back to calling her *lady* again, but I couldn't stop myself. The purple coffee had saved me from wormhood, and it had also made me loquacious. "I can keep a secret."

Still looking me dead in the eye, she said, "Two witches can keep a secret, if both are dead."

Sternly, Bentley said, "That's enough, Dr. Ankh. Ms. Riddle will have your respect, if I am around."

Dr. Ankh didn't flinch. "What I meant was, now that Ubaid O'Connor has activated her elf bloodline, it is important that the appropriate parties are aware of what they may be dealing with. At least until she is apprehended."

Persephone perked up. "I do like tracking people," she said. To Bentley, she said, "We'd better hit the trail before it gets cold."

He agreed.

"Speaking of hitting the trail, my work here is done," I said.

"I'll walk you home," Bentley said.

I put my hand on his shoulder. "I should be fine crossing the street, but I appreciate your chivalry. You stay here and finish up what you need to do. You know where to find me."

As I left Xavier's place, I heard Dr. Ankh telling the detectives what she knew about Ubaid O'Connor, and where the fugitive doctor might have been headed after leaving town.

I did manage to cross the street on my own without incidents or surprises.

I walked into my house and called out, "Mom? Are you ready yet?"

She called down, "Five more minutes!"

Five more minutes. Yeah, right.

I threw my blood-soaked clothes—black turtleneck and dark jeans—into the washing machine, had a quick shower, and put on fresh clothes.

I knocked on my mother's door. "Are we going to go belt shopping, or what?"

"Come in," she said. I found her sitting on the couch, leafing through a brand new architectural magazine. "I've been waiting for *you*," she said. "Did you really need to shower? You looked fine at breakfast."

"I like to keep people waiting," I said. "It's kind of a power move."

"Always with the jokes," she said, getting up and gathering her purse and gloves. "I'm not *that* slow." She gave me a worried look. "Am I?"

"Don't worry about it," I said. "Things have a way of working out."

CHAPTER 37

Sunday Morning

"This wasn't my idea," Bentley said.

We were standing outside on the porch, even though the weather had turned inhospitable. The porch was much more private than the interior of my house.

I shivered as a breeze cut through my clothes. A blizzard was forecast for later that day.

Bentley was in a rush to beat the weather out of town. He was going, along with Persephone, to track down Ubaid O'Connor and the missing vials of Activator X, Y, and Z. For the sake of simplicity, and to not sound ridiculous, everyone referred to the three-injection treatment simply as Activator X.

The tracking job would take him out of town for a while. Neither of us knew for how long.

"I never implied it was your idea," I said. "The timing is suspicious. That's all. I mean, even you have to admit the timing is rather convenient. You're always on some special assignment when my mother's in town."

He glanced at the door, then back at me. "It's not the worst time for me to be going out of town," he admitted. "Your mother can be intense. And then she makes you..."

I held my finger to his lips. "Don't say crazy. Don't you dare."

"Equally intense," he said.

I frowned. I'd rather be called crazy than share an adjective with Zirconia Cristata Riddle.

He kissed my furrowed forehead. "At least you're cute when you're annoyed."

I pretended to angrily shove him away as I took a step back. "I liked our relationship a lot better when I was the one making *you* cuter by annoying you."

"I know you did," he said. "I remember your games with the rainbow sprinkle donuts. But what we have now isn't bad."

"It's not half bad," I agreed.

He gave me one of his sexy, smoldering looks. "You'll miss me."

"I'll try to miss you, if I can find the time. My mother is obsessed with picking snowberries. She wants to drive to every mountain in the area looking for a late-fruiting crop."

"She wants to spend time with you."

"Why do you insist on trying to find a positive motivation for the things people do? What kind of detective are you?"

"A good one." His eyes darkened from bright silver to dull iron. "Though not as good as you."

"Dumb luck is not the same as solid investigative work. You and I both know it was pure coincidence that I showed up at Xavier's door at the right moment. Maybe Mrs. Pinkman had something to do with it. But if she did, it was subtle." I paused and frowned. "And if she did, how dare she? What kind of an atheist would play God in the lives of the living?"

"Mrs. Pinkman didn't do anything," he said. "She's still here, isn't she?"

I nodded. "Drinking her ghost tea and dropping things," I said. "She busted my sugar bowl."

"You'll figure out what she's here for. You always do. You figured out what Ubaid did to Nick, based on a pair of boots."

"They were great boots. When you track that young lady down, I'll take the boots, and the Department can fight over the rest."

"Zara..."

"Fine. They can have the boots, too. I'm not that shallow."

He gazed into my eyes. "I'll be back in time for Christmas. I promise. My word is my bond."

"Even if you don't make it back, I'll be okay. I have the other Riddles, plus Mrs. Pinkman. She's out here on the porch, by the way. She's sitting on the rocking chair, watching us, and knitting something."

"Good," he said decisively. "She can keep an eye on you in my absence." He gave me a peck on the cheek, then turned and trotted down the stairs.

I put my hands on my hips. "That's it? A peck on the cheek?"

He turned and looked up at me from the sidewalk. He nodded in the direction of the rocking chair. "I can't do what I want right now. Not in front of a nice little old lady."

"You owe me double when you get back," I said.

"Double, plus interest." He gave a hint of a smile, turned, got in his car, and left.

I stared at the red tail lights as he disappeared.

He was right about me missing him. I already did.

I was about to head inside when another car pulled up into the spot where Bentley's sedan had been.

The driver made eye contact with me, waved, and quickly got out.

The driver was a stranger, a woman. She was stocky, mid-thirties, with short, curly hair and full, round cheeks. She wore a masculine overcoat and trousers.

"Ms. Riddle? Ms. Zarabella Diamante Riddle?" She had a confident voice and walked toward me with certainty, hand extended. "My name is Boomer."

I stepped down off the porch, met her on the walkway, and shook her hand. "Boomer? Is that your first name or last name?"

"My full name is Blythe Boomer. Blythe Delores Boomer, but everyone just calls me Boomer. If you're ever around when I holler for my supper, you'll see why."

"Nice to meet you, Boomer." She had a firm handshake.

"I won't take up your whole Sunday," she said. "I do need your signature on a few documents, but all that boring lawyer stuff will be done in a jiffy."

"You're a lawyer?"

"That's what the certificates on the walls back home say."

"What is this regarding?"

She had her back to me, and was unloading something from the passenger seat of her vehicle.

"The estate," she called over her shoulder. "Sorry I didn't get here sooner, but I hit some weather on the road. First I was on a bus, but that broke down. I got this rental car, and then one of my tires blew out. It's been a real humdinger of a road trip, but don't you worry. I kept the little guy safe and warm the whole time, and he's doing just fine."

She turned to face me, holding what she'd been taking from her car. It was a bird cage. It was covered in quilted fabric, to protect its occupant from the cold wind, but it was, without a doubt, a bird cage.

"Marzipants," I said, with absolute certainty.

The budgie inside the padded cage squawked in recognition of its name. Exactly like a being of pure evil would.

"We need to get him inside right away," Boomer said, making a straight line for my door.

I raced up the steps ahead of her, opened the door, and quickly shouted in, "We have a visitor. Best behavior, everyone."

Boomer chuckled as she walked past me. She kicked off her snowy galoshes and continued all the way into the living room, all the way to the bare spot where we'd been planning to put up a Christmas tree.

"Perfect location," Boomer said, setting down the cage. "There's a pedestal in my car for hanging it up. That way little Marzipants can look out the window all day." She brushed off her hands and glanced around the room. "Nice place you got here. When I helped Minerva draw up her will, she said you were the only person she could trust with her budgie, should he outlive her. I thought she was a nutter, offering to pay me personally to drive him over here to you, but now I can see you were the best person." She stretched, cracking her back, then worked both hands all the way around her stocky midsection, tucking her shirt into her trousers. "I wouldn't mind living here myself, if you've got a spare room." She chuckled again. "That's a joke. I wouldn't put you out."

"Thank you for going to all the trouble," I said. "I'm not sure this is the best home for a small bird. The last small bird who visited had a bad experience." Clockbird had been eaten by Boa.

The confident lawyer held up a hand. "Budgies are very easy to care for," she said.

"I have a cat. She doesn't look that threatening, but she can grab a bird out of mid-air."

"Ms. Riddle, I am a pet lover, and I do care what you do with the bird, but, after a certain point, it's out of my hands. You can coat the little guy in buttermilk and bread crumbs and serve him for Christmas dinner, but I must warn you it wouldn't make much of a snack, let alone a meal, and I'd rather not know about it if you do."

Mrs. Pinkman, who had joined us in the living room, made a horrified look. The ghost could understand what was going on sometimes, and she'd been getting better at it over the week.

"I won't do that," I said. "I'll honor Mrs. Pinkman's wishes. I'll honor them like she was right here with us, watching me like a hawk."

"Marzipants is an old man," Boomer said. "Budgies don't live much past the age he already is. Once or twice when we were on the road, I thought I was going to have to give him mouth to beak, but he was just playing dead."

"Playing dead," I said, nodding. "Yes. I remember. That is one of his many budgie tricks."

Boomer drew a paper from her overcoat pocket, a pen from the other, and handed both to me. Switching to formal lawyer mode, she said, "Please sign to acknowledge your receipt of the asset."

I took the pen and paper, quickly read over the document, and signed.

Boomer shook my hand again. "Wow. This whole thing went down a lot better than I expected," she said. "I'll be on my way."

"You're not driving out today, are you? There's a blizzard warning. If you head east, you'll be heading straight for it."

"Thanks for your concern, ma'am. I'm going to stick around for a day or two, maybe longer. I've got an old friend who lives around here. I'll take a break, shack up in a motel, see the local sights, and then, who knows?" She held her hand to the side of her mouth and whispered. "I might look at some real estate while I'm out here. Looks like the move west was good for you."

Marzipants shrieked inside his cage.

Boomer excused herself to go get the rest of the budgie's cage, as well as some food and other supplies.

The lawyer and I spent another ten minutes setting up the pedestal and going over care and feeding, then Boomer left.

I was alone with the budgie in the living room for no more than a minute when both of the other animal residents entered.

Boa was absolutely silent. She jumped onto the back of a chair, where she watched the tiny bird inside the hanging cage with great interest.

Ribbons landed on a bookcase and peered down.

He asked, "Where's the other one, Zed? You need at least two for breeding. This one is not even female. It will not produce eggs."

"This isn't livestock. It's a pet. His name is Marzipants."

"That is not a good name. That is the same one used by the devil bird that Zoey often speaks of."

"This is the devil bird," I said. "He was left to us in Mrs. Pinkman's will."

Ribbons chittered with evil delight.

Mrs. Pinkman was bent over the cage, cooing at the companion pet who had outlived her. The bird pranced around proudly, responding to his mistress, even though she was a ghost.

"At least now we know why Mrs. Pinkman is here," I said, mostly to myself, since Ribbons wasn't very good at listening to people talk through their boring human problems. "Something tells me she's going to stick around a bit longer."

Over on the chair, Boa made a chattering sound and licked her lips.

"Or maybe not that long," I said.

My mother came into the room, her magazine in hand. She walked past the bird cage without comment, and took a seat by the window. "Why don't you have a copy of the New York Times delivered here? It would be nice to have something to keep one informed of current events in the world at large. There's something about this town that's so insular. It's as though nothing outside town limits matters to anyone here."

"You're not going to say anything about this?" I waved at the cage. "Our new addition to the family?"

"It doesn't look very new to me. That poor thing is nearly as old as the cage."

Marzipants squawked.

"It's Mrs. Pinkman's bird," I said. "That's why she's been hanging around all week. The budgie is her unfinished business."

"Not for long, by the look of those feathers," my mother said. "How did it get here?"

"There was a lawyer here. She drove across the country, just to bring the bird here."

My mother smacked her lips. "That reminds me. I'd like to have something lean served at dinner tonight. Zinnia has returned to her regular size, but with the way she's been eating, she will easily exceed her goals. I'm thinking about grilled chicken."

The bird squawked again.

My mother looked up at the budgie in its cage. "What a dreadful noise it makes. So shrill and annoying. Who would ever choose to be in the same room with it?"

I said nothing.

She looked at me. "Where's Teddy B? I thought I felt his energy. Is he not joining us for dinner?"

"He's going out of town with Persephone. They're tracking down the O'Connor woman, and the missing vials."

"Who will protect you when he is gone?"

I sighed. "I can protect myself."

"Don't worry. I'll be here," she said. "I know I seem like a soft, sweet pushover, but I can be assertive when the situation calls for it."

"Mom, I've seen you choke people like you're Darth Vader."

"Who? Is that one of your colorful friends?"

"Never mind. Thanks for offering to protect me," I said. "I'll try not to need it."

She licked her lips. "I could bite that genie again, if you'd like. He was tasty."

"Please don't bite anyone."

She gave me an enigmatic smile, opened her magazine, and started flipping the pages. "It should be a memorable Christmas this year," she said.

"I'm sure it will be," I said.

For a full list of books in this
series and other titles by
Angela Pepper, visit

www.angelapepper.com

9 781990 367137